'A joyfully warm and witty read with real sparkle and knowing' – Helen Lederer

'Engaging characters, heart-warming, inspirational storyline with witty dialogue and loads of laughs. I loved it!' – Carol Wyer

'A novel about starting over and living life to the full – I loved *The Mercury Travel Club*' – Mandy Baggott

'A truly wonderful and exciting debut, *The Mercury Travel Club* is crammed full of warmth, wit and poignancy. A lovely, witty story about life, love and winning at starting over. I loved it' – Alex Brown

'*Bridget Jones's Diary* meets *Last Tango in Halifax* in this moving, funny and warm novel about falling apart, putting yourself back together, and living life to the full' – Laura Lockington

'Entertaining and uplifting' – Lorelei Mathias

D1638877

WHERE THE CHAOS COMES FREE

The Mercury Travel Club

HELEN BRIDGETT

RedDoor

Published by RedDoor
www.reddoorpublishing.com

ISBN 978-1-910453-28-5

A CIP catalogue record for this book is available
from the British Library

Cover design: Anna Morrison
www.annamorrison.com

Typesetting: Tutis Innovative E-Solutions Pte. Ltd

Printed in Great Britain by Bell and Bain Ltd, Glasgow

For my wonderful family and friends – you're always an inspiration!

A Fresh Start

A hearse drives out of the cul-de-sac as I drive in. I hope that's not an omen.

Cross Road: genuinely the name of this street. I didn't pick the place because of the address but I have to confess to enjoying the irony. I couldn't bear to stay in our old house during the sale; it wasn't just the thought of people traipsing round judging my taste and rifling through my memories (which would have been bad enough), but no, he brought her into our house.

'Never in our bedroom,' he yelled at me when I found out, as if bedding your mistress in the spare room somehow puts you on a higher moral plane.

The thing that annoyed me most was that she burned our only Jo Malone candle. It lived in the spare room, never actually meant to be lit – just to sit there and tell anyone visiting we had impeccable taste. Every woman knows this; I'd never set fire to a £40 candle in anyone else's house, but she did it in mine. She lit the match that started the row and eventually brought us here.

So here I am; I think they used to call these 'starter homes', small boxes for young couples. Given the obvious funeral taking place, maybe things have come full circle and they're 'finishing off homes' now, last stop before the old fogey centre.

I can't see a single person peeking through the blinds to have a nosey at the new neighbour. I might have caught someone's eye, maybe made a new friend and have someone to talk to. Maybe I'd even get invited to an impromptu party – but nothing. Probably for the best, I'm not sure I'm ready to start explaining myself yet.

Hi, I'm Angela. My husband ran off with the caterer we hired for our daughter's graduation party – pleased to meet you.

It's New Year's Eve and I start wondering why they chose today to hold a funeral; I guess because no one is working tomorrow. It's always best to schedule your exit around the bank holidays.

They're funny things, funerals; like all the big moments of life and death they take no time at all. A couple of words and that's it, next please. I remember when Patty's husband died, she looked at her watch as the congregation were leaving and said, 'A few thousand pounds for twenty minutes? He wouldn't have been happy with that.'

It made us smile because she was right, he wouldn't have been.

Right then, Mrs (or I suppose its Ms now), stop this and perk up; this place is carefully designed to cause no offence: neutral magnolia walls, teal carpet and white gloss doors. The air has a whiff of industrial cleaning about it; the landlord probably bought the 'new tenant' package. Everything is packaged nowadays.

Wash that man right outta your life? Certainly madam – would you like the bronze, silver or gold package? The gold comes with free mistress removal.

I've bought a new bed and sofa, which were thankfully delivered on time, and I've unpacked what I need to: a ready meal, bottle of wine and a pint of milk. At the moment it still feels as if I'm staying in a holiday cottage for a few days. But this is it. This silent, easy to maintain house is all I have to show for twenty-four years and eleven months of marriage (yep, I didn't even get a silver wedding anniversary bash). I mustn't get morose. It's over, but my life isn't.

Despite hankering after a party invitation, I do want to be alone on my first night here. I thought it would be a good time to reflect and make plans for the future; sitting here now, I'm not sure what I'm going to do. It's a funny night to spend on your own. Ordinarily I'd just watch television, but tonight it's all people having a wonderful time. I must definitely avoid alcohol at all costs: do not open the wine, do not get drunk or maudlin. Have a bath, an early night and wake up gloriously refreshed for a dignified start to the next stage of my life.

The single years.

Oh Lord, what just happened? I wake up with that scary sensation; I have no idea where I am or what I've done to get here and I don't recognise the room at first glance. Out of habit, I peer across the bed at the next pillow but there's still no one there. At least I didn't throw myself on any random passer-by or accost a new neighbour. Or if I did, the vision of me drowning in my own drool wasn't particularly attractive and he didn't stay. I also bypassed the bath last night and collapsed fully dressed with a full face of make-up; my pillow case looks as if Robert Smith has slept on it.

I remember switching on the TV and then convincing myself I'd stick to one glass of wine if I opened the bottle. There are some lessons you don't learn no matter how old you get.

Although every brain cell is begging me not to, I have to lift my concrete head up and take it downstairs to find the paracetamol. The kitchen is like a crime scene. I could imagine *CSI* dissecting the evidence.

'Wine rack empty and lasagne not cooked,' they'd note in their authoritative way.

'Drinking on an empty stomach, nasty. How much wine?'

They'd shine one of their torches into the recycling corner (even when plastered I seem to be environmentally responsible).

'Looks like two empties – a champagne and a cab sauv.'

(Did I really open the champagne too? And not just open but consume?)

'Good taste, but a lot for one little lady.'

They'd nod in knowing agreement.

My phone is sitting on the worktop and with trepidation I check I didn't make any drunken calls to my ex; I sigh with relief when I'm assured otherwise. It lights up with Patty's daft photo and I realise I've had it on silent all night. I tell myself I wanted to avoid well-wishers, but the truth is I was more afraid that no one would ring. I hug my little phone as I see lots of missed calls around midnight and just as many text messages with kisses on the bottom; it's like a virtual embrace and I'm so relieved that people care. Zoe tried to call so many times before and after midnight; she would have been working the room at the anointed hour.

I feel terrible for not being sober enough to pick up the phone to my one and only daughter. Discarded wife and neglectful mother; the accolades are piling up this year. Zoe will be my first call as soon as Patty gets off the line. In my hungover state, the saving grace is that Patty talks so much I don't usually need to think or say anything.

4

'What did you get up to last night?' asks Patty. 'An orgy with the new neighbours?'

I snort; it counts as an answer.

'Guess where I ended up?' she continues. 'Onstage at the Rose & Crown. Guess what I sang? "Like a Virgin". It was absolutely hilarious…'

This is what a conversation with Patty is like. I can drift off for hours and she doesn't notice. It's very soothing, almost like being in a coma yet knowing that there's someone on the outside trying to make contact.

I've known Patty (she was actually christened Patience – it doesn't fit at all) for over thirty years (ouch). She's four years older than me and was my supervisor when I joined the airline (being a stewardess was a glamorous career back then, before budget flights). Patty has always been the biggest personality in the room. I'm sure if we were ever invited to the White House, all eyes would be on her. She'd also get the President singing; an ex-drama school student, she gets everyone singing and if *The X Factor* had been around when we were young, she'd have won. She frequently tells me that she still has time to be the next Susan Boyle.

She usually does Cyndi Lauper numbers, but I suppose 'Time After Time' isn't really a New Year crowd-pleaser. Also the Rose & Crown doesn't have a stage, so she was in all likelihood standing on a table. I don't mention this.

'So have you?' she asks.

Blimey, a break in conversation, and I'm expected to reply.

'Have I what?' I say.

'Made any resolutions? New Year, fresh start etc., there must be loads you want to do now you've lost all that baggage.'

Invent a way of drinking wine without having a hangover? That's the first thought to enter my head and I'd probably win the Nobel Prize for it. I drift mentally to the prize-giving where the room raises a glass of champagne to me; the imaginary smell of it makes me gag.

'I'm not ready yet,' I sigh. 'I just want to unpack, recover and get my bearings first.'

'I'm not going to let you stew,' she replies. 'No wasting your life away as divorce debris.'

'Give me until the end of the month,' I say. 'You know what I'm like.'

'You must be the only person who makes their New Year's resolutions in February,' says Patty. 'OK, you've got till then or I'll come round and sort you out myself.'

Heaven forbid.

With a final, 'I'm always here for you', she's gone and the house is silent again.

Years ago I came to the conclusion that January 1st is the very worst day to start any resolutions as you're always too tired or hungover. So I give myself a month of grace and start in February. It's worked so far; just as everyone else is giving up, I'm just getting going. And you only have to stick to them for eleven months. Well, ten months, because let's face it no one sticks to anything in December.

Now I have to redeem myself on behalf of all other errant mothers in the world and phone my daughter.

Meet the Family

Toad. What a complete and utter toad.

Here I am, a fortnight in and doing just fine. I've been to the sales, I've bought cushions, I've bought some microwaveable vegetables, made healthy meals for one and I haven't had a drink. I'm being mature and sensible; you might even say, acting my age. Then, I open the bloody paper and there they are:

The A-Team: Alan Hargreaves and partner Amanda winning a luxury holiday at the glittering New Year Charity Ball.

They are *not* the A-team: we were the A-Team – Alan and Angie. Doing everything together and sticking by each other no matter what. That was our nickname, I made it up. How dare he give it to his new slut.

They're obviously deliriously happy in the photo; all glammed up in black tie, sipping the champagne and nibbling hors d'oeuvres, no doubt. I bet she took her make-up off before she went to bed. That should have been me? How did we get here? The doorbell rings.

'You've seen it?' asks my daughter.

Zoe can see me holding the offending article but has a copy with her just in case I'm the last to find out. She always was a daddy's girl and was devastated when this first happened, especially as her graduation party had been the incendiary event.

Since the divorce finalised she has tried her best to be neutral, but she knows the photograph and him using our family nickname can only hurt me.

'Why didn't you mention it when we spoke?' I ask.

'I didn't want you to think that I'd chosen to spend New Year with them; I didn't have a choice. You know that, don't you?' she pleads.

'*Et tu, Brute,*' I think to myself, rather unfairly.

She's the hotel assistant manager, so I knew she would be there, but still I feel the knife twisting.

'You've got this place looking nice,' she says looking round.

I'm not going to change the subject or do small talk. I really can't. Not with my daughter. It must come across as surly and she lets out an exasperated sigh.

'It's happened, Mum. He's a bastard…'

Yippee.

'… but it's happened. Dad's getting on with his life, you need to now.'

Three thoughts enter my head:

1. What the hell does 'getting on with your life' actually mean? (What precisely do I get on with?)
2. Why do people say it when the life you knew is over? And…
3. I'm getting advice from a twenty-three-year-old. Shouldn't she be having the relationship crises and turning to me?

'… come on, Mum, forget him. Let's go to lunch, I'll drive,' says Zoe.

I find myself drifting in and out of most conversations these days, then suddenly they're over and, like today, I've agreed to something.

'I'll wait until you've had a shower, you'll feel better,' she adds. I must look worse than I realise.

Half an hour later I'm refreshed and presentable. I get into Zoe's stylish Fiat 500 and giggle to myself as I see many residents of Cross Road being picked up by their kids. The old folks' weekly outing; I hope they've all remembered their teeth.

When we get to the restaurant, Zoe insists on a table by the window. I watch her as she glances through the menu and then asks about the provenance of the beef. I know this isn't a vanity: she loves her food and the hotel she manages is gaining a reputation for dining since she joined it. She checks that I'd be happy with a chateaubriand before ordering it.

'After all, we're celebrating a new start,' she says when I try to insist she doesn't need to spend this much on me.

I can see that an assertive young woman has taken over my baby girl's body and I approve wholeheartedly.

It shouldn't surprise me. When she was five years old she took hold of a menu and very calmly ordered 'soup then peas' from the waiter who was offering her fish fingers. At eleven, she made her sports teacher go through the rules of hockey while she wrote them down before the game. She then held them out to the referee each time she thought there'd been an error.

At university she got a first in hospitality management and now she's on a fast track programme with the DeWynter Hotel chain, looking every inch the professional that she is.

Yes, my daughter has grown into a very kind but serious young woman, the image of her father with her hazel eyes, dark blonde hair and dimples. I haven't seen the dimples much recently as she's all but stopped smiling since the divorce.

I think back to my twenties with Patty, all the fun we had, and just hope Alan and I haven't destroyed her chances of that.

'Work is fun,' she replies when I ask her about it.

'What about laughing, dancing, friends and boyfriends?'

'The last thing I want is a relationship,' she says.

'We did have some good times you know. I did love him,' I remind her.

'It's not enough though, is it?' she whispers and I take her hand.

She looks up at me and smiles with her mouth but not her eyes.

* * *

I'm back in the office today and Charlie has the same article open on his desk.

'Any chance of your Alan spending those holiday vouchers with us,' he asks.

'You're not suggesting I ask him?' I say.

'You could get Zoe to drop a hint,' he suggests. 'It'd be nice to get a few thousand pounds worth of sales in the till. Didn't you want to do a few more days' work?'

And that's the truth; right now I work part-time, which was fine as a second income, but I could do with a bit more now I'm an independent woman.

Charlie started Mercury Travel ten years ago when he finally realised that his Rep days were over. I joined eighteen months ago and there's also a young Australian girl, Josie, working here. She came to England backpacking hoping that one day she'd meet the perfect English gent; the business is a bit like a sanctuary for losers in love.

I used to help Alan with his business, then one day he persuaded me I should have my own interests and perhaps find a job which would *get me out of the house*. Now that I think about it, that was probably the start of the disintegration and he was lining things up to leave. I shake the thoughts away – can't dwell on that now.

We're a boutique agency in a bohemian suburb of Manchester where independent shops tend to thrive. We specialise in a more personalised service for older clientele but that doesn't protect us from the internet completely. Our customers like something a bit different, so we're often searching out empty-nester adventures, but they could replace us with their teenage kids if said children could be prised away from games and social media for long enough. We tell our clients, 'Yes you could do this online but you can also afford to let us do the dreary searching.'

I suppose we're the travel equivalent of the help and it seems to work.

We've spent the morning putting up posters advertising our 'Tanuary Sale'. Anyone who books their holiday with us this week gets chauffeur driven to the airport. It's my idea; Charlie wanted to give them a course of sunbed sessions before their trip (hence Tanuary) but I persuaded him that exposing our customers to potential melanoma isn't the best way of securing repeat business. Anyway, the drive to the airport is something people will value; parking costs a fortune and it's a lovely way to start a trip, something the big companies just wouldn't offer.

We need to do something to compete with the bigger agencies as January is a crucial month for travel; everyone gets sick of the British weather and books something to look forward to. Hence the non-stop holiday adverts on TV. People tend to think that the bigger companies can offer better prices than us and don't bother coming in. Here's hoping the offer helps and I can avoid begging Alan for his business.

As a bribe, Charlie is sending me to investigate afternoon teas at an exclusive hotel. I ponder why everyone so far this year feels the need to feed me. Are they afraid I'll poison myself with my cooking? Anyway, it's time to call my mum, a woman who definitely knows her choux buns from her millefeuille.

On my way out I take some of our brochures. I still can't get used to the idea that he'll be picking a holiday without me. I wonder what they'll choose. What would we have picked if we'd still been together?

It's a good day to be out and about, a stunning winter's day – the type children draw, where a clear blue sky is dotted with perfectly formed clouds and complemented by a serene frost across the land – beautiful. Manchester is a wonderful city to live in and an easy city to escape from; within half an hour of leaving the office, I'll be driving through the glorious Cheshire countryside. Later this afternoon, the sun will set with a warm smile and we'll feel blessed by Mother Nature. I love this type of weather.

I pick up my mum on the way out.

'Now, this is work; you need to behave yourself,' I warn her.

'When do I not?' is her shocked reply.

For as long as I can remember my mother has promised to spend her dotage personifying the poem by Jenny Joseph, 'Warning'. She particularly likes the part about gobbling up samples in shops. I swear that she knows when M&S are about to start their cake tasting. Dad has long given up trying to tame her and sits quietly in the background.

Anything free and she goes for it, so I firmly expect to hear extra cake requests for her 'poorly friend who couldn't come'.

We arrive at the hotel and are seated in a beautiful parlour where a dozen tables are waiting pristine in their white linen and silver cutlery. Oh to have lived in an era when one always 'took tea' in rooms like this. I turn to say this to my mother and find that she has taken on the alter ego of food critic; she has armed herself with a notepad and half-moon glasses, which she peers over every time the waiter arrives with something.

'They'll give us more if they think I'm going to rate them,' she conspires with a wink.

I shake my head and choose not remind her that the hotel already knows we're from the travel agents. In an attempt to stop her checking each piece of cutlery for smudges, I start a conversation proving that I'm getting on with my life in a mature, sophisticated way.

'I've seen a poster for a book club,' I say. 'I thought it might help me meet people.'

'Are there men there?' she asks without looking up from a teaspoon.

'I don't want a man, Mum, I was thinking of maybe getting a cat for company.'

'Well at least a cat won't walk out because of your cooking.'

So they do think I'll give myself gastroenteritis if left to my own devices.

'I can cook,' I protest, 'and besides which Alan didn't leave because of my cooking.'

'Of course not, dear. What's that old saying? Oh yes, the way to a man's stomach is through a microwave. She can cook you know.'

I know she can cook, everyone knows she can cook. Alan bloody well met her because of her cooking. I mean what sort of woman makes a pass at a bloke buying a cake for his twenty-two-year-old daughter? What did she think? The daughter has flown the nest so she might as well move in? And we gave her a bloody round of applause at the party.

I bite my tongue and catch the eye of the manager to agree the deal we'll offer our customers. He then signals the waiter.

'Thank you that was lovely,' I say as he starts clearing the table.

He nods politely and tries to escape, but Mum is in there before he can get away.

'I don't suppose you could put another one of those éclairs in a doggy bag?' she smiles. 'It's for my friend who's very poorly at the moment.'

She never fails.

Ever.

Mid-life Crisis

It's my fifty-third birthday and I've taken the day off to celebrate.

I spread my birthday cards out along the mantelpiece (so that it looks like I got more than I did) and arrange the beautiful bouquet from Zoe.

Patty is ranting away.

'A cat and a book club?' she asks. 'How old are you today – ninety?'

She's brought birthday bubbly and olives, both of which she is quaffing voraciously.

'So he gets to bonk and you get a book? He gets pussy and you get a cat?'

I grimace at the unsavoury connotations.

'He gets a trollop and you get Trollope?'

We both nod acknowledgement of that one.

'Any more?' I ask.

'No, I've run out for now. But seriously, that's your plan?' says Patty.

'It's a start,' I reply.

'It's not a start, it's a finish,' she warns. 'You're saying, "Just walk all over me; I'll hide in the corner and keep out of your way." Cats, books and cardies? That's your fresh start?'

I'm about to protest about the cardigan-swipe but then I look down at my sensible knitwear and close my mouth. Patty hands me an article.

'Here read this. Fifty is the new forty and, get this: fifty-three is the new middle age. You're perfectly entitled to a mid-life crisis. Get a Porsche, a toy boy, even a vibrator – but please not a cat.'

After briefly considering that I doubt I'll live to 106, I have to admit I've always fancied a mid-life crisis but was never sure what to do. I don't want a toy boy; I'd have to have a Brazilian (I imagine). And I don't want a Porsche; I like my Mini.

In fact, I've never considered what I do want out of life; Alan and Zoe always came first.

'Come on girl, don't go maudlin on me,' says Patty, 'tonight, we are going to party.'

And we do.

Patty pours us both a glass and puts on *Now That's What I Call Music 1983*; she turns up my ancient CD player as high as it will go and 'True' by Spandau Ballet fills the house. Tony Hadley serenades me as I take off the cardie and put some lipstick on (daring stuff, I know). I empty my glass of Prosecco for courage and put myself in Patty's hands.

We're lucky enough to have every type of restaurant you could ever want within walking distance, but Patty reminds me that there's more danger of bumping into someone we know if we stay locally, so we get the tram into the city centre. We start at a tapas bar I've read about but never visited. We enjoy copious cava along with tortilla, serrano, chorizo, patatas bravas and Manchego – even the words make your mouth water – and we're soon reliving our stewardess days. We do the spoof safety talk for the gorgeous waiter and then torture the poor guy by making him pose for selfie after selfie, which Patty posts on her Facebook page to prove to the world we're having a good time. The waiter doesn't realise how lucky he is: Patty used to be in charge of mouth-to-mouth training so it could have been far worse.

We get a cab home and Patty serenades the poor driver with 'Joe Le Taxi' for most of the journey despite knowing only those three words of the song. Thanks to the bubbly, I find this hilariously funny and my jaw is aching through smiling when I eventually turn the key in the door. There are worse injuries.

My birthday continues into the next day. Still high on life I go to work and find the shop decked out to celebrate my special day.

Charlie likes to back the underdog, and since the divorce that's me. After being reassured the cake is not from Amanda's shop, I blow out the candles and make a wish to my fresh start – whatever that might be.

Maybe fifty-three is the new thirty-three after all.

It takes a phone call from my daughter when I get home to bring me crashing down to earth.

'Who was that on Facebook?' she asks. 'He looks young enough to be your son.'

I'm slightly offended. On the night I didn't feel the age gap was that big (I wonder if it ever does) but have to confess that if I'd met the poor waiter while sober, I'd have been more tempted to give him a hot meal and iron his shirts. Fortunately Patty has mainly posted pictures of herself and him; I'm only peeking out of the corner of a couple. Surely this is some recompense for Zoe.

'I was just having some fun, getting on with my life like everyone tells me to,' I protest.

'You need to stay away from that Patty,' she says. 'Everyone can see those pictures, you know; once things are uploaded to the internet, they're there for ever. What will Dad think?'

I hope he thinks, 'Wow, she's having fun with a hot young guy' or even 'Dammit, I want her back', but I suspect he hasn't even seen them.

I put the phone on speaker and go to make a coffee while my daughter continues to tell me about the perils of the internet.

'I do know how the internet works,' I tell her. 'I've only been using it for twenty-odd years.'

She wouldn't be the first person I've heard saying over fifties don't understand technology and while I'm not Einstein, I'm not Joey Essex either.

'Then you should know better,' scolds Zoe.

I'm so dumbfounded, I tell her I'm sorry and promise not to do it again.

The Book Club

I've been reading all day while outside it pours down.

In order to restore my daughter's faith in me, I've decided to go to the book club after all. I'm cramming in *A Thousand Splendid Suns* before tonight and although I wouldn't have picked this title if it weren't for the club, I love it. It's about a woman in Afghanistan in the seventies. She's married off to an older man when she's fifteen and is completely trapped but eventually her spirit breaks free. I know how she feels.

Zoe's call has been playing in the back of my mind. Of course I knew that it was a cheeky thing to do – that was the point of it. Am I too old for a night out? It doesn't seem so long ago since I was a carefree stewardess travelling the world. If I'd been in the restaurant watching, would I have disowned the two women taking pictures? I'd probably envy their courage wishing I could let it rip with good friends.

And asking: 'What will Dad think?' was unfair of her. He lost his right to comment on my lifestyle a few months ago, but then again, maybe he did look at them and recall the fun-loving woman he originally fell for. From Zoe's response I imagine he'd be more likely to recoil and think, 'Thank God I got away from her when I did.' Is this not what they all meant by 'getting on with my life'? If not, then what?

I sigh and snuggle down. Today, I just don't care; no one can get to me. I'm cosy, have a lovely mug of coffee and a good book. What more could I want?

It's funny, if I tell people I've spent all day on the sofa reading a book, they'll say, 'Oh I couldn't sit still for that long' or 'What a waste of a day' and yet all week long, I sell trips to people who spend thousands of pounds, buy holiday clothes, queue at airports and then lie on loungers for two weeks reading.

I guess I won't have to persuade this crowd of that. I don't quite finish but I have to leave if I'm going to get there on time. It's dark and the street lights shine down on to the wet pavement but there are no raindrops reflected in their glow, a small break in the weather to help me get to the pub without looking like a wet dog. I pull on a raincoat and armed with umbrella cross the small park to reach The Crown.

I'm hit with a blast of warm air as I walk in and I feel my cheeks ripen. I look around and see a group of a dozen people sitting at one of the dining tables. Many are holding the book, so I inhale some confidence and walk over.

'I guess this is the book club,' I chirp.

'That's us,' replies one of the women and pulls out a chair so that I can join them easily.

I'm told there are more people here than usual because of everyone's New Year's resolutions to get a life. As I look around the table I see a very definite 'type' of person, probably every bookish stereotype you could imagine. Amongst our numbers we have the quiet intellect (Ed), the twinkly-eyed flirt (Peter), the eccentric bookshop owner (Caroline) and of course the divorcee (me!).

As soon as the drinks arrive, Caroline asks if anyone would like to start.

'I enjoyed finding out some of the history of the region,' I offer – not quite knowing what you're supposed to say at book clubs.

'She was so young to go through all that. I just wanted to rescue her,' adds Caroline.

'Like Lawrence of Arabia, whisking her off her feet and riding away on his trusty steed.' Peter's comments come with an elaborate sweep of his scarf.

'You do realise T E Lawrence never went to Afghanistan?' Ed corrects.

Peter responds with a huge open-mouthed exclamation, 'Reeaaally.'

Ed smiles graciously and we all relax a little more into the evening.

Conversation flows easily considering we've never met before and it occurs to me that the book is just a focal point or excuse; we could be talking about anything. I could have joined a wine club or a flower club, the point is to just get out and meet people.

'Are you local?' asks Caroline as the evening draws to a close and a small number of us start drifting into more personal conversations.

I tell her that I live and work less than ten minutes away.

'It's amazing how many people we must see every day and yet never meet,' she comments, 'although I'm ashamed to confess that I book my travel online.'

'Thank God for that,' I laugh. 'I didn't want to admit I'd used Amazon.'

'That's perhaps why none of us ever meet. What made you come tonight?' she asks.

'Recently divorced,' I answer without further explanation and she seems to understand.

'So starting over,' she says.

'Whatever that means,' I shrug. 'I'm sure I don't.'

In films, the newly divorced or bereaved tend to rediscover their childhood passion for painting or playing the piano then make a fortune out of it. I was never any good at either of them. Caroline sits quietly while I ponder.

Needing to break the silence, I offer, 'I thought I might have my hair done.'

'It's always a good start,' she says, then adds, 'I might be able to help.'

She tells me she's training to be a life coach. I've never heard of them and as she's explaining what she does, I can't imagine how you train to be one. It seems to consist of getting people to make lists and stick to them. But…nothing ventured and all that. I agree to let her practise on me. As we're getting dressed to leave the pub, we arrange to meet at my house on Sunday. I'm going to make lunch and then I'm going to have my first life-coaching session. Somehow I think Zoe might approve of this; it's her type of thing.

'Do I need to do anything in advance?' I ask.

'Just one thing,' says Caroline, switching to the soft therapist-style voice which I think comes free with the training, 'and I don't want you to think too hard about the answer to this question – just day dream.'

I get butterflies and wonder if I should be writing this down.

'On Sunday I'll bring a magic wand with me and on Monday when you wake up – your life will be perfect. What does that perfect life look like?'

And with that she gives me a peck on the cheek and heads off into the rain like a Disney fairy godmother. I put my umbrella up and start to head home feeling quite elated. After a few steps I take the brolly down and let the rain fall over my face; rather than soaking me, it seems instead to be washing away some of my woes.

I've made a new friend for the first time in years.

Perhaps I will be OK after all.

Magic Wand

The checklist under the fridge magnet has today planned to such military precision that even I can't fail:

12.30 put chicken in oven
1 p.m. parboil spuds
1.20 roast spuds
1.40 steam veg
1.45 pour sneaky glass of courage before Caroline arrives
2 p.m. eat and drink heartily
3 p.m. relax and sort life out

I haven't been able to stop thinking about the question all week and, dreading that I'd get the answer wrong when she asked, I decided to question everyone at work.

'If you had a magic wand, what would your perfect life look like?' I asked them realising how stupid the question sounded out of context.

It didn't put Charlie off and he was straight in there. 'Ooh – I'd run a beach bar like Tom Cruise in *Cocktail*. Maybe even with the man himself; people would come for miles for my Slippery Nipple.'

Josie chipped in twirling her shoulder length earrings. 'I'd move to the Bahamas with James Bond. He'd have been ship-wrecked without his suitcases and have nothing to wear but those little speedos all day, every day.'

I wasn't surprised by this: Daniel Craig emerging from the ocean in his trunks is Josie's screensaver.

'This isn't helping,' I said to them, looking for a little more inspiration than this.

'OK then, Little Miss Serious. Making what I have perfect?' said Charlie.

I nodded.

'Well I started working in travel to have adventures and yet I'm in a shop all day worrying about keeping it open. So I'd get out more – join people on their trips and make sure they had a good time; that way, they'd book again.'

'You'd be good at that,' piped Josie, and he would.

'I'd also have someone who loved me, we'd have the best dinner parties and you'd both be invited.'

Great, I thought, I have somewhere to eat in Charlie's fantasy life.

'Hubby and I would be pillars of the community – we'd raise money for charity and live happily ever after.' He bowed theatrically and we gave him a round of applause before cutting it short as a customer walked in.

Throughout the week I found myself pondering the circumstances of everyone who sat in front of me, just wondering whether they were living their perfect lives, whether this trip around the Black Forest or to a Greek Island was part of that. In the end, Charlie's hadn't been that much of a stretch; I wonder why he hasn't done it.

I thought Patty might be slightly more ambitious when I ask her the same question but she ducks it by saying she wants 'constant gratuitous sex'. As far as I know she hasn't had sex since her hubby died four years ago, although she talks about it a lot.

Anyway, back to today and my checklist. I glance at the clock; bugger, 1.30 and I've missed spuds-in time – so much for foolproof. I increase the temperature to compensate, not sure whether this is the right thing to do. My mother was annoyingly accurate about my cooking prowess; I've been on a prod-prod ping-ping diet since moving here. Anyway, the chicken is starting to smell wonderful – I hope she's not a veggie. The doorbell rings.

'Too late to ask now,' I tell myself.

Caroline is carrying a large hessian shopping bag and pulls out a bottle of Pinot Grigio.

'I thought this might go,' she says handing the bottle to me.

'It will indeed,' I reply, 'follow me.' We head into the kitchen and I pour us each a glass.

'Nearly ready,' I say, pretending to know what I'm doing.

Caroline peers into the oven glancing at the temperature.

'Smells delicious; shall I cover the chicken so it doesn't dry out?' she asks.

'Just what I was about to do,' I lie handing her the roll of foil. 'Why don't you supervise the oven while I tackle the veg?'

Caroline happily accepts her new responsibility and I spy her turning the temperature down as I check the microwave instructions on the ready-prepared veg.

After a pretty perfect lunch, we move into the living room.

'Shall we start?' asks Caroline and I nod.

She reaches into her bag again and this time pulls out a magic wand.

'Do you have a hatstand in there too?' I ask as she hands the wand to me. It's very pink and sparkly, not something I'd expect Caroline to own, but I'm happy to play along.

Next out of the bag is a chart with different aspects of my life listed: my love life, career, finances, social life, and body and mind. Caroline lays it out in front of me.

'I want you to think about each aspect of your life separately,' she explains. 'Tell me how you feel about your current situation and give it a mark out of ten. We'll jot that number down in this box.' She points at the chart.

'Then you'll close your eyes and wave your magic wand. You'll tell me how you wish things were in a perfect scenario and what you would have to do to score ten for each aspect. We'll jot down these actions here.'

'Can I say "whoosh" every time I wave it?' I ask.

'It's compulsory,' she smiles. 'Now where would you like to start?'

I beg her to leave my love life to the end; I don't want to start with such a low score.

'No problem, let's start by transforming your career, what would perfect look like?'

I give it a six out of ten right now. I love travel, love the shop and the guys. They've been my salvation and it fills me with dread that one day they might not be there.

And what would I do to get to ten out of ten? I have to confess, Charlie's dream struck a chord. Travel should be a lot more fun – we have to put the pizzazz back into it and I want to play a bigger role in it all, somehow secure our futures.

Whoosh – it will happen.

'And your finances, how would they improve?'

I give this seven out of ten as money isn't an issue but the source of it is. I have a healthy divorce settlement and when the house sells I'll have another lump sum. We've lived there since we were married and in that time the value of our big family house has risen so much that neither Alan nor I will struggle to buy a smaller place. If we'd still been together, we might have downsized and bought an apartment in Spain when we retired. Not that we ever discussed that; it's just another thing *we* won't do but *they* might.

'I have enough, I just wish I'd earned it myself,' I tell Caroline.

I spent the many years of our marriage helping Alan set up his now thriving business, although I doubt he credits me with anything. He sells security systems and I persuaded him to aim for business contracts rather than domestic ones. I didn't take a salary at the time or a share when we split up. I suppose I didn't really believe it was actually happening to me. Now I can't stop thinking about Amanda and her business; Alan probably respects her as a real businesswoman and she'll never be waiting for a divorce settlement. I wave the wand.

'In a perfect world, I'd like to prove my independence,' I say with my eyes still closed. 'I'm a successful businesswoman. Also, I'm not used to spending on myself, so in my perfect world, I'd not cling to every penny as if it were my last. I'd make my own money and enjoy it a bit more.'

I open my eyes and wave the wand once more for luck – *whoosh* – oh this transformation lark is so easy.

'Excellent,' says Caroline as she notes down what I say. 'Social life next?'

I give this an eight out of ten as it's not going too badly and if I keep up what I've started I'll get to ten. Then we move on to body and mind.

'Do you have a full-length mirror anywhere?' asks Caroline.

We head upstairs to my bedroom and Caroline guides me in with my eyes closed.

'Before you score this aspect,' she says, 'I want you to picture what you look like right now.'

I try to remember when I last looked at myself properly, probably my birthday night when I got dressed up to go out with Patty. I had to put on a little more make-up than I used to but I don't recall looking too bad so I give myself a six out of ten.

'Now keep that picture in your mind,' instructs Caroline, 'and open your eyes.'

I gasp as I compare the real reflection with the imaginary one: the woman in front of me is at least ten years older. When did I get so old? And thin? No wonder people send me out for cake all the time. The clothes I'm wearing don't help. When I threw on the grey marl sweater, I thought it said *casual and carefree*; instead it says *cast aside and careless*. I take it all in. My once glossy brown hair has stopped shining and now has a grey landing strip that a 747 could land on. I have a mono-brow that Frida Kahlo would be proud of and which scowls down hiding the green eyes that Alan used to love.

After leaving the airline and having Zoe, I always carried a little extra weight on my tall frame but argued that it suited me, and anyway, it was recompense for having to fit into a stewardess uniform all those years. In my heyday, Alan once told me I looked like Catherine Zeta-Jones; now I look like her husband, pre-op.

Why has no one told me I look this bad? Have they got used to it? I promise to take myself in hand, although aiming for ten out of ten might be a bit too ambitious right now – I'll aim for seven.

'Shall we go back downstairs and look at your love life now?' asks Caroline.

As we leave the bedroom, I glance back at myself and reflect that it's not surprising he left me. After all, I committed that most heinous of crimes: *letting myself go*. Caroline pulls me away from the mirror, trying to reassure me that the break-up resulted in my shambolic appearance and it was not the other way round. I wish I could believe her.

'The question is do you want a relationship in the future?' she asks when we're safely back in the living room.

I can't contemplate having to find another man yet equally cannot envisage every day for the rest of my life being spent alone. I never thought I'd be facing this at my age.

'If my magic wand life is perfect,' I say, 'then yes – there is someone who loves me.'

'Then we'll plan a few activities to get you out there – gently,' she reassures.

Caroline leaves me with my chart and tells me that she'll be checking up on me. After saying goodbye, I go back upstairs and put on my old jeans. They are way too big now; I guess six months of divorce does that to a girl.

'Time to sort yourself out,' I tell my rather forlorn reflection.

Arise Bo Peep

Today I take myself into my favourite department store, House of Fraser. There are more upmarket places I could go but I'm not quite ready for the uber-confident sales ladies of either Selfridges or Harvey Nichols. This store is more my level at the moment and I'm on a mission to try out one of their 'eyebrow bars'; I've seen other people do it and let's face it, Frida has to go.

I pay my money and lean back in the chair as instructed hoping that my legs are not in an unladylike display. I let the beautician ply her trade. Wow it hurts; I'm not sure when being tortured in public became acceptable but these bars seem to be everywhere and no one seems to be screaming or cringing quite as much as I am. I now completely understand the notion that Beauty = Pain. I hope it's worth it when the raging red soreness calms down.

I thank her for torturing me and work my way through the beauty booths being sprayed with every fragrance available. I'm persuaded to buy an excruciatingly expensive moisturiser which contains plankton and guarantees to plump my skin and turn back the aging process, both of which I am in dire need of. I silence the inner voices who scream at me throughout the sales speech, *'How are they allowed to get away with saying this? You know it's impossible.'* Although in fairness, I have never seen a wrinkled whale and I believe they eat loads of the stuff. Yes, I do know that's entirely down to the fact I've never actually seen any whales.

Next, the hairdresser works her magic and achieves this without inflicting any pain at all. She dyes the landing strip and restores a bounce I haven't seen in a long time. I get in the lift to go home but can't stop staring at the reflection of a woman with shiny chestnut hair and perky eyebrows. She looks so good; she deserves some new clothes. Although the comfy knitwear department is calling out my name, I resist and press the button for the trendy floor. I splurge on a wardrobe Patty might approve of in a size smaller than either of us has ever worn.

On the way home, I catch a glimpse of this new woman in shop windows; she looks like a stranger, a happy stranger. She looks a lot more confident than I feel.

To help complete the metamorphosis, when I get home I take a bin liner to the contents of my wardrobe: all in all, a totally cathartic experience.

I lie in bed happy that I've started on my magic wand list. I have one brief crisis of confidence where I hope I don't look like mutton at work tomorrow, but then relax and will the moisturiser to work its miracles by dawn.

I guess it does as I get second glances on my way in to the shop and it's not just in my imagination. Even Josie notices something; she admires the new clothes and puzzles over what else has changed.

Of course Charlie gets it straight away: 'The caterpillars are gone – oh thank you sweet angels; I've been dying to take a waxing strip to you for ages. And the bird's nest, you've said goodbye to that too.'

I hadn't realised I had so much wildlife about me (Patty would probably intervene right now with a 'bush' joke but I don't have any – jokes that is). I hope to see Patty later on and can't wait to show her the new look.

Meanwhile, the shop is buzzing. You would not believe the knock-on effect one person's life has on others; because I've had my hair done, Josie has hers done and emerges with a pixy crop that only someone with her cheekbones could carry. Then because he now has two gorgeous new 'girls', Charlie perks up and gives every customer a glass of Prosecco with their booking. Because all the customers feel very special and spread the word, we sell more holidays and so it turns out that because I had a hair colouring and my eyebrows plucked, we hit our January targets.

Karma I think – or something similar.

Later that evening, Patty listens while I fizz about my transformational day.

'I always say, "Put yourself out there and the world is your oyster,"' she reminds me.

I haven't always trusted her on that one but now I see what she means.

I dig out some old photos and we look through them together over a takeaway. It is funny how you always remember more than is captured in the picture. I recall all the insecurities I had while posing for them. I remember us standing sideways trying to look thinner. I can remember all the emotions I had then: terror, embarrassment and probably guilt for having slipped on some ridiculous diet. Seeing them now, they show two beautiful young women in the prime of their lives – if I could go back and talk to the younger me, I'd tell her she was gorgeous. Of course she wouldn't believe me.

'You always posed like that.' I pick up a picture and point it out to Patty.

She was the blonde to my brunette; she had the boobs and I had the legs. She never stopped smiling and laughing; you'd have thought she was on commission to prove the saying that 'Blondes have More Fun'.

'Tits and teeth,' she replies, immediately replicating the pose. We'd been taught that at training – the key to having a good portrait shot; I can't imagine anyone getting away with that advice these days.

I look again at the pictures of me, smiling, with my whole life ahead of me. I had gorgeous long chestnut hair back then; later, when I got married, I had it cropped in a very sensible 'Diana' style which matched the awful pussy-bow blouses I took to wearing. I felt the need to be sensible and grown up like a proper wife. Patty came round to dinner shortly after I married and was horrified to hear me discuss the virtues of a Kenwood Chef we'd received as a wedding present; she told me that I'd gone from twenty-nine to forty-nine overnight. We fell out over that but she was right. I hadn't even unpacked the damn thing anyway.

I look more like the young me now. The hair's not as thick but it's long and wavy, not at all sensible older woman. I want to be rid of her and have the adventures I always said I would. I haven't been dumped, I've been liberated.

'I'm no longer going to be dull old Angela Hargreaves,' I declare.

Patty waits.

'From now on I'm Angie Shepherd – back from the ashes.'

'Bo Peep returns, hurrah,' toasts Patty.

I'd forgotten about that nickname.

Wonderwoman

My mum is delighted to hear I've ditched Hargreaves and re-taken the family name.

'It tells him you've moved on,' she asserts.

Patty and I nod at her sage words. They've both come round to help me assemble two bedside tables which turned out to be flat pack. Patty brought a screwdriver and Mum a packet of chocolate digestives.

'I tell you what else you should do now you're a single woman in the modern world,' Mum continues.

We wait for the oracle to speak.

'That thing Stephen Fry does…what's it called again… twerking.'

Patty snorts her coffee.

'I don't think you mean that, Mum,' I say.

'Yes I do; all the celebrities do it, including her with the huge bum. Go on, look it up.'

I try to stop Patty but she's having too much fun. She pulls up a video and we stare at the rather instructional video.

'Stephen Fry never does that does he?' asks my horrified mother.

Of course Patty has to give it a go and it isn't pleasant.

'You mean tweeting, Mum,' I explain and yank the tablet from Patty to show her our National Treasure's Twitter account.

I've never bothered with social media but sign up just to keep Mum happy. I'm @AngieShepherd53 and have a picture of little Bo Beep as my avatar. I follow Josie, Charlie, Sarah Millican and the bookstore. Patty and Mum also join up and start following me. Now I must think of a witty first tweet. Patty doesn't want to be seen following dullards so I must not just say Hello. Here goes…

@AngieShepherd53 *Hello everyone out there*

Oh well – it's a start.

February is fast drawing to a close and I need to get a move on with the rest of my magic wand actions. I really want to start helping Charlie with the business. You'd think with it being so cold and dark, people would want to book holidays and get away. However, many of our customers are already away at their winter retreats and the store was a bit too quiet today.

The new dynamic Angie Shepherd wouldn't settle for that: she'd be thinking of ideas to drum up trade, she'd put down the remainder of the choccy biccies and leaflet the streets or something. She'd save the travel industry single-handedly and be showered with business awards. That's the type of woman I imagine her to be.

I put the TV on mute and start scribbling some ideas down. Gradually though, I get more and more engrossed in the crime drama unfolding. I love a good murder mystery even if it's a twenty-year-old episode of *Columbo* like this one. Perhaps I'll be dynamic from tomorrow.

My phone rings mid-biscuit and I have to leave the good detective to his work; Caroline is giving me no choice in the matter.

'Well, the month is nearly over,' she reminds me. 'How are you getting on with your magic wand life?'

'Really well,' I try to convince her, mumbling through crumbs.

'I went straight out and had my hair done, bought new clothes. The mirror exercise shocked me into action and everyone's noticed the difference.'

She isn't fooled.

'That's fabulous but let's be honest, it's easy to sit in a chair and let someone make a fuss over you. Anything else to report? What about your career? Meeting people?'

I get over the gentle scolding and tell Caroline about signing on to internet dating next month and the work idea I have but need to discuss with Charlie. It seems too simple to work, so I'm sure someone else must have tried it and failed.

'You're giving up before you start then?' asks Caroline.

I can now see that life coaches have to be benevolent bullies as well as magic-wand wavers.

'Who do you know who has tried your idea?' she continues to challenge.

My silence leads to her next question.

'So it follows that you know no one who has failed either?'

'No – I guess not,' I squirm.

'And would it feel good to succeed, would it be fun?' she asks.

'Yes, it would be brilliant.'

'Louder.'

'YES, IT WOULD BE BRILLIANT,' I yell leaping up.

'Then go do it,' she tells me, 'and no excuses.'

Whoo-hoo, Angie Shepherd has left the sofa.

I practise my 'pitch' overnight and on the way to work, but I'm still nervous when I present the idea, even though it's only to Charlie.

'OK then, here's the thought…' I take a deep breath. 'There are lots of single people – like us – and older couples, empty nesters too. They've got time on their hands now but they're not sure what to do with it. The same old beach trips bore them. The single people don't know anyone to take and the couples have run out of conversation. We could bring people together with themed getaways, sophisticated but fun, like wine tastings in Bordeaux. On our trips there'd always be something to talk about and it doesn't matter if you don't know anyone at the start, you will do by the end.'

I pause and watch the cogs whirring across the table.

'And we could go along and make sure they're fun – enjoy ourselves a bit more,' I add.

Charlie beams.

'My Redcoat days return.'

He gives me a big kiss on the forehead.

'I love the new you,' he says.

I feel tingles of excitement. We get straight to work on the idea. As a trial run, I ask Caroline if we could do a themed weekend with the book club.

'I hope this doesn't look like I'm taking advantage of you because you're my life coach,' I tell her.

'Not at all,' she says, 'I love it. We could both advertise it in our shops; it might drum up trade for me too.'

I hadn't thought of that, but it might also work for other local shops too. First things first. We're reading a classic next time, Wilkie Collins' *The Woman in White*. This calls for a gothic castle getaway I think, so I leave Charlie to it. It doesn't take him long to find a perfect venue.

Josie designs some posters and rushes over to the print shop to have them produced; I take some copies to Caroline and we all tweet the idea. Fortunately everyone else has more than three followers. Caroline contacts all the book-club members with the idea, they re-tweet and now we just wait to see what they say.

We don't have to wait long. Social media works its magic and people seem keen to have a little escapism. Before long we're fully booked up and Charlie hugs me with delight as we confirm the final place.

I'm on a high too as I walk home. So far this year has been non-stop and I've done so much more than I ever would have done in my pre-divorce days. I've joined a book club, seen a life coach, changed my looks and become more dynamic at work. From the outside, it must look as if I'm some kind of superwoman.

This must be what they mean by getting on with it. I even have the theme tune to *Wonder Woman* running through my head as I trot along the street.

Best Friends

The post-adrenaline crash hits me as soon I as get home.

In the office, I'd been on a real high celebrating the bookings with Charlie, but now I'm back in this empty house with no one to tell. There's no one watching the sports too loudly, no one grunting a distracted 'well done' without looking up, no one waiting for dinner although he could have started it himself. All the niggles you think you'll never miss, but you do. I miss having someone to come home to.

It hits me so hard and I slump down on the sofa. This is it.

It isn't some temporary blip; this is the long term. This is how every day will be.

Some people love living alone, they even enjoy it, but I'm not sure I'll get ever used to it. It's so hard to imagine the rest of my life alone. The house is so quiet and having the radio on constantly to try and hide the fact just isn't working. They say life is short, but on the days I'm not working and don't speak to a soul, it feels very long.

I promised Caroline I'd work on my love life tonight and Patty is coming round later to look through the lonely hearts with me. Could I honestly face dating or getting to know someone new? I've heard that even online, the fifty-year-old men are looking for thirty-year-old women.

It would be so much easier if things could go back to how they were. Did I try hard enough to keep the family together and get Alan back or did I just let her take him like the last loaf on the shelf?

'No please, you have him, I insist.'

I wonder if Alan knows how much I've changed. I wonder if the new dynamic me is what he was looking for when he went off with Amanda.

Perhaps I should just let him know that we could give it another go.

'Don't you even think about it,' is the warning I get from Ms P.

She starts flicking through the dating ads.

'See,' she points out, 'there are plenty of fish still in the sea without you having to go back to that washed-up walrus.'

She divides the ads between us putting a little 'A' alongside some and a 'P' alongside others. I take a look through her selections; she's allocated herself the handsome twenty-somethings and given me the retirees who like long walks and sunsets.

'You like nature,' she says by way of explanation before pouncing on one ad and circling it twice. 'Look at this: handsome, sports car, own business. He could shake this cougar's cage any day.'

On behalf of all mothers of twenty-year-old men, I show my distaste. It's ignored.

'Or how about this one? Slightly older, likes fine wines, managing director. I'd keep him for best.'

Exasperated, I ask, 'What would you do if any guy actually asked you out?'

A Mata Hari style swish of the hair and a deep throaty voice declares, 'I'd have him covered in chocolate and sent to my room.'

'No you wouldn't, you haven't accepted a date in four years. You're a femme-fatale fraud Ms P.'

'What did you expect? He did die, you know,' she cries while stuffing everything in her bag and leaving.

'Pats, wait, I'm sorry.'

But she's gone.

The house falls silent again and I don't know what to do. I can't lose Patty too. I'd rather have her back than any man; after all, I've known her longer. I'll date the retirees if that's what it takes.

I try to call her but it goes straight to voicemail. I say I'm sorry for being so insensitive and ask her to call me back. By the time I go to bed, she still hasn't called. I leave one more message with another apology and say that I'll stay out of the way until she wants to speak to me again. I hope it sounds understanding rather than dismissive.

I fret about the tone of that message all night and am exhausted when I get up for work. I have a tediously long day waiting for some news. I try to focus and show a real interest in each customer but my heart isn't in it knowing what I've done to her.

This is worse than dating. Two days on and she still hasn't been in touch. I'm pacing the shop floor, I must have cleaned the brochure shelves a hundred times. We've got a lot to organise for this book weekend and I also want to speak to the wine merchants to see if they'd be interested in designing a tour, but I won't make a good impression like this. I have to do something because this is torture. Whatever happens next, I know that if someone had hurt me, I'd want them to keep saying sorry. So although I said I'd wait, I've sent a text to apologise. I've even put a little x on the bottom. I leave the phone at the office so that I'm not constantly checking it and trek over to the wine merchants to do my best to talk business, filling in the time until she calls me.

When I get back, I'm relieved to see that she's replied: 'SRY – BEING DAFT – WILL CALL ROUND TMRW x'

I will go to sleep happy tonight.

Come the morning, I can't focus on anything until I see Patty, so I decide to start unpacking some of the boxes I brought with me. It's a fairly random selection, packed when I wasn't thinking straight, so I have to smile to myself when I open one of them and find it full of my old fitness videos – yes tape and everything. Lord knows why I kept them in the first place never mind transporting them from house to house; I'm glad I did and I'm glad I kept our ancient video player for all our old family films.

First of all I pull out the incredible Jane Fonda – all leotards and leggings – *'feel the burn'* and *'if it ain't hurtin, it ain't workin'*. Like most people, I bought the video, but it turned out that you had to do the exercises, not just watch them. I remember Patty and I giggling at it while drinking a bottle of Frascati; we were yelling 'clench that butt Jane' at every sip. Not surprisingly, it didn't work for us.

I bought others hoping they'd suit me better. And I seem to remember every husband in the country buying their wives Cindy Crawford's video; they obviously thought that the sight of a supermodel frolicking on the beach in a swimsuit would make their other halves feel motivated and good about themselves. It didn't even have a good sound track – not like the one I find now: Paula Abdul's video. I loved this one.

I put it on and am immediately in full flow: Paula, 'Straight Up' and a rather energetic grapevine. I was always good at this aerobics step; I could put a bit of rhythm into it.

Next I find Cher. This one is insane. She's doing exercise in a dominatrix outfit! At least they play 'Addicted to Love'.

I have the broom handle slung low and am at one with Robert Palmer's backing singers when there is a knock on the door:

'Patty – I was just…'

'I know, I've been watching you through the window for ten minutes. Pass me that mop, Bo Peep.'

For the rest of the night Robert Palmer has two extra backing singers making him look good. Lucky man.

Blimey, I'm stiff the next day.

Several hours of 1980s fitness videos can do that to you. I creak my way to work grimacing with every movement. I'm sure someone is going to rush up to me any time soon and offer to oil my joints. When did I become this unfit? Surely once upon a time I was a fitness goddess? I shake that ridiculous notion away. That was never the case; I was just young.

Patty rings the office the moment I lower my damaged body into my chair. I put her on speaker to avoid having to lift anything.

'How are your thighs this morning?' she asks.

Not even a 'hello' then.

'Mine feel as if I've done twelve rounds on a bucking bronco – either the horse or sugar-daddy version.'

'Straddling the sofa arm doing an impression of Cher riding a cannon might do that to a girl,' I remind her.

The dirtiest laugh you'll ever hear fills the office. When she recovers she remembers why she called.

'I think we should go to a karaoke bar tomorrow night.'

My heart sinks.

'Oh Pats, I can't. Zoe will disown me,' I protest.

'Oh, she'll never know and anyway, you don't have to get up – just stand in the audience and applaud me. Come on, it'll be a laugh.'

I've opened Pandora's Box by getting those videos out. I weigh up my options and they seem to be:

1. Turn Patty down and risk hurting her just when I've re-gained her friendship.

2. Agree to go along, stay sober and applaud Patty's efforts all night, thereby eradicating all memory of whatever I did to offend her.

I have to go with the second option and Patty's right, Zoe will never know.

The Granny-Okes

Patty has chosen Valentine's Day for our night out arguing that the married men will be in restaurants so anyone we find in a karaoke bar is fair game; here was I thinking we were going for a singalong.

I wonder what Alan is getting his new woman today. He always used to get me 'one red rose for my one English rose'. I used to find it romantic but when I think about it now, he was probably just too cheapskate to buy me a dozen. Still, I'd have been ecstatic if either the postman or the flower store had knocked on my door this morning. I wonder if they can tell from the flower selections which bouquet is for a wife and which for a mistress?

I have a flick through the local paper smiling at all the romantic messages in the classifieds; it's a strange place to declare your love.

My jaw drops.

Amanda, A Single Rose for My English Rose, Alan xx

I've always known he could be pretty thoughtless but does he not have an original idea in his head? Is it any wonder middle-aged women are turning to alcohol in droves? Our husbands and ex-husbands are practically pouring it down our necks with their thoughtlessness.

Furious, I call Patty. I don't give a damn what anyone thinks. I was demure and wife-like for years – look where it got me.

'Can we leave now?' I ask her.

Come the early evening, we're in the karaoke bar having already enjoyed a glass or two en route. Despite the fact that I know I'm tone deaf, I start to feel the bravery that comes free with every bottle of wine.

'Let's do it,' I whisper much to Patty's delight.

'True Colours' follows 'Material Girl', which follows 'Hey Mickey'. We have to be forced off the stage in the end.

A century of womanhood being thoroughly shameless and we feel not a shred of embarrassment about any of it. It is a truly wonderful night.

The morning after...

Patty came back here last night but I can't remember much more and I think we went to bed pretty quickly after a bloody good night out. I'm still smiling as I put the kettle on and my phone beeps to tell me that I have lots of texts and emails.

I flick through the messages. Some people lament that texting is very impersonal, but let's face it – it saves conversations you don't want. Anyway lots of people are telling me I was hilarious last night, not sure how they know that. One from Charlie says: **WAY TO GO CYNDI!!;)** How bizarre.

I pop the phone in my dressing gown pocket then fill two cups and take them up to Patty.

'Wakey, wakey,' I call.

Patty is already awake, staring at her phone with her mouth wide open.

'What's up?' I ask.

'We're only bloody trending.'

I know this means there are lots of people talking about us on the internet, but why would people want to talk about us?

I sit down beside Patty and look at all the comments. It's not just us they're talking about; after all, there are two other members of the new singing sensations – the Granny-Okes.

The finer details of last night start coming back to me, and with each memory, I die a little; Zoe will surely disown me. The karaoke bar turned out to be quite sophisticated and hi-tech with a live YouTube stream (and to think a stream used to be a lovely babbling brook not a source of live humiliation).

So I know for sure that we did blast out our favourite tunes and now it appears that we did this with two other fifty-somethings, Sheila and Kath (who were actually rather good), according to their morning messages. YouTube is a wonderful invention: not only can people watch us plastered but they can comment on our efforts too – hence the new band name.

Our bleeding hearts followed 'Don't You Want Me' (which I do remember) with 'Tainted Love', which involved lots of slurring and a big chorus. The crescendo of the night was no less than that female anthem, 'I will Survive' or 'Sh-ur-vive' as we sang it.

Well having seen this I'm not sure that I will survive.

I don't go outdoors or take any calls over Sunday and manage to avoid speaking to anyone. I have a very long bath to try to wash my embarrassment away. I eat salad and drink herbal tea as penance for any humiliation I may have caused and when I go to bed unscathed, I pray that my daughter hasn't had time to watch YouTube.

Monday unfortunately arrives and I can hide no more; I have to go into work knowing that Charlie and Josie have already viewed my performance because they've commented. I'm dreading it, really dreading it.

I walk in and smile as if nothing has happened.

'Morning – lovely day,' I call out and for those first five minutes, I think I might have got away with it as they just politely nod back.

I'm about to sit down when Charlie beckons me over.

'Could you just take a look at this?' he asks as he hunches over the PC with Josie, their backs to me.

I walk up to them and they spin around, whipping off their jackets to reveal T-shirts printed with downloaded photographs of the Granny-Okes stage performance. Oh Lord, can something be horrifying and hilarious at the same time?

'You were so funny, I've told everyone that I know you,' gushes Josie.

'Why didn't you do any Culture Club?' asks Charlie doing his best Boy George sway.

'That's not about heartache,' explains Josie earnestly. 'We felt your pain you know.'

'Her pain? What about mine? My bloody eardrums were bleeding.'

I bash Charlie over the head with a brochure. He ribs me all day long, but then he always does. Everything is back to normal and I did survive.

I guess the song was right after all.

Well almost.

'Video this time, Mum, video the whole world can see. What were you thinking?' Zoe is fuming. 'I begged you not to do something like this. I mean four old women trying to recapture their youth. Why not go the whole hog, get four old bald blokes and form a boy band too? No wonder he left you.'

I go from sorry to angry with this last remark. I don't get angry very often; I think most wives and mothers learn to grit their teeth at an early stage otherwise we'd explode on a daily basis.

What I want to say is: 'I did this BECAUSE he left me. I'm hurting too you know. And I'm not old; I'm only fifty-three. Hell, we lived through some of the most hedonistic years ever. None of this austerity for us; we were punks, new romantics, glam rockers and ska-kids. We brought the banking system down way before you did. We had yuppies, huge mobile phones, political protests AND the boys wore more make-up than the women. We knew how to party.'

But what I actually say is, 'Oh come on Zoe, it was only a bit of fun; it'll be forgotten about by tomorrow. Anyway, I bet The Bangles look like us now.'

Getting on with It

I'm in a department store with Alan and Zoe; they're choosing Hawaiian shirts of all things.

They're discussing each gaudy option with great gusto but ignoring my desperate protests. I keep telling them the shirts are awful but they just won't listen; it's as if I'm not there.

Then I notice that I'm on the outside of the store shouting through the windowpane.

'Alan would never wear these monstrosities,' I yell, hammering on the glass.

Then Amanda comes into the shop and they all turn round to face me. I see that I'm in black and white while they're in colour.

'You don't belong here any more,' mouths Alan. 'Go away.'

Smiling, he puts his arms around both women and turns them away from me.

And with that I'm banished from my own dream.

I wake myself up feeling shattered and newly bereft.

I have to make it up to Zoe otherwise she'll end up being ashamed to see me. I call her and invite her for Sunday lunch.

She's reluctant to accept but I plead, saying that I have to apologise somehow. When she agrees I breathe a sigh of relief.

Rescued.

I make a real effort and Zoe looks surprised when I open the door to her. Following THAT video, I think she was expecting me to look like a text-book relationship car crash, but I put my makeover into full throttle and I can see she's impressed.

'Wow – you look amazing,' she declares as she walks in, 'really amazing. I wasn't expecting this at all.'

For the rest of the day I keep noticing her looking me up and down.

After my dream I'd been ready to throw myself into Zoe's arms and beg her to come and live with me for ever. I'd ask her to speak to Alan and tell him it had all been a dreadful mistake; we all needed to be together. That was the natural order and it had to be restored.

Instead, I feel a sense of pride in Zoe's voice and decide to live up to my image.

'Thanks, a quick G&T before dinner?' asks my fake confident self.

I feel as if I'm working in First Class again; I'm the perfect hostess making polite conversation. Zoe tells me all about her work. The hotel is doing well but taking up all of her time.

'A new career always takes up all your time,' I tell her. 'When people talk about work-life balance they mean that you get your first twenty years to yourself and then your last twenty years – but the forty in between you have to slog it out.'

'Oh well, at least I'm enjoying it,' she answers raising her drink to me.

I tell her about the book-club weekend away and our idea to try to do more events to boost sales. My daughter and I are having a grown-up conversation.

Rioja follows the G&T.

'Don't you want to know how Dad is?' Zoe is very tentative in introducing the elephant to the room.

Thinks: *'Of course I do, despite everything I'm desperate to hear that he's missing me and that it's not working out with that floozy or that he looks awful, is going bald and getting flabby. It's all I've wanted to talk about since you got here.'*

Says: 'How is he?'

With a gulp of wine Zoe sighs.

'He's fine, put on a bit of weight with all that baking, but fine. Amanda takes the lead in most things. She's got him entering this Entrepreneur of the Year competition and even ballroom dancing of all things. She probably takes the lead in that too.'

I smile picturing poor Alan being dragged around a glitter ballroom – serves him right.

'Their apartment is nice.' Her voice lowers. 'But it's not home…when the house sells, nowhere will be.'

And then it comes: the tears, the hugs, the relief.

We don't have to pretend any more. I am no longer the professional hostess, the got-it-together divorcee. I'm Mum again and for a moment, Zoe is my little girl. It feels so good as I hold her close and inhale her very being. We eventually let go of each other when the snot threatens to subsume us.

'I know it's not much but wherever I am, you have a home. You can move in with me any time, right now if you like,' I say.

'I'm assistant manager, I can't move back in with my mother. Besides, look at you, there's no way you want me cramping your style. You've moved on, I can see that.'

I reassure Zoe that she can move in or stay or squat whenever she wants and promise to buy her some PJs that will always be here ready for her.

She's staying the night now and as I clear away our dishes, I can't help wondering just what people want me to do.

When I was a physical wreck, I was told to pull myself together. Now that I've camouflaged the broken bits, I'm told that I've moved on too much to share a home with. Do I have to fix everyone around me before I'm allowed to fix myself?

Come morning, I despatch my daughter back to work and within ten minutes of saying goodbye to her, Patty appears. I must get a security guard; no wait, that'll encourage her even more.

'How was prodigal daughter?' Patty makes a beeline for the kitchen and helps herself to the cheesecake Zoe brought round. It is common knowledge that Zoe always brings a home-made dessert when she goes anywhere for dinner and I imagine Patty has been camping outside waiting for her to go so that she can get stuck in.

I sigh and let loose.

'She thinks I don't need her any more. Apparently, I look as if I've got it together and I've done all of these new things and… well I'm not old Mum I guess. She was quite upset.'

I pause for a reaction, but her mouth is full so I continue.

'I don't know what I'm supposed to do. Fade away into the background in case I offend anyone? Give up, wear sweatpants and appear on *Jeremy Kyle*? I didn't ask for this; I wanted to stay married. I can't go back, I have to move on and I'm doing it the only way I know how – I'm not an expert in "how to be divorced" after all.'

I breathe and wait for the reply. Nothing.

'Patty. Say something.'

'Blimey. Just waiting for a gap. Nobody wants you to appear on *Jeremy Kyle*. We want you to be happy but you've got to admit that your transformation from housewife to hotty has been fairly rapid. Zoe isn't used to thinking of her mum as a woman with a life of her own.'

'Hotty? Me? That's ludicrous.'

'Remember Martin?' asks Patty.

'Plumber Martin, the one you wanted to look at your pipes?'

She nods. 'That's the one; he asked me out for a drink a few weeks back.'

'Wow, tell all.'

'Just before Valentine's Day. I actually went out on a date for the night, one that didn't involve you for a change.'

She laughs in despair.

'I got dolled up, new clothes, underwear – the works. Got there fashionably late thinking, "Look at me in a fancy wine bar with a new man." Honestly, I was the proverbial cat with the cream.'

'What happened?' I ask.

'He wanted *your* number.' She prods me painfully as she says it.

My jaw and then the penny drops.

'Surely we didn't fall out over that?' I ask.

'I know,' replies Patty, 'I was being daft, but I'd plucked up the courage to have my first date in four years, as you kindly reminded me, and all he wanted was your number.'

Patty starts laughing and although I was trying to be sympathetic, I do the same.

'Anyway, I thought about setting up a new business pimping you out: "*Ancient but well-preserved skinny bird available for hire*". I could hand out leaflets on the street or build a website with a link to YouTube – no, on second thoughts your singing would put them off straight away.'

'Cheeky cow.'

We wipe our tears.

'So we're good now?' I venture.

'We're fabulous dahling, always have been.' She embraces me in a bear hug and gives me a big kiss.

'Why don't you come with me next weekend?' I ask. 'It's the book-club trip.'

'Do I have to read something?' she asks and I give her a sarcastic look in return.

'It's a ghost story, you'll enjoy it,' I tell her. 'We're taking everyone to a gothic castle. It'll be nice and spooky.'

'Well, I always did enjoy having the willies…' she starts.

'Stop now,' I despair.

'I'll behave, I promise,' she smiles. 'And yes I'd love to come; you probably couldn't manage without me anyway.'

'True,' I surrender. 'Here's the book you need.'

I hold out the copy I've just finished reading.

'Is there a DVD I can watch instead?'

I throw the book at her and she catches it before sauntering out.

Having restored two of my closest relationships, I think I deserve some me time. That means a little *Murder She Wrote* with a bar of Galaxy. I pop to the corner shop and when I get back my new best friend is waiting on the doorstep.

She's a tortoiseshell with little white paws. She seemed to adopt me a couple of weeks ago and I call her Socks (yes, I know – hardly imaginative) as she doesn't wear a collar. I don't think she's a stray but she's the only one who doesn't seem to have an opinion on my state of being, so she's a very welcome visitor. I invite her in to solve the crime with me and give her some tuna. In return I receive a grateful purr and a snuggle on the sofa.

Girl Power restored.

Let Me Out...

What a whirlwind. I'm officially hot (well according to one middle-aged plumber) and I've managed to upset those around me as a result. I could decide to keep my head down, and in fact that might be safer for all concerned. These thoughts are running through my mind as I sit in the office getting ready for the weekend. I determine to host this book-club retreat professionally but otherwise keep myself to myself. I picture myself as an elegant and respected hostess.

The only flaw in this plan is that I'm quite flattered. Me, hot. It doesn't matter who pays the compliment, I'd defy anyone not to have a spring in their step after hearing that. I don't want to retreat back into my shell; when I stop to notice, I realise I've started to enjoy myself.

I do so want this weekend to be good, for everyone to have fun, to tell other people and for it to lead to lots more business. Patty and I are heading up tonight so that I can check things out before Charlie and the guests arrive on Saturday. I have time to do something to make it extra special, I just need some ideas. I've already written welcome cards, had a little gift pack made and sent out the directions. It all looks great, but I'm wondering whether there is some icing missing from the cake.

A search around the internet and I have what I'm looking for: the hotel is apparently haunted. A tour of the cellars will be a perfect way to start the reading.

I'm on fire now, so I book myself a wee treat at the spa – a hot stone massage. Well you might as well give it a go – she who dares and all that.

I must remember to shave my legs before I venture into the spa. For a brief second I am lost in thought trying to remember the last time I did that. I think it may have been nearly a year ago.

I start by smearing a whole tube of extra-strong hair-removing cream on my legs and leaving it on for slightly longer than the packet advised. I shower it off and still look like Chewbacca; I'll be making a case under the Trades Description Act tomorrow.

After that I try to master the art of waxing. 'Simple, easy to use strips' – no they're not. Heat wax up, smother over leg and rip it off? It mentions nothing about how you get it off the towels and carpet when it drips everywhere. Who would do this regularly? And I know they don't stop at their legs. Having cried out in pain trying to rip one strip off, I cannot imagine who decided this would be a good thing to apply to your privates. I cringe even thinking about it.

In the end I decide to go back to the old-fashioned method and take an industrial-strength razor with me to wield when I get to the hotel; my legs are already crying out for their human rights. The razor isn't a girly pink one but a Macho Glide, the type I used to steal from Alan (light-bulb moment: that might be the last time I shaved them). Men don't realise how lucky they are not having to do this; apart from Olympic cyclists and drag queens, of course.

It's a long drive up to the Eden Valley, so Patty has come equipped with the contents of Willy Wonka's factory.

'We'll have diabetes by the time we get there with that lot,' I say.

'Rubbish,' replies Patty. 'Here, have a gobstopper.'

After a singalong to Absolute 80s radio, we hit a signal black-spot and no amount of twiddling with the knob helps to restore sound.

'What shall we do now?' asks Patty like a needy child.

'We could play a game,' I suggest. 'When I was a kid, we used to try to make words out of the last three letters on a car registration.'

'Sounds a bit dull.'

'Well you come up with something better then,' I tell her.

'OK Bo, keep your knickers on, we'll give it a go,' says Patty scanning the cars that drive past.

'Here you go – XPT – make a word out of that.'

We both sit silently for a moment.

'Got one,' exclaims Patty, 'Sexy-Pants.'

'That's not one word,' I say.

'I hyphenated it,' she tells me. 'Anyway, you do better.'

'Exasperated,' I sigh.

At which point we leave the signal blackspot and Patty starts a duet with Billy Idol.

We turn off the M6, go through Kirkby Stephen and before long we turn into the long driveway of Craghill Castle. I tingle with anticipation as the building comes into view; it is stunning. I have a feeling that this is going to be a very good weekend.

We check in and are shown our rooms. The whole place looks perfect. We drop Patty off first and then I get to my room. The concierge opens the door on to a suite with a huge four-poster bed; they obviously want to impress the organisers. They've taken care with the décor, using contemporary colours and fabrics that complement the age of the building without being simply chintzy.

'My room is FABULOUS,' declares Patty as she bursts into mine. 'Much bigger than this. I could get an entire rugby squad in there.'

It's a big relief that the hotel is so wonderful because the March weather is awful: dark and stormy, yet perfect for a ghost story I suppose. If the sky could summon up some thunder and lightning when people are safely here, that would be perfect.

Patty and I have a calm evening of good food and warming wine. I check a few details with the manager and we both retire to our bedrooms.

When I open my eyes and remember where I am this morning, a surge of happiness flows through me. I now know how cats feel when they do that big stretch. I snuggle down to enjoy the moment and drink it all in; the softest pillows, the firmest mattress, most luxurious linen and knowing that I don't have to wash or iron any of it, I could live like this for ever. Eventually I have to get up, if only to take full advantage of further luxury, a breakfast beyond Weetabix.

'Here's to the magic wand.' I raise a glass of freshly squeezed orange juice to Patty. 'We wouldn't be here without it.'

Patty picks up a silver fork. 'I hereby command this wand to bring me the perfect book-club stud tonight: brains and brawn, handsome and humorous, charming and cheerful.' She skewers a sausage on to it and waves it in the air just to ensure the spell is cast.

'So just stay out the way missus.' And she chomps off a warning-sized bite.

I'd love Patty to meet someone but I can't remember anyone like that at the book club, maybe flirty Peter at a push.

The book-club members arrive throughout the day and Charlie calls me at lunchtime to tell me he's in his room. From the joy in his voice, his room is every bit as gorgeous as ours.

We all gather together for drinks at six in the gothic dining room. Everyone's delight over the accommodation is followed by excitement at the appearance of the hotel manager looking every inch the Victorian undertaker; this is my surprise for them.

'We're here to read about a haunting; a woman in white I believe,' he declares as the book club hangs on his every word. 'And while you may feel safe when the undead are confined to the pages of a book...'

Dramatic pause.

'How will you feel when a troubled soul walks amongst you?'

Nervous laughter all round – this guy should be on the stage.

We're given a lantern between two and the tour of the hotel vaults begins. Dark and draughty, it sees me clinging on to Caroline and I can see that Patty is doing the same with Peter (she grabbed him rather quickly). I can't see Charlie anywhere; I hope he's not going to miss this.

Our guide stops by a huge wooden door.

'Many years ago these vaults were sealed...to hide a terrible crime...Mary Argyll, a young woman betrothed to the Old Laird but in love with another, was imprisoned here until she denounced that love. Locked up in her long white wedding gown she refused to name her true love and so the Laird threw away the key.'

We're on tenterhooks.

'Sometimes you can still hear her calling, "Let me out, please let me out", and rapping on the door of her prison cell. But here she died. Many years later, her body was taken and given a Christian burial, still wearing that fateful white gown. Let's go and pay our respects to her now.'

We turn away from the door and start moving forward – but then it begins: a slow hammering on the door, louder and louder, then a cry, 'Let me out, please let me out.' We scream and I dodge behind Caroline, coward that I am. Our guide raises his lantern.

'Mary is that you?'

At this point there is a pulse-raising scream and the door bursts open – a bloodied woman in a tattered white wedding dress. We scatter then eventually turn to check out our ghost.

'Charlie!'

Top marks for effort; he arranged this with the manager when he heard we were touring the vaults. I wouldn't have hidden in that room all night. The club members loved it and over dinner as everyone discusses the book, the castle and the *'definite eerie atmosphere in the vaults'*, I relax a little. Our first venture has gone well, even if it does feel as if I'm in an episode of *Scooby-Doo*. I wonder which character I am.

On Sunday morning we're free to relax and enjoy the grounds; the rain has mercifully stopped and the lawns are luminous green as they always are after a spring downpour. Daffodils are starting to bloom and I feel as if the heavens have conspired to make things as perfect as they could be for me. I say a little 'thank you' under my breath. I bump into Charlie on the way to the spa and arrange to meet in the car park before we go our separate ways. The massage is a little strange. I hadn't known what to expect (maybe the stones were used to warm up the room like in a sauna?), but it turns out that in a hot stone massage they actually heat up some pebbles and rub them over your back. I ask myself, who was the first person that thought this might be something people would pay to have done?

Anyway, it's time to leave this wonderful place so I head to our rendezvous where Charlie is already waiting.

'Has Patty surfaced yet?' I ask.

Charlie nods to the hotel entrance where Patty is giggling and leaning into Peter. He's jotting something down.

'Blimey – he's giving her his number.'

'Hardly likely, sweetie,' he assures me.

At that point Patty storms towards us and thrusts the note into Charlie's hand.

'First her and now you; apparently I'm a gay pimp-too.'

I clasp my mouth to hide the laughter. Charlie gets out his mobile phone and starts scanning Patty's body up and down making beeping noises as he does it; she bats him away.

'Yes,' he says, 'I can confirm that there is no gaydar fitted to this vintage model; I repeat, no gaydar.'

Charlie gets pelted with a mint humbug from Patty's pocket.

'Didn't fancy him anyway,' says Patty.

Necker Island, Here I Come

I'm lying in bed reminiscing about the weekend and feeling just a bit chuffed; maybe this is my thing? Perhaps I could have been a hot-shot entrepreneur if I hadn't got married or poured all of my now obvious talent into Alan's business. As I savour my coffee and toast, I imagine my ascension to Richard Branson's inner circle and the fame it brings. I'm profiled in all the top business magazines, the former stewardess who turns around high street travel. I'd be photographed in my old uniform – or maybe the title of the article would be 'From Stewardess to Captain of Industry' and I'd be in a pilot's uniform. I'd look assertive and serious – no maybe not, maybe the exact opposite of that – I'd be relaxing on Necker Island, cocktail in hand, enjoying the fruits of my success. Perhaps both; after all, it'd run to more than one page. In the interview, I'd make very pertinent points:

> *Society forgets that over fifties were the wild childs of the 1980s. We applaud the vigour of Mick Jagger and Madonna but somehow we forget the ordinary man and woman. My business keeps the adventure of youth going.*

I like that last line and say it over and over again in my head, just to get the perfect tone. Of course they'll profile me, say I have a daughter and that I'm divorced. Now, shall I tell them Alan dumped me for a younger model or should I stay magnanimous? Definitely magnanimous; in fact I won't mention him at all.

Ooh, now there's an idea. I grab my phone and search for the local business awards; I remember Zoe saying Alan was entering them this year. What if I entered too and beat him? They say that the best revenge is a life well lived, but sometimes it's also nice to take a swipe at your ex along the way. I find the Entrepreneur of the Year awards and see that Amanda has been a runner-up three years running. I feel vindicated for some reason (cruelly thinking that she always seems to end up with seconds) and know that I have to enter and I have to win. The A-team with their black-tie dinners; I'll show them. I can see myself floating between the tables, getting to the stage to rounds of applause. It's just like the Oscars and I look fabulous in a full-length gown, the type Julia Roberts would wear. I look intelligent and classy. My nemesis will have to grin and bear it as Richard Branson congratulates me on my achievements and wishes every community had someone as dynamic as me. I raise a toast to thank those who've helped me along the way:

'To Caroline for believing in me and to Charlie – for helping me take those first steps…'

As I thrust my imaginary champagne glass up for a toast, I forget that I'm holding a rather full mug and so manage to throw tepid coffee all over myself and my favourite jammies.

'Aargh.'

Naturally, I leap up causing the plate to overturn and buttered toast to smear all over the duvet – it couldn't fall dry-side down, could it?

Award ceremony over I guess as I extract myself from the mess. My spirit is not dampened, though.

I'm going to win this.

I don't have to persuade Charlie as last week's success has given him a new lease of life, too. When I walk into the shop today, I can see he's been dying for us to get there. He has transformed himself into the host with the most with a new blazer, buttonhole and if that isn't a dab of fake tan, he must be extremely flushed with excitement.

'My Angels,' he declares, 'we know we can just make it up and make it happen; we can give people a good time.'

All of a sudden we're his Angels and he's a visionary leader but nothing wrong with that.

'We've seen that if we have an idea, we can get people booking those holidays, soooo…'

Quiet anticipation from Josie and me.

'I hereby announce the very first Big Ideas Night. We'll get together after work, I'll supply snacks and brain juice, then we'll come up with loads of great ideas for trips.'

I don't like to point out that his brainstorming acronym is BIN as I'm quite happy to have something to do in the evening and who knows, it might get me closer to Richard.

For the rest of the day, Charlie and I manage to talk about everything but Peter and then just as we shut up the shop he breaks.

'Come on, ask me.'

'Ask you what?' I say innocently.

'You know full well and the answer is yes – I called him.'

Josie's ears prick up and she joins us. 'Called who?'

Josie baulked at the idea of spending a weekend talking about books, but if she'd thought there could be romance on offer she might have taken up the invitation to join us.

'Charlie picked up a hot date at the weekend,' I tell her, 'a twinkly-eyed Irishman.'

'Good one, boss,' she high-fives him in appreciation.

'He's invited me round for dinner next week.'

Josie squeals, 'A dinner party? Charlie, he's your magic wand man, he must be.'

'What will you wear?' she adds in a serious tone.

This is the most important question of the day and with the gravity of debate that now ensues, I'm surprised Radio 2 haven't debated it on the *Jeremy Vine* show: '*Call in and tell us what you think. It's a first date scenario, do you go casual or smart?*'

I leave them to it and decide it might be useful to invite Patty and Caroline to the BIN. I'm just about to do so when Patty must have read my mind. My mobile starts singing 'Material Girl' (I've surprised myself by learning how to change ringtones and this is especially for Ms P).

'Patty, I was just about to call you. Do you fancy coming to a brainstorming we're having for work?'

'Never mind that; we won't have time for such trivial matters soon. You'll never guess what's happened,' she gushes.

'George Clooney has declared that his human rights lawyer wife is too intense for him and he'd rather spend his life with a karaoke singer?' I suggest.

'He might just say that in a few months' time. Go on – guess,' she urges.

'I can't – just tell me.'

'You and I are going to be famous,' she gushes. 'We're re-forming the Granny-Okes.'

After our drunken performance, the karaoke club had lots of people asking when we'd be back. They got hold of Sheila and Kath through their Facebook pages and have asked us to do a few sessions to get the crowd singing.

'They're going to put a banner up to advertise us, too.'

I'm truly horrified at the very idea.

My first thought is, 'What will Richard Branson think of that?'

I don't want to see myself plastered across a banner. A few hours ago I was an award-winning entrepreneur and now I'm a karaoke attraction?

Zoe will definitely disown me this time.

'Why don't I just stay backstage and manage you instead?' I proffer. 'After all, the highly successful Bananarama were a trio.'

There are howls of protest from Ms P.

'Noooo…I have big plans for you. Don't worry, it'll be fabulous.'

My heart and soul plummet.

BIN

To distract myself from the inevitable humiliation of the first practice session this weekend, I get back to my goal of becoming an award-winning entrepreneur with the inaugural BIN session.

I've been to Charlie's before but the place never ceases to enthral me; I could get lost here for days. Books, books and more books, and not the tasteful classic literature that you find on many a middle-aged bookshelf but ream upon ream of general knowledge. Travel books of course, piles of them, but 'how to' guides too. How to Hypnotise, Bluff Your Way in Wine, Decorate Like a Pro, Train Dogs, Escape an Avalanche, Speak Portuguese; you name it, he has a book for it. I'm sure I could take a holiday in Charlie's house and come out a fortnight later a qualified surgeon. I love it.

Caroline has brought along Ed, although from our very brief meeting, I wouldn't have thought this was his type of thing. She volunteers to lead the session and kicks off by giving us each a book and a random object. We have to think of a trip inspired by these objects. I'm given *The Goldfinch* and a pencil sharpener, and pulling a face, I start.

'Goldfinch, golden triangle, Bermuda Triangle, Bermuda,' I start, 'sharp, harp, carp – deep-sea fishing in Bermuda.'

Ed has *The Dice Man* and a teabag; Caroline obviously spent an absolute fortune on these props. He goes for it, too.

'Dice, black-jack, casinos; tea, cups, win the cup,' he says, 'winning weekends – Ascot then the World Cup with a casino in the evening.'

He might be quiet but he has something there.

'And we could also draw one of the customers out of a hat at the end and they get a bottle of champagne. It could be our thing, when you book with us you might win something,' adds Charlie.

We all like this concept – you book up for a few trips with us and it becomes a sort of a social group with surprises thrown in. Customers would get to know each other and eventually start to book up together.

'Charlie,' I think out loud, 'we could call it the Mercury Travel Club. Customers sign up for a year and every quarter we take a week away. We could add wine themes to the book weekends and then the prize would be a case; for example, we might go to France for the Bordeaux and Bovary.'

'It's not only wine, but cocktails are making a comeback too. They're being served in jam jars now.' Josie knows these things.

'Ooh, that might be a bit different – where did cocktails originate?' I ask.

'London,' Ed tells us in a dour but factual voice, 'but most people would associate them with New York, manhattans and all that.'

'Now we're talking, manhattans in Manhattan; I'd go for that,' declares Patty.

'Reading *Breakfast at Tiffany's*; that has to be your Christmas trip,' adds Caroline.

By now the room is buzzing and Charlie looks rather gobsmacked. We all stop talking and he starts asking lots of questions like, 'Won't that be expensive?' and 'Will people sign up for a full year?' None of us knows the answers but it would be an amazing club to join.

We have to give it a go.

Testing, Testing

The day of reckoning has arrived: the Granny-Okes have their first practice session tonight. I haven't been able to concentrate all day and now, in precisely one hour, I will be humiliated beyond recovery. Let's look on the bright side – there's a good chance I might be dropped from the group when they hear me sing sober.

Nevertheless, I don't want to be *told* that I'm awful; it's one thing knowing but quite another to be informed of the fact. It would be like netball team selections during PE lessons all over again. A girl of my height had to be spectacularly dreadful not to get picked until they were dividing up the last resorts.

I'm not sure how to prepare, whether to take a lozenge or something. Maybe do some scales? I put on some music to get me in the mood; a little 'Like a Virgin' I think.

Now, I have never thought this a challenging track to sing; in fact in either the shower or the car, I manage a spectacular rendition. However, when I have to stay in tune for the duration, well let's just say that even the *X Factor* singing coaches would have their work cut out for them. I will have that lozenge.

I arrive first, so get my excuses in early.

'Patty,' I whimper, 'I do know that I can't sing. You don't have to protect me. I'll go now.'

'That's utter rubbish, Bo,' she replies.

She is incredibly officious tonight. There is no wine in sight; instead glasses of water and lyric sheets are neatly arranged on the table. Sheila and Kath arrive and the room is filled with an excited buzz – I feel such a fraud. Patty takes charge.

'I think we need to start with a set list so that we're only practising numbers that we'll do.'

We all nod at the sensible suggestion; as long as Patty keeps talking, I delay the moment of humiliation.

'I thought that we should have songs from throughout the decade so I've compiled this list of top 10 hits from every year.'

She hands out the lists and instantly we start reminiscing over each track.

'Ah, "When Doves Cry", I went camping with Peter Matthews to that one,' says Sheila.

'"Ebony and Ivory", the dullest song ever made,' adds Kath.

'"Mull of Kintyre" is probably joint dullest; McCartney had a knack for them,' I say.

'There are some tracks we wouldn't have thought of that might be good,' suggests Patty.

We wait to hear…

'Like The Clash.'

Our raised eyebrows prompt her on.

'"Should I Stay or Should I Go" would be a brilliant Granny-Oke song. We have to think about the whole performance and that could be our finale.'

Patty has been working on this quite seriously. When I have my day with Richard Branson, I imagine she'll be having a similar session with Simon Cowell.

She then gives us her suggested shortlist:

1. 'Like a Virgin' (Madonna – 1985)
2. 'Push It' (Salt-N-Pepa – 1987)
3. 'Livin' On A Prayer' (Bon Jovi – 1986)
4. 'Karma Chameleon' (Culture Club – 1983)
5. 'Girls Just Wanna Have Fun' (Cyndi Lauper – 1984)
6. 'Should I Stay or Should I Go' (The Clash – 1982)
7. '9 to 5' (Dolly Parton – 1981)
8. 'I'm In The Mood For Dancing' (The Nolans – 1980)
9. 'Pink Cadillac' (Natalie Cole – 1988)
10. 'Love Shack' (B-52's – 1989)

My first thought was 'I wonder how Joe Strummer feels being sandwiched between Cyndi and Dolly', and the second was, 'Yep, I'd listen to this set.'

'No one wants to hear a pitch-perfect bore belting out power ballads time after time,' Patty continues. 'Anyone can do that. We've got to entertain, have some character, make people laugh without showing ourselves up. So I've got a few more ideas…'

Patty used to be in charge of the cabin crew and it shows now. She's conducting her orchestra again and as I take a sideways glance at Sheila and Kath, I can see they're enthralled.

'I mean, if you were going to see the Granny-Okes, what would you expect?' she asks.

'Blue rinses and cardigans,' suggests Kath.

I don't counter that cardigans are perfectly stylish knitwear for any age group. I seem to be defending them too often.

'They'd forget the words or be doing some knitting,' adds Sheila

'Precisely.' Patty is triumphant. 'We need a look, we need characters and we need to ham it up a bit. It's not just about the singing.'

She puts a reassuring arm around me, which instantly has the opposite effect; what is she planning now?

'Which is why we need you, Bo Peep.'

She's thought it all through: while the trio carry the song, I carry the act with granny-isms to entertain the audience. I offer them boiled sweets, tell them they'll catch their death of cold and occasionally do a granny dance to tunes that 'take me back'.

'You'll be like Bez to our Happy Mondays.'

Oh Lord.

Having established the set list, Patty moves on to discuss costumes.

'I have some ideas, just wait here,' she says and leaves the room.

This week seems to have been all about clothes, from Granny-Oke costumes to Charlie's dating outfits. Could there be a more diverse spectrum?

This is also the week of Charlie's first dinner date and the debate with Josie has continued every day. I don't know why there is a debate, as men always look the same: trousers and shirt. The colour might change but that's about it. We used to have training days at the airline where the dress code was 'smart casual'; for women this is impossible to interpret but for men? Trousers and shirt-top button undone. Formal occasions? Trousers and shirt-top button fastened and tie on top. Black tie? Well, that's self-explanatory. I suppose they might think that we just throw on a black dress or a blue dress according to the event. They don't, however, understand the complex underwear partnering with any outfit. I've never yet heard a man discuss the difficulty of getting out of Spanx when you desperately need to get to the loo.

Anyway, despite me thinking that there was an obvious solution for Charlie (and his eyes are a beautiful blue, so even the colour of shirt isn't up for debate), I was happier discussing his outfit dilemma than I am sitting here waiting to see what Patty has conjured up for me.

'You should wear a soft tactile fabric,' Josie had enthused, 'so that if he just brushes against you when he's pouring wine or something, he'll want to do it again.'

'Great idea.' Charlie was taking notes.

'It has to be an expensive material,' I'd added in jest. 'You don't want him getting an electric shock.'

'No, that's not the sort of memorable night I was aiming for,' he laughed.

'And no cheap nylon,' warned Josie, 'just in case the place is candle-lit.'

Then we were in free-flow imagining the disasters that could avail Charlie if he wore the wrong shirt. I thought I'd managed to keep the conversation away from me but no chance.

'And then just as I've electrocuted my date with a nylon shirt, the Granny-Okes turn up and the sparks land on their blue-rinse wigs,' said Charlie.

'… and fire spreads to the cardigans and surgical stockings,' from Josie.

'… while they're singing *Eternal Flame!*' Charlie burst into song.

I cringed. 'Please don't make me dread this more than I already am.'

'You'll be great,' Charlie wiped his eyes.

'It'll be too hilarious,' added Josie.

'I know it'll be funny,' I said, 'but here's the question: will people be laughing with me or *at* me?'

And by people, I meant Richard Branson of course.

But back to the current costume dilemma…

Patty brings out four suit bags and hangs them on the wall. The bags hang from the picture rail like the corpses of my entrepreneurial career as Patty builds up the tension for the grand-reveal.

As each bag opens, I can see that she's done herself proud; she's taken the costumes as seriously as the set list. I'd expected fancy-dress shop leg warmers and tutus, but Ms P has more ambitious plans.

'We're like the Spice Girls,' she explains. 'We each have our own character and personality.'

'Kath – Granny Ant.'

There's a military jacket and frilly shirt to go with Kath's black curls and no doubt suitable face make-up.

'Sheila, my little rock chick, Gran Bon Jovi', and she pulls out ripped jeans, leather jacket, a big wig and a bandana. I hadn't seen that coming but Sheila loves it.

'Bo...' It's my turn, what on earth has she chosen for me? My heart is thumping as she opens the bag.

'Granny goes to Hollywood.' Inside the bag is a big white T-shirt with 'GRANNY SAYS RELAX' emblazoned across it. I'm quite relieved, it could have been much more embarrassing.

'And what about yours?' asks Kath, but I already know the answer.

With a delighted flourish, Patty unveils the final costume bag, and there they hang, the wig, the jewellery and the multi-coloured layers of lace that will transform one mid-fifties widow into the one and only Granny Lauper.

'Nothing can stop us now,' she declares.

That's what I'm afraid of.

Love is in the Air

As we reach closing time on Saturday, we're given a preview of tonight's date outfit. Charlie has decided on a new slate blue shirt and designer jeans (told you so).

'I think this says casual but classy.' We nod as if this combo was not entirely predictable from the start.

'I'm almost sick with nerves,' he tells us.

A tad melodramatic but Charlie does look terrified.

'You needn't worry, your stars are fantastic.' Josie reassures him by reading out today's words of wisdom from the *Metro*: 'Although you'll feel uncomfortable at first, your surest route to success is put yourself out there with confidence and courage.'

They nod sagely at the advice of the oracle; most things work out better if you approach them with confidence but I don't like to point this out. I'm the one with the life coach after all.

'Think about something else,' I advise. 'Do you want to see more on the travel-club idea?'

The ploy works and both Charlie and Josie are instantly animated. We sit down together and I pull out the scrapbook I've been doodling in.

'The Mercury Travel Club – Global Adventures, Local Service' reads the front cover.

I've taken all of the ideas we developed and I've drawn a calendar of trips. If you join our club, you become a Mercurian member and you'll be going somewhere new each month. There are plenty of book weekends to keep Caroline happy and I've combined bigger holidays with weekend trips. Each one supports a local business, so there's a wine safari with a tasting at a local wine merchants before we go and the chance to win a case of wine when you get back, and a trip to Belgium with prizes from the local chocolatier, as well as all the ideas we came up with on the BIN. Over time, my thinking is that you get to know people (although I do realise that many people can't wait to get rid of anyone they've met on holiday, despite the promises to keep in touch). I guess that even in a small town like this you can avoid them if you want to. I've been very creative with the scrapbook: each month has a picture of the destination and the ideal prize to give at the end. The pretty pictures seem to have Josie enthralled.

'Oh I love February's trip to the home of Aphrodite,' she enthuses.

'I thought it was a bit less obvious than Paris and, of course, there's a Greek restaurant over the road that might donate a meal for a prize.'

'It's gorgeous,' adds Charlie. 'Can I take it with me tonight? To see what people think?'

And, of course, it gives Charlie something easy to talk about. My mind wanders to the Entrepreneur of the Year award speech where I tell the audience that of course I tested the idea with local people before going ahead. *After all,* I'd say, *customer feedback is essential to entrepreneurs.*

My scrapbook method will probably be taught in all the top universities.

'Brilliant idea,' I answer, 'and see if you can get any of them to book a trip.'

With Charlie despatched to get ready for his date, Josie and I get ready for ours. I decided to start doing something; after all I did put it on my plan and so far it's the only area of my life I've neglected. Last week I mentioned that I might start internet dating and it sent Josie into a frenzy of excitement.

'Oh you have to let me choose someone,' she said.

'You have to be able to read between the lines,' she told me. 'Stocky build means short and fat; masculine appearance means bald with tattoos.'

'Rubbish,' I exclaim.

'I'm telling you. And you have to check out the hobbies, like this one – "enjoys watching TV" aka "has no life at all and is extremely dull".'

'I like watching TV,' I protest.

'But that wouldn't be the highlight of your profile would it? You'd say – "*successful businesswoman*" or "*mature lady who loves to travel*".'

'Less of the mature, that's not how most people describe me.'

'You're right; mature in a woman's profile means forty and in a man's means seventy.'

'You've done this before, then?' I ask and she nods.

'Oh yes, many years ago; no one is what they claim to be. I started writing a glossary to help people navigate the BS', she tells me.

'You should publish it.'

'It makes you look too cynical: "Hi, I published a book about the crap men say" isn't a good conversation starter,' she sighs.

'So what should I do?' I ask.

'Speed dating,' she asserts and that's why we're now both getting glammed up in the toilets at work, nervous as hell but on our way to a wine-tasting event organised by 'Love in the Fast Lane'.

Love in the Fast Lane

We found a plethora of speed-dating events you can go to. I'd envisaged a room above a pub where you sit at a table and the men circulate every five minutes. That's old school and nowadays, speed-dating events can be anything from dinner parties (too difficult to escape, according to Josie), to salsa classes (too much touching) and diving holidays (too much flesh on show). We chose wine tasting in the Italian wine café off Albert Square. I love the idea of a wine café; we thought it might be the safe speed-date option and reasoned that at least we'd have the distraction of a good Barolo if the conversation wilted.

'I can't imagine you needing to do internet dating,' I say to Josie. 'You're young, attractive, good fun.'

'It's not really a last-resort thing like it used to be,' she explains. 'I might meet someone when I'm out with mates and if I do, that's cool, but he might not want to commit or something. So if I want a relationship and not just a one-nighter then I get online and filter out all the time-wasters. You kiss fewer toads.'

It seems rather cold but I can imagine Zoe doing just that, ordering a man to meet her specific specification: six foot, professional, own teeth and happy never to watch golf or fart in her presence. I must tell Patty.

'We need a code,' Josie tells me; she goes on to give me some signals for '*rescue me*', '*steer clear*' and '*this one's perfect for you*'.

'I rarely use the last one,' she adds optimistically as we get out of the cab.

Once more unto the breach.

'To start with,' begins the sommelier, 'an elegant Gavi from the Piedmont region.'

'Not bad at all,' says a voice behind me. 'I was there last summer; stayed in a delightful *casolare* – sorry, cottage, just can't help falling into the lingo. Anyway, had a lovely time exploring the vineyards. Of course it's all more authentic out there, they don't export their best, well why would you? And as for the food we heathens call Italian...'

Just as I think that I'm only going to be bored to death, I realise that I might also drown in splash back as he gargles the mouthful of wine, squirts it from cheek to cheek and then expels it vigorously into the spittoon.

I tug my right ear so much that my lobe is six foot long by the end of his exhibition. Josie waits at least ten minutes before coming over and I sigh with relief as I excuse myself.

'That was our "*rescue me*" signal,' I hiss.

'I know but your face was a picture when he started all that gargoyle stuff,' she laughs.

OK missy – game on.

We change wines and partners; for the Fiano I have a divorced lawyer who boasts that his ex-wife didn't stand a chance with the settlement; he'd made her sign a watertight pre-nup.

'That doesn't seem very fair,' I comment.

'If I'd been fair to all of them, I'd have nothing left,' he tells me.

'All of them? How many times have you been married?' I ask.

'Er, three...no, four times. Don't get me wrong, I'm a romantic at heart, just get bored easily. Did I see you come in with the ripe little Aussie over there?'

Forefinger pressed on end of nose '*steer clear of this one*'. This signal also has the fortunate effect of making you look so ridiculous that the guy leaves you alone anyway.

Josie doesn't seem to be doing any of these signals; I'm sure she's set me up. There are six wines to taste and six men to accompany them. I attempt to pair the wine with the men but the Gavi wasn't fresh or fruity and the Fiano was a little too acidic for my taste.

The Pinot Grigio, however, does seem very easy going if not a little young.

'So which wines do you like?' I ask him.

'To be honest – anything on special offer.' We both laugh. 'I won't pretend to know anything about it.'

'That's refreshing, there are a few know-it-alls in the room tonight.'

'Amongst the women too,' he tells me. 'I'm not cultured enough for most of them.'

Across the room, Josie is scratching the top of her head like a primate; our '*perfect for you*' signal. Damn, why now when I'm finally having a decent conversation?

I ignore her but she continues, adding a glare and a sideways nod at the guy she's with. Pinot Grigio notices it.

'Is that one of your little signals?' He smiles when I look surprised.

'I noticed the ear tugging and nose pointing, not that subtle,' he explains. 'So what does the gorilla impression mean?'

'That the guy she's with might be perfect for me,' I confess.

He laughs out loud.

'She's having you on,' he says, 'unless you like BO.'

I look at her again and she's still at it, signalling me to come over.

'Seriously,' continues Pinot Grigio, 'I stood next to him a while ago, it's not easy to smell the wine around him.'

'I'll get her,' I say.

Just as the sommelier is about to suggest we change partners and I see Josie trying to make her excuses, I start asking questions to delay the move around.

'Could we just try this one again?' I ask.

'Yes, it's more complex than I've had before. Maybe we could talk about it for a bit longer with our current partners,' follows Pinot.

'Maybe have another glass together?' I add.

The sommelier agrees and we stick with our partners for one more. Pinot and I start scratching our heads, tugging our earlobes and pointing at our noses while loudly discussing the wine.

'Huge aroma,' he says, 'overpowering at times.'

'Could be served with something quite bold and brassy, like an Aussie barbecue,' I suggest.

Eventually Josie escapes and confronts the giggling duo that we've become.

'Very funny,' she says.

'We thought so,' answers Pinot. 'I'm Matt by the way.'

And so it passed that my speed-dating session ended successfully – for Josie anyway.

Mothers' Day

Mothering Sunday – the day that mothers across the land are waking up to partially cooked breakfasts and egg boxes transformed into daffodils.

I smile as I recall Zoe's childhood efforts. I loved seeing what my completely unartistic daughter would produce; she was always better with practical ideas and every year she'd be more concerned about where I'd keep the eggs if she took all the boxes. 'They make the boxes to fit the egg shape,' she'd explain to me earnestly.

And now look at her, graciously helping her Gran out of the taxi and into the restaurant. Three generations of women celebrating family together.

As we sit down and clink a toast with our complimentary glass of Prosecco, I relax. After our goat's cheese starter, we order a bottle of Sauvignon Blanc, which I can now bluff my way in appreciating. This is going to be a good day I think to myself as a delicious salmon en croute is followed by a fluffy chocolate soufflé.

I am in heaven but Zoe looks a little agitated, almost as if she's going to make a speech. Instead, she takes a quick gulp of wine and turns to my mum, 'Aren't you going to tell her?' she asks.

I look quizzically at Mum. 'What have you done now?'

'It's not what she's done, it's who she's seen,' says Zoe.

I can't for the life of me imagine where this is going and Mum is giving nothing away; I have never seen such concentration on petit fours.

'Come on then, someone tell me,' I plead.

'Dad,' pronounces Zoe.

I'm confused at first.

'Alan? When? Why? You're not even his mother,' I say.

I'd be hurt by this if I wasn't so astounded. Without even looking up she mumbles:

'He says I was like a mother to him and he doesn't want to lose touch.'

I swear a halo has just appeared over her head. Who the hell does she think she is? Mother Teresa? I'm now livid.

'It's a bloody shame he wasn't more like a husband to me then. Mum, honestly how could you?'

'I was curious and besides it was a Wednesday and Jackie had cancelled on me.'

I shake my head in disbelief; a lovely lunch ruined (and a daughter betrayed) because my mum's chiropodist couldn't make her usual house call.

'Wait, Mum, listen to what happened.' Zoe takes hold of my hand tenderly.

'Go on, Gran.'

Under orders from her granddaughter, Mum shrugs like a spoiled child.

'All he did was talk about you, it was quite boring.'

'Gee thanks, Mum.'

'Said he'd seen you in town and saw that you'd had your hair done. He heard about the book-club weekend and fancies going on one himself.'

News to me – he only ever read the sports section.

'Even heard that you've been out on the town enjoying yourself; he said it was like seeing the old Angela again, that you had some good times together.'

I'm not sure what to say, especially as my daughter is seeing this as a ray of light.

'He misses you, Mum. He's made a mistake but realises it now,' she tells me.

'He didn't say that, did he?'

I'm numb. Is this why everyone else is getting a date but not me? Are the heavens working to reunite us? Zoe obviously thinks so.

'No, but he might next time.' Then Mum realises she's said too much.

'Next time?' I ask.

'He's invited me round for lunch. I won't go if you don't want me to,' replies Mum.

Three thoughts enter my head simultaneously:

1. She will go anyway.
2. I'm as nosy as Mum and need to know what's really happening here.
3. The new woman definitely won't want the ex-wife's mother in her house, especially if she asks for a doggy bag.

'Go,' I sigh, 'but I want to know every last detail and do NOT get seduced by her cupcakes.'

We nod and seal our sacred pact.

No Place Like Gnome

With Mum and Zoe despatched to investigate his new love nest, this morning I start to wonder whether Alan will ever visit this house.

I find myself looking around objectively. If Alan ever falls on bended knee, does penance and begs forgiveness so that I deign to invite him over, what will he think of this place?

He might be expecting something more homely, more like we used to have. It's not as if I haven't tried; I painted, put up photos and bought some throws, but it's difficult to stay enthusiastic when you're only doing it for yourself and I have been rather busy with work.

I imagine Amanda launched herself into the full throes of romantic nest-building. I know that they've gone for an ultra-modern city apartment and I envisage it spotless yet filled with the aroma of baking. They've probably got an island in the kitchen and they stand chatting with a glass of wine while she 'throws together' something wonderful despite having been at work all day.

In my imagination, they've both got perfect white teeth too. This jars with the vision of them drinking lots of red wine but it happens on American TV shows. How does that work? On TV, they're always drinking huge glasses of red wine before eating and yet they never get plastered and they never have stained teeth when they smile lovingly at each other. I must buy some of that magic wine.

Back to their love nest. I wonder if she makes him take his shoes off before he's allowed near her perfect cream rugs and cushions (which I bet she has). They'll have a balcony not a garden but she's bound to grow herbs somewhere and they'll all be perfect, not scraggy weeds like mine always seem to end up. Alan was always the gardener in our house, so I wonder how he's coping with a balcony.

I look out at the scraps of lawn and earth that comprise my front garden and feeling guilty, I decide to take action. Two hours and an unjustifiable amount of money later, I return from the garden centre with plants, tools and a new doormat which shouts *Welcome*.

I know how ironic that is.

I get to work and am soon transformed into Angela Titchmarsh. Or Angela Sackville-West, because I don't imagine that Mr Titchmarsh wears flowery gardening gloves or carries a lilac-handled trowel. I have the concentration of a surgeon as I plant the ready-flowering spring bulbs and shrubs that will transform this scrap of land into Kew Gardens. If I'd planned ahead, I wouldn't have picked a very muddy day to start this and I might have tackled it in stages, but as it is, I'm filthy and groaning in agony when I eventually struggle up to survey my achievement.

Not bad at all. Alan will be impressed when he makes his inaugural visit.

One of my neighbours walks past and nods at my efforts.

'You've got that looking good,' he says as he strolls past.

I thank him, head indoors and then end the day by resting my weary body in a bubbling oasis of ylang-ylang – whatever that is.

The next morning I'm driven to ask myself why anyone bothers with gardening? One minute I have a perfectly potted green space and the next something resembling a rubbish dump.

I know exactly when it happened; at 4 a.m. this morning I was dragged from my dreams by a raging storm. Outside the forecast gales had arrived a day early; wheelie bins were hurtling down the road in a bizarre break for freedom while fence panels and sheds battled to stay upright. There was nothing I could do at that time in the morning, so just turned over and lay awake while the cacophony raged on.

Now, on my way to work, I am exhausted through lack of sleep and truly hacked off to see several recycling bags and their contents flattening my recent efforts.

The 'witty' gnome I added to the welcoming décor looks as if he's had a night on the town with several Stella cans at his feet and an empty hanging basket sitting on his head at a jaunty angle.

I give up and holding my lapels tight to my chest, I stomp into work; my hair also decides to get angry in the storm.

'Love the Scissorhands look,' says Charlie, admiring the coiffured rage on my head.

He is far too chirpy and in danger of wearing that coffee. I ignore him, sort out my troublesome hair, have a caffeine intake and calm down.

The gnome looked as if he'd had a really good night on the tiles I smile to myself. I think I'll call him Norman – spelled Gnorman of course.

Today's conversation is all about the dinner party; we want to know the details and fortunately Charlie is bursting to tell. We wait until the post-lunch slump and seat ourselves comfortably so the storyteller can begin.

'He's nice.'

Hardly a glowing reference, and not quite matching Charlie's serene faraway smile.

'Really nice, lovely. I feel as if I've known him all my life.'

This is sounding like love and as Charlie takes us through a night that ended with a little peck on the cheek and a promise of a 'next time', he looks like a puppy that's just had his belly stroked. I think we'll see much more of Peter; in fact, very soon, as it turns out that he's offered to help us with the Mercury Travel Club.

'They all liked the idea,' Charlie says, 'but Peter couldn't see where we'd make any money.'

Peter is in banking, which is not something many people confess to these days. He helps people with ideas to secure funding, so knows his way around a business plan. He thinks my scrapbook needs 'fleshing out a little' – a very polite way of putting it. So, if I'm up for it, he's going to help us work out whether the Mercury Travel Club could be profitable.

I never even considered that it might not be and all of a sudden I feel really stupid; it's a scrapbook of pictures, that's all. Peter wants me to bring along the costs and prices but I haven't even thought about them or anything else that you might put on a spreadsheet. I'm sensing an evening of humiliation ahead – so much for Entrepreneur of the Year.

My guts are churning as much as they did when Patty told me the Grannies were reforming; now I'm thinking that a night onstage sounds a far easier option.

I feel a bit deflated as I walk home, but then I notice something rather bizarre as I approach the house. The debris from last night's storm has gone. At first I think it must have blown on down to someone else's garden but then I see that the plants have been tidied up and, most bizarrely of all, Gnorman has been joined by a female gnome. I look around to see if anyone is filming for *You've Been Framed*, but nothing. I sigh and go inside; I don't know why I find anything unusual any more.

I'll call her Gnora.

Pedal Faster

Perspective is a strange thing; one person's disaster zone is another's Shangri-La.

I meet Caroline in the hope that she'll give me permission to get back into comfy clothes and hibernate for the rest of my life. I've done a little bit of everything on my wish list but seem to have ended up more terrified and confused than when I started. She's having none of it.

'So you're saying that a top financier, who's a good friend and very nice, is going to look at your business idea and that you're having a real laugh with your girlfriends?'

Actually, what I think I said was that I was about to be humiliated by and in front of everyone I know, but she doesn't seem to see it this way.

'Isn't this what you wanted? Some fun? Friends? An exciting time at work? That magic wand was working overtime on the day you waved it.'

'Part of me wishes I hadn't asked for all of this, it's too scary,' I tell her. 'I need to know how it all turns out. If this were a movie, I could fast forward to the end just to check it ends happily.'

And that's the truth. I am scared and the really scary part is that I'm doing it on my own. If I knew someone had my back, someone was cheering me on, it might be easier.

'I wish I'd asked to go back to how it was, when things were dull but safe.'

'Close your eyes,' Caroline instructs and I do as I'm told.

'Remember when you got your first bike, how did it feel?'

'Exciting, incredibly exciting.'

I can picture our family room on Christmas morning. I'm seven years old and beside the tree is a brand new gold Raleigh bike with a huge bow attached. I remember wondering how on earth Santa got that down the chimney.

'And when you first rode that bike?' asks Caroline.

'My dad held on to the back and I wobbled along the street. Then he let me go and I was on my own. I was terrified.'

'So what did you do?' coaxes Caroline.

'Just kept holding on and turning the pedals until I realised I was actually cycling all by myself,' I say.

'And how did that feel?'

I'm taken back to the moment and can feel the bike stabilising then speeding up beneath me. I'm doing it, I'm really doing it. A breeze is blowing my face and a smile is spreading throughout my body. I go faster, panic when I wobble a bit then regain my balance. I feel as if nothing can stop me now.

'It felt amazing,' I tell her, 'just amazing.'

I open my eyes and that moment is with me still.

'And it will do again, Angela. You just have to keep faith and keep turning the pedals. You'll get there.'

* * *

That sensation of finally achieving it has been with me all week. I've been turning the pedals as fast as I can and although I've hit some bumps in the road, I'm still upright.

First of all, we meet with Peter and I confess from the outset that I didn't know how to do a business plan and that I feel a bit foolish. He dismisses my concerns kindly.

'The important part is the idea,' he says, 'and you have that in spades.'

I now know why Charlie is smitten; Peter truly is the nicest man in the world and very clever. He shows us how to get started and answers every stupid question we're brave enough to ask. Charlie and I are now working on the Mercury Travel Club together and will soon have a concept that Richard Branson will be proud of.

Second, I tell Zoe that I have to appear with the Granny-Okes just once more. She hates the idea but I tell her that it's important to Patty and I just can't let her down. Zoe asks me to try to stay in the background. I'm not sure how easy that will be; Patty has bought us all inflatable Zimmer frames to walk on to the stage with before casting them aside as we launch into song. Nevertheless, I promise to try to minimise the humiliation. I'll think of a way.

The third event had me reaching for the stabilisers: I came face to face with Alan. He walked into the pub where Charlie and I were hunched over the laptop puzzling our way through the business plan. When I play this video back in my mind, I'm sure I look intelligent frowning over numbers with my glasses perched on the end of my nose. In reality, I probably looked short-sighted and confused.

'I hope he's paying you for the out-of-hours work,' he says.

It's his attempt at a joke but my foot comes off the pedal and I'm wobbling. Charlie jumps in.

'Oh, she'll be paying me if this joint venture comes off, she's an amazing woman.'

He ignores the compliment but is staring at me, and despite the slight paunch forming around his midriff, he still looks good. Come on girl, pedal.

'She always has been,' Alan says. 'I've heard good things about the book weekend you ran. Any chance of you giving me a call when you run the next one?'

Is he really asking me to call him? PEDAL! With calmness I do not feel at all, I hand him a piece of paper.

'If you jot down your details, we'll add you to our mailing list,' I tell him.

He is stunned but does as he's told then nods a goodbye.

Charlie high-fives me, or he would have done if my hand wasn't shaking so much.

I take a deep breath and a gulp of wine; I didn't fall off after all.

The Sprinkler

I've been playing back my encounter with Alan over and over again; did I look confident or cocky? Did I look like a woman who wanted her ex back or one who'd moved on completely? Should I have invited him to join us and been friendlier? Who knows? It's done now, but I know that not even meeting the girls for practice will distract me enough to forget about it.

Anyway, off to Patty's. As I drive up to her house, I'm astonished to see she's cleared her garage out and this is now our rehearsal 'studio'. It's huge, has a concrete floor to absorb the dancing and is far enough away from anyone to risk disturbing the spring birdsong. It's also freezing cold, so I don't care how much I'm mocked today, this cardigan does not come off.

Patty's hubby died four years ago of cancer; he was diagnosed in the January and gone by summer. He was older than Patty but you wouldn't know it – jogging, tennis, golf – he did it all. Larger than life, people used to say. That's probably why the gap he left was so huge; Patty and Nige would feed off each other constantly – like Morecambe and Wise or Ant and Dec.

Patty hasn't touched the place since then. She moved into the spare room and time stood still in the rest of this colossal house. So clearing out the garage is quite a big step for her and I've also noticed that she's moved his old stereo equipment out of the den.

'You set this up yourself?' I ask nodding at the stereo.

'The sound system?' she says.

(*Blimey it's not just a garage and a CD player; we have a studio and a sound system now.*)

'I moved it but got the lads next door to show me where all the cables went. I'm convinced cable sockets are taught to boys in secret school lessons.'

'Along with advanced TV programming and leaving clothes on the bathroom floor,' I add.

I don't know when it happened but at some point in Alan's affair, he started picking up after himself. Every morning for the past twenty years, I'd find last night's undies discarded on the bathroom floor. Then suddenly, there was nothing. At first I thought he must finally be taking notice of my nagging but later I realised that he was tidying them up himself because they were new. Otherwise, it would stand out too much. Stupidly he thought he could still bury them in the washing basket and I wouldn't notice them there.

It's funny the things that really anger you when you find out your husband has been unfaithful:

He took her to dinner – that was annoying.

He slept with her – that was hurtful.

He bought new underwear to impress her – quite frankly astounding.

He left me to bloody wash his FILTHY WHORING PANTS – INFURIATING.

Remembering this puts all thoughts of being nice to him out of my head.

Come on, let's rehearse.

Blimey they're good, Sheila and Kath can sing and Patty has real stage presence – she's funny without being ridiculous.

I've been trying out the classic 1980s dance moves; Moonwalking is far too hard and the Robot is for men who really don't have any rhythm, but there are a couple I can suggest.

'This one's called the Cabbage Patch.' I do the move – circling my rib cage in one direction and arms in the other – I get a round of applause from the girls.

'And this one's the Electric Slide,' I say. Sliding one foot along and following with the other – very easy even for me.

'The Clone made famous by Molly Ringwald, a classic 1980s combination,' I continue.

'From *The Breakfast Club*. I know this one,' says Kath as she joins in.

'And of course the one and only, Flashdance.'

Patty flicks on the music and the rehearsal becomes a free-for-all. The title track belts out and Irene Cara-style moves are attempted randomly and badly. No one tries the knee slide on the concrete floor but we're all exhausted by the end of the track.

'Someone should put together an eighties aerobics class, it would be brilliant,' suggests Sheila.

'As long as it's in the upstairs room of a pub, I'm knackered.' Patty is a lovely shade of pink. 'Energy drink anyone?'

I hadn't realised that a large Chardonnay counted as an energy drink, but it must be true as it certainly perks all of us up.

As I get older and try new experiences, I like to think I am gathering wisdom to pass on to my dearest daughter. The first lesson I must bestow is that one should not drink wine in the afternoon before any food (I think I knew this but must have been testing it out).

The second lesson is that attempting The Sprinkler (it's a real dance move – honestly) after said copious amount of wine can only lead to trouble. I will probably have a scab on my knee from falling over. How awful, getting a scab on your knee at the age of fifty-three.

My dearest daughter is already far wiser than me.

April Fool

Oh what a wag my boss is, completely hilarious; he'll tell you as much himself.

My phone wakes me up at 7 a.m., number unknown. I answer to a very deep male voice. 'Am I speaking to one of the original Granny-Okes?'

'I think so,' I say.

'Then I'd like to book you as my support act, are you free at the weekend?' asks the voice.

It's turning into a bad Sean Connery impression with each word. This should alert me but I'm still half asleep so I tell him that we are.

'Great, you'll need to do Spandau Ballet tracks. Can you sing me any lyrics?'

Why I start doing this I don't know but in my best Tony Hadley voice I start warbling.

'Hmm, that's a bit quiet. Can you do it any louder?' asks the caller.

Stupidly, I sit up and project the song full force.

'What were the last few words,' says the voice, 'I couldn't quite catch them.'

I really belt it out this time: '... *I'VE LOST MY MIND.*'

Charlie and Peter burst out laughing at the end of the line and yell in unison, 'You certainly have – April Fool.'

'You will pay for this,' I warn them before slumping back into my pillow, smiling all the same.

So Charlie and Peter were together at 7 a.m., then? Wait until I tell Josie.

I don't have to tell her; the post-coital glow across Charlie's face would outshine the Blackpool Illuminations.

'Ooh, someone's happy,' chirps Josie. 'Come on, we want details.'

'Ask him who he woke up with,' I prompt, but Charlie gets in first.

'Or what I woke up to,' he flicks on his phone to a recording of my morning performance. I give him a shove but Josie is not distracted.

'We've heard Granny Hollywood squawking before, that's not news…'

Moi? Squawk? I'd be offended if I didn't want the lowdown on Charlie's love life.

'… but Charlie's big romance,' says Josie, 'now that needs serious tea and biscuits.'

A customer rather inconveniently walks in to book a holiday (the cheek of it), so Josie heads off to help, wagging her finger at our Blushing Boss.

'Post lunch,' he says, 'I promise all the details.'

The morning goes quite quickly. It's the right time to grab a bank holiday break and we have a steady flow of people doing just that. Every now and then someone will also ask if we're doing one of those 'haunted book weekends', so we add their names to the list of prospects for the travel club.

Which in itself turns out to be the reason for Charlie's sleepover; Peter came round to review the plan we'd written. Of course they did all of this over food and wine. How come I never get this kind of service at the bank?

'He thinks we've got something here,' gushes Charlie. 'For a business like ours, it's all about establishing a niche in the market and serving it well. Peter thinks we can do that. He looked at our plan, then gazed into my eyes and said, "Handsome and talented, how will I keep you to myself?" I tell you, I just melted.'

Josie and Charlie are gazing into the distance, lost in a world of princes and ponies. I surprise myself by being more interested in the idea.

'So it could work?' I ask.

'If we really give it a go,' nods Charlie.

Mr Branson, hold that spot on Necker Island, I might be coming after all.

Drowning not Waving

Dearest daughter calls me to say that the dinner with Alan and my mother has been arranged. He called to fix a date immediately after bumping into me at the pub. That can't be a coincidence? I must start feeding some lines to Mum; I won't tell her to be on her best behaviour, she can be as outrageous as she likes.

So my family and ex-family will shortly gather around another woman's table. I can't decide whether to shun alcohol and the inevitable maudlin chorus of 'All By Myself' or whether to get a crate in and succumb. The latter would save me a late-night trip to the corner shop in my jammies I suppose.

I was once in the supermarket buying one of their more upmarket ready meals (as well the obligatory bag of salad to prove that I'm no heathen in the kitchen, the one that eventually gets thrown away looking like a compost heap), when the cashier turned to me and said 'Hmm that looks lovely, I bet you'll enjoy that.'

I remember thinking at the time, 'How does she know?' but smiling politely anyway. Now I find myself doing exactly the same thing. Whenever a couple book a holiday, I stare at them while they're not watching and work out whether I think they're going to enjoy it. You can always tell if it's one person's dream and another's nightmare.

Ten-day tour of the silent fjords with a group of people sporting Fair Isle jumpers, a bus I can't get off and more herring than you can fit in a camper van? Sounds wonderful, darling – sign us up. Next time can we go to Vegas?

It works better if they're open about it and take turns in who chooses the break; I've just sold one couple a weekend break to Rome. He loves the sights, she hates walking; I suggested that she go for an upgrade to a rooftop spa hotel so that if she prefers not to trek to the Trevi, she can just absorb the ambience from the whirlpool. They were delighted and we put a few extra pennies in the Mercury pot.

I have to say, the spa looked wonderful; maybe not Rome but perhaps a little home-based luxury might just be in order.

At the end of a pretty busy day, I give Patty a call.

'Aha, Bo, the very woman I wanted to speak to,' she declares. 'I've booked us a weekend away.'

'You must be psychic,' I say. 'That's just what I was about to suggest, maybe a nice spa break. No work, just us relaxing.'

'I've got something even better.' My warning lights have turned amber and I expect that red is a sentence away.

'It's an eighties night, tribute act, dancing; this hotel does them all the time.'

'Oh Patty, please tell me we're not singing.'

'No – just enjoying ourselves and of course checking out the competition.'

I sigh but agree; there is no arguing with Patty when she's on a mission.

'And if you're not doing anything tonight,' she continues, 'I've downloaded the whole series of *Poldark*.'

A rather tame suggestion from Ms P, but it will keep me off the wine for the evening, and one thing is certain, I won't be thinking about Alan's dinner party while I'm watching Ross Poldark sweeping Demelza off her feet on the windswept Cornish coast.

* * *

'Are you still in bed?'

'Morning, Mum, of course I am,' I yawn. 'Why aren't you? I didn't think you emerged before eleven?'

It's 7 a.m. Sunday morning and I remember the dinner party was last night.

'You need to call Zoe,' Mum tells me.

'Why what's happened?' I panic.

I hop out of bed pulling on my tracksuit in case a 999 visit is required.

'She got a bit upset last night,' says Mum.

The bastard, what did he say to my daughter? I put the phone down on Mum and call Zoe; I can tell from her voice that she's weary.

'Did I wake you?' I ask.

'No,' she sighs, 'I haven't really slept.'

I tell her to stay where she is and that an emergency supply of croissants is on its way round.

When I get to her house, via local shop for as many pastries as I can find, she's already up and brewing the coffee.

She looks sad and I am heartbroken to see it, my baby bird vulnerable and wounded. If I don't do something, I will not be able to hold back the tears I feel forming.

'I'm supposed to be looking after you,' I smile, taking over the coffee pot. We can both tell the smile is fake, but it is holding back Niagara.

I busy myself pouring drinks, putting out pastries and jam and then we sit down to eat, silently. After the first cup, she looks up at me.

'It was awful, Mum.'

I let her speak.

'I don't know what I was expecting; maybe that it would just be like old times. Four of us around the table, laughing at Gran. But there was no laughter, it was the wrong four,' she sighs. 'It was so polite. He even kissed me on both cheeks as if I were some *business* associate.'

She spits out the word 'business'; I pour more coffee and sit waiting.

'All she talked about was herself, her interior design, her cooking, her ballroom-dancing. I kept looking at Dad and thinking, "You gave us up for this?" Because he didn't just leave you, I see that now, he left *all* of us and sold *our* home. I'm furious, Mum, I really am.'

And she is; that croissant has been shredded so efficiently, it wouldn't feed a sparrow.

'He didn't leave you,' I say trying to soothe her angst, 'and although the meal was a bit awkward, this is his way of trying to tell you that.'

She just shakes her head, 'No, he made the wrong decision; that was not the Dad I used to know.'

I don't want Zoe hating her father so I try to change the subject.

'Did Gran behave?' I ask.

Despite herself she lets out a snort, 'Oh yes, she was outrageous.'

'Spill.'

'There was one point when Amanda wouldn't let Dad get any salt out; she said the food was perfect and didn't need seasoning. This was like a red rag to Gran, so she gets out the condiment packets she steals from cafés and hands a few to Dad.

'She nudges him so indiscreetly and says, "I've got a bit of ketchup as well if you want me to leave you some. It's all a bit bland."'

Hurrah for Mum.

'And then when we leave, Amanda holds out this cake box and says to Gran, "I'm told that you love a doggy bag, so I've put in some of my cupcakes for you." Gran grimaces like she's being poisoned and actually turns it down.'

Blimey, now that is loyalty.

'She's entering the Great Cheshire Bake-Off later this year.'

It takes me a second to realise that she means Amanda not Mum.

'She can't win it, Mum, we can't let her. I'll show Dad anyone can bake.'

Zoe has decided to hit Amanda where it will hurt most, her ego, or make that her Aga.

To achieve this, she tells me, she wants us to do an intensive baking course and has found an evening class for us to do together. It promises to turn even the worst cooks into master chefs; I imagine she emphasised this part because of my famous close relationship with the smoke alarm.

I can't say no, can I?

Charlie also has plans for me.

'Sweetie, we need to really go for this travel club soon or it'll be too late. Peter wants to take us through the finances later on today, is that OK with you?'

I nod and Charlie calls him to agree the time. That soft focus look falls over his face when he hears Peter's voice; I hope he remembers why he's calling.

My phone rings and Patty gushes the details for my other commitment – our tribute weekend.

I think there was a time shortly after my divorce when I wondered how I was going to fill the days; I remember looking at the empty calendar on the wall in dismay. Now it's almost too full: a quick break checking out tribute bands, come back revitalised, meet with our business advisor to become an amazing holiday entrepreneur, somehow learn to cook, win baking competition, save friends and family from a life of drudgery and kick my ex's butt, in the process making him regret his decisions and come crawling back.

How hard can it be?

Peter is going to meet us after work and in the meantime, I'm so hyped up, not wanting to drop any of the plates I'm spinning, that I don't let anyone leave the shop without booking something. Later, we sit at Charlie's dining table with coffee rather than wine and Peter takes us through an example business plan, explaining each section:

'What I'd be looking for, if I were going to lend to a business, would be a very clear answer to each of these questions.'

I feel as if I'm going to get an exam at the end.

'Who is the target audience?'

I look to Charlie to see if we should be answering but Peter continues. 'You're quite clear on this: older empty nesters, have a bit of disposable income, classic baby boomers.'

It's odd to hear yourself classified and to learn that you're a 'valuable market segment' but there you go, I'm worth something at last.

'The key question is how you want to structure this business.'

I don't understand at first; Charlie picks up the conversation.

'Technically, Mercury Travel is my business and so this would just be an off-shoot if we kept things the way they are…'

How many emotions is it possible to feel in a single moment? Terror, fear, hurt, anxiety, humiliation; I can't believe Charlie would use the idea without me?

'So I was wondering…' He continues to speak, although the nervous heartbeat pounding through my head makes it difficult to hear. '… would you be interested in becoming my business partner?' His eyebrows rise hopefully.

It takes a while for this to sink in and eventually I give the same rubbish response as I gave when Alan asked me to marry him: 'Who, me?'

* * *

Five days later, Patty and I book into our hotel mid-afternoon. It's an unassuming place on the outskirts of town and whereas some hotels are set up for business, this one is set up for partying. The notice in reception shows there are tribute acts almost every weekend of the year, not just eighties nights but Rat Pack, Disco and Abba of course. You name it and there's someone here pretending to be it, presumably making a decent living.

I've had the business plan clutched to my bosom since Tuesday. I don't know why but it hadn't hit home that in order to win Entrepreneur of the Year, I'd actually have to run a business. Otherwise I'll have to aim for employee of the year, which doesn't sound nearly as impressive.

I'm excited and scared. What if it doesn't work? It's a lot of money, most of what I have left over from the divorce. It's more than money though, it's me. Can I do it? Am I all talk? I couldn't bear the gruesome twosome to know I'd failed.

I head to the spa and lie in the steam room soaking in the self-doubt. Within half an hour, I notice the place is really filling up. I'm knocked out of my thoughts by a group of women jostling for space on the tiled seating. I've probably cooked enough so get up and leave them to it.

Later, I meet Patty for a G&T before we head to the function room. It's like a slow-motion scene from a movie: two women push open double doors into a ballroom filled with people who turn to stare at them. It's crammed. They're not actually staring at us just taking the measure of anyone who comes in: are we all surprised at just how many have turned up? A couple of people are in fancy dress but most are dressed for a night out; some would have definitely been wearing the same outfit in the eighties but others are far too young to remember, so it would just be a decade that they've heard about.

We eat a fairly standard meal but no one is here for the food. The music cranks up and for this mild-mannered throng, a switch flicks and they go back in time.

It's great fun, just dancing the night away with people my own age; I didn't even think this was still possible. The band is pretty good, going through all the classics. Of course Patty watches them with a critical eye.

'Our set list is better,' she concludes, 'and we've thought more about the costumes.'

I don't argue; I don't get the chance because suddenly she squeals and runs off to give a full-force hug to a very-well-dressed guy standing quietly in the corner. Fortunately, he seems equally pleased to see her and reciprocates. She drags him over to meet me.

'Meet Craig,' she beams. 'He was one of my absolute favourite stewards.'

Craig shakes my hand and tells me that Patty taught him everything he knows, poor chap.

Her former protégé explains that he is now a bookings agent for retro and tribute acts. Patty just about explodes with excitement.

'You should see our act, Craig. We sing, you should check us out on YouTube.'

'I'll do that,' he says, 'good acts can work pretty much every week of the year all around the world.'

He swaps numbers with Patty and then disappears backstage.

'Wow, fancy meeting him,' declares Patty. 'It must be fate; we are destined to be onstage, don't you think?'

Alas, it seems as if we are. Craig didn't take long to check the video and despite it, seems to be offering us the chance to appear at a gig next weekend. We'll be supporting a tribute called Double Duran. It's a charity event and they need people who will play for free, so I suppose I can claim to just be doing my bit.

I hope against hope that no one I know comes along.

The following week, I know I need to rehearse, rehearse and rehearse again. If I have to get on that stage (and I do now), I'm going to give it my best shot so I don't look too ridiculous. Nothing can distract me, absolutely nothing.

No chance of that. Someone has decided to play silly beggars with the gnomes. They're in a different place every time I come home; at first I think they've just fallen over and perhaps the postman has stood them back up but it's more mischievous than that. When I get back this evening, I find a gerbera wedged between them as if Gnorman were courting Gnora. It looks ridiculously cute but I have to wonder who on earth has the energy to do this type of thing?

And what are they trying to say?

No time to think about it. Patty, on a mission to perfect this first gig, has us choreographed and word-perfect. We have time for four songs (or tracks as I'm told to call them now), so they're all the crowd pleasers. Costumes are ready and inflatable Zimmer frames are tested for punctures.

Zoe hasn't dropped her ambition either; she's gone ahead and signed us up for 'Baking like a Pro'. I can't even bake like an amateur so I'm dreading this more than the stage appearance; at least there I can hide behind the others. I've tried to suggest that perhaps Zoe doesn't need me with her, but she's as bad as Patty, determined that I'm going to join in. When did all the women I know become so bossy?

One day to go: this time tomorrow night, the performance will be over, thank goodness. That's the good news; the bad news is that Patty, Craig and Double Duran, in fact everyone I know, has been tweeting about this gig. Maybe it'll rain tomorrow and no one will turn up. Oh Lord, that would be worse, wouldn't it? Charity left destitute by failing Granny-Okes.

* * *

The day of reckoning and needless to say, I awake having not slept much at all. But there's no turning back, we have to get on with it.

Costume – check; Zimmer frame – check; wig – check. I am ready.

We arrive and the club is heaving, although that isn't much of an achievement as it is quite small. I am quietly relieved that it's busy; empty would have been humiliating and the charity will make some money at least. Backstage, the girls are buzzing and soon it's time to go on.

We go on in our big cardigans and Zimmer frames, thick support tights drooping around our ankles and spectacles draped around our necks. We look a bit fragile and puzzled by the audience as 'There's No One Quite Like Grandma' plays in the background. The three singers line up behind the mikes; I sit down on a stool at the side of the stage and take up my knitting.

'Ooh, look at all these lovely people,' says Patty. 'Shall we sing something for them?'

We Granny-Okes nod enthusiastically and pull our tights up.

The opening chords of 'Like a Virgin' start up; the girls bob up and down like little pistons then Kath shouts, 'Ooh I think I know this one.'

They throw off their cardigans to reveal their outfits and launch into the first track of our first gig. I watch and am absurdly proud of my friends.

The audience get into the spirit; it's a bit of fun and everyone can see that. I don't do much to this track, just knit and bob my head.

The next track is another eighties classic with an intro that everyone knows, Bon Jovi's 'Livin' On A Prayer'.

This is Sheila's big number; she lets it start, gets very animated, and as we reach the chorus, she lifts her Zimmer and starts playing it like an air guitar. The crowd love it, everyone is joining in and I can see mobile phones flashing away.

I'm supposed to get up and join her in a granny rock duet but quite frankly the act doesn't need it, so I stand up and do a little twerk (as instructed by the video we watched). I then sit back down and mop my brow. I don't think anyone even noticed me, thank God.

My heart is pounding; I got up and survived. I get out a bag of mint imperials and offer them to a couple of people in the front row. As I'm having a little look around, I see Charlie who smiles and waves at me. I give a quick wave back but my attention is drawn to the back of the room where Alan is standing with Amanda; he seems to be enjoying things and raises his glass to me, at which point Amanda walks away. He doesn't follow; he looks at me and shrugs his shoulders. I don't know what this means and I don't have time to react as the girls are on their final number. It's 'Girls Just Want to Have Fun' and all of us are swaying along with Granny Lauper taking the lead and enjoying her moment thoroughly. She'll be back, I can tell.

We finish, take our bows and leave the stage buzzing. Craig is beaming as he embraces Patty. He suggests going to watch Duran and having a nightcap together. I don't want to risk bumping into Alan so tell everyone that I've had enough excitement for one night.

And I have. As I lie in bed reliving the evening, I'm so relieved that it went well but would feel even better if I knew I never had to do it again.

There seems little chance of that; my phone hasn't stopped buzzing with congratulatory text messages, including one from Alan which doesn't have an x on the end, but I imagine he wouldn't want something like that to be found out. I've deleted it anyway. Patty calls and is beside herself; Craig has told her he can definitely find us more gigs so I think she's now planning festival domination.

Fortunately Zoe wasn't there; unfortunately she's still focused on baking domination.

What's that expression? Out of the frying pan, into the fire?

And on We Go

I've been utterly exhausted this week, a real come-down after the gig. Charlie has been asking me about the business venture and I feel awful that I haven't looked over it properly. I don't ever seem to get the time.

Tonight was baking night, and not just baking but 'baking like a pro'. These people are demons, so competitive with their cupcakes. I can't understand when baking became an Olympic event. It was something we did with our mums to pass the time on a Sunday; it wasn't a source of conflict. If your cake didn't rise, it got covered in custard and became a trifle – simple.

The teacher is talking about glycerine and I seem to be the only one confused.

'Isn't that what you make explosives with?' I whisper to Zoe. 'This is getting a bit serious.'

'That's nitro-glycerine, Mum.' She doesn't take her eyes from the tutor.

As we whisk our Victoria sponge mixtures, I spot the pupils eyeing each other up trying to work out who will be the worst, and needless to say, it's me. My cake comes out as flat and hard as a Frisbee and although I'm tempted to skim it across the class to lighten the mood, they force me to ice it.

When we get home, I open the back door and throw it out, declaring, 'Here you go birds, an evening treat.'

I throw it at the bird table expecting it to shatter into spongy pieces; instead, the weight of it knocks the whole table over and even the fattest pigeons scarper in fear.

'You'll be better at the crumbles,' Zoe reassures me through a mouthful of her own feather-light creation.

My heart sinks like the centre of my cakes at the thought of going again.

It's late when Patty rings with the great news that we have another gig. This is followed by Zoe confirming that she has the application form for the competition. I murmur meekly at both and wonder how on earth I'm going to extricate myself without hurting anyone's feelings?

It's raining, a spring shower heavy enough to force a day indoors. It doesn't seem to matter how many years pass, this type of weather always takes me right back to being twelve years old. Watching the drops race down my bedroom window, making mental bets as to which raindrop would win; the chill that falls both because of the weather and the end of the weekend. School lay ahead and there'd be no more playing out today.

There was always a Western on TV, or it seemed that way. I flick through the TV channels now and find one amongst the plethora of murder mysteries and paranormal dramas. Nowadays if you're not investigating the dead, you're romancing the undead.

For the first time this week, I don't have to be anywhere or do anything: no singing and no baking. I'm glad; this is good thinking weather. I curl up on the sofa and surround myself with everything I'm likely to need for the next few hours: a throw, hot chocolate, a notebook and pen.

It's so good to have this moment after the rollercoaster of last week. Can it really all have happened in such a short space of time? It seems like someone else's life.

I read through the business plan we've written. To achieve this would mean giving up everything, all the other distractions, as I can't do another week as exhausting as this. I'd have to say no to Patty and spend less time with Zoe. I may be letting them both down badly, but on the other hand, I could let myself down even more if I don't.

Rather simplistically, I decide to make a list of pros and cons; I don't get far and wake up two hours later from the deepest sleep in weeks. I'm lying in the exact same position and my notebook and pen are still in hand; I've written nothing but I know who I need to speak to.

When I call Mum, she asks why I'm not consulting my 'life-coach-thingy'.

'I'm impressed you've heard of them,' I answer.

'Of course I have. I've been to the self-harm section of the bookstore too,' she tuts.

'I think you mean self-help, Mum.'

'Whatever you say; it's still my advice you want.'

I have to meet her in a department store café as Monday is 'free coffee for pensioners' day and as she likes to say, 'If they're giving it away, who am I to say no?'

We don't talk until she's comfortably seated, able to watch all of the regulars and comment upon their consumption.

'See her over there? Been ordered to lose two stone and yet still gets a cream cake every Monday, someone should tell her doctor.'

I glance at the lady in question; the place is full of seventy-year-olds getting their free cuppa.

'And he lost his wife last year, poor soul.' She waves and he waves back. 'Nice man.'

She takes a sip of coffee and then sits back in her chair, like an oracle on her throne.

'So what's wrong, sweetheart?'

This year spills out – it's been great, I've done so many new things and met lots of new people. Now, Patty wants me to sing with her, Zoe wants me to become chef of the year, Charlie wants me to go into business and I seem to be saying yes to all of them. I've tried on so many hats this year and now I'm not sure which one I want to wear.

'You sound like Mr Ben,' she laughs. 'Remember him? Used to go into the changing rooms and come out as something different every week. I quite fancied doing that.'

It wasn't quite the sympathetic advice I was looking for from my mother but she has a point.

'And even Alan came to the gig. I'm not sure if that means he might want to come back?' I add.

'I bloody well hope not, after all he's inflicted on my girls.'

She pushes her cup and cream scone to one side then fixes a look.

'It seems like he's going through one of them man-o-pause things. Needs to realise his mistake by himself, not have you trying to work out what he wants. Forget him,' she says.

'And if you're thinking that Patty will disown you for not singing, you're wrong. There'll be more room on the stage for her if you get off; she'll thank you in the end. And as for being less of a mother for not going to cookery classes, think again; that ship sailed a long time ago.'

'Gee thanks,' I reply.

She takes a sip of coffee and wipes her mouth; mine is still ajar from all the tough love just dispensed. She has a remarkable insight into my entourage.

'All I'm saying is that these things are what other people want to do, and good for them. Having you there alongside them makes it less scary for them but at the end of the day it's their dream not yours. Now tell me about Charlie.'

I tell her all about the travel club and Charlie's offer. I'm surprised how excited I am when describing it and how I'm sure it could work.

'So what's stopping you?' asks Mum.

When I think about this question, the answer is very simple: after so many years of being in a couple and having someone to make decisions with, I just want someone to tell me I should do it. I need permission.

'Tell me to go for it, Mum,' I say.

'As long as there are some cheap deals for pensioners.' She goes back to her scone and gives half to me. 'I don't dish out this advice for free you know.'

I'm definitely not drowning any more.

Howdy Partner

I give Patty the news that I can't sing any more but I promise to advertise their gigs in the store and then I beg Zoe not to make me go to any more cookery classes. Given the nerves I feel before telling them both, I'm surprised when they both take the news rather well. Too well. Mum was right about Patty – she tells me that my departure is no problem as *'to be honest, Bo, it's quite difficult to fit four people on the small stages we get offered'*. The act (i.e. my dearest friend) has more room to breathe now.

Most importantly, I tell Charlie that I want to give the business a go. He has the paperwork drawn up and it's there waiting for me to sign. It's still strange seeing the name Angela Shepherd staring back at me, it still looks like someone else. I practise my signature a few times and warm the pen up so that the ink flows smoothly. I don't want to look back on this document and see hesitation or uncertainty. After a few attempts, I'm ready and I swirl my given name boldly, as large as the space allows. The final full stop is a promise to myself to give this all I have.

I'm an entrepreneur.

Within a few weeks, we have launched our new partnership.

I feel very different as I walk to the shop, *my* shop, on launch day. I am definitely walking on sunshine – so the song goes. I have new shoes, businesswoman shoes, pointy and shiny with killer heels, and today they don't hamper my ability to skip down the high street one iota.

Charlie is already there and gives me a big hug.

'Howdy partner,' he says.

I just smile; it feels good.

We work flat out for the next fortnight. First of all, we give the place a spruce up and nearly come to blows with the 'decorator slash designer' (who uses these inverted commas and the slash while talking about himself).

'What colour says adventure to you?' he begins, getting out his swatches.

'Blue?' I venture. 'As in ocean.'

'To me it's the colour of the Sahara, the earth, the spices of India.'

He goes off on one and whisks out a selection of colours for me to approve; they're exotically named, 'Turmeric', 'Distant Lands', 'Moroccan Dust', 'Toasted Maiden'. OK so I made the last one up, but I bet it exists in some paint collection.

'Lovely names, but at the end of the day – they're all brown,' I tell him.

I know by bitter experience that you can be seduced by the names and the fashions in the magazines but if you paint your room brown, you'll hate it by the end of the week, month if you're the patient type. Besides which, the shop is orange at the moment (yes, the colour of the sun seemed a good idea back then) and brown isn't enough of a change.

I insist that he explores the adventure to be found in the oceans and the skies because I know that he won't settle for being told to paint it blue, especially when he has to get it all done in a week. We find a compromise having spent far too long agreeing that the oceans of the Caribbean are turquoise-green. We settle on Pantone 319.

Next, I have to develop the calendar of holidays; we decide the calendar will change every year and culminate in a big New Year trip. Charlie thinks that having customers on a high in December will ensure that they book up for the next year. So Charlie, Caroline and I sit down one evening and finalise trips for each month of the year. I watch them laughing away at one point and feel the most enormous sense of pride; I'm one of them now, a local businesswoman struggling against the tide of globalism. Or a passionate individual making ends meet by sharing the thing that brings them most joy; that sounds better. Globalism always makes everyone feel guilty: we like the idea of small businesses but supermarkets are always a damn sight cheaper. I can only hope that they don't start selling holidays.

And so on to the launch of the Mercury Travel Club. In an hour or so Charlie and I are doing a ribbon cut for the *Chronicle*. We've raised some money to send some local carers on a weekend break and everyone who comes in will get a little brochure explaining the club. Caroline is doing the same in her shop, Peter is telling all of his businesses and Josie is putting it on Twitter, Pinterest and Facebook. We're all doing our bit, so fingers crossed.

All morning I answer messages asking how things are going; customers tell us it looks interesting and we get lots of good luck messages from friends. It feels very exciting and although I know there's no chance of being fully booked up by lunchtime, I hope to have one booking at least. And a booking from one of us wouldn't count.

I am so anxious for someone to book up today; it's completely illogical but I keep thinking that if we get a booking on the first day, it will mean that everything will go well. Now, who can I get to book something?

I scour our local directory to try to find clubs that might be interested; there are an incredible number of social groups around here. Mum's groups obviously but also Men In Sheds – for men to discuss their problems (like how to keep the remote from their wives, I imagine) – folk dancing and knitting groups.

There is also a local wine school. Now why didn't I know about that earlier and why doesn't Patty know about it? You can take qualifications in wine drinking; I can't wait to tell her, she'll probably qualify as a professor in no time at all.

They have to be a good target for the travel club, so I ring up the organiser then email through the calendar of events. I tell her we have just launched today and that we have an opening offer for members of the school. She promises to email everyone she knows and when we've finished talking I get straight on to the wine merchants and blag the discounted case of Bordeaux I've just promised.

I can't keep hitting 'refresh' to see if anyone has booked or I'll do nothing else all day. I focus and get on with the day job. In the end we have quite a successful morning with late bank holiday bookings. It isn't until late afternoon that Charlie looks up cautiously.

'Well, we've got a booking,' he says.

I run over to his desk, wondering why he's not more excited. I scan the screen for the details.

It's the very name I'd prefer not to see: Alan Hargreaves + 1.

Crystal Balls

'Oh forget him, just take his money and treat him like any other customer,' is Patty's practical but harshly given advice.

'Let's talk about me instead,' she adds.

I can't help but smile. When did we stop?

'I've decided where we're going for my birthday.' She pauses for dramatic effect.

'The Chippendales, a karaoke or the Firemen's Benevolent Ball?' I ask.

'Hmm, not bad suggestions, maybe next time. No, we're going here.' Patty pushes a leaflet towards me.

'Cleo Castanello, Clairvoyant to the Stars. Which stars, then?' It strikes me that most of the 'stars' I have ever seen grinning from black and white photographs on restaurant walls are now either disgraced, discredited or dead.

'That's not the point. I'm going to ask her about the Granny-Okes, whether we'll find fame and fortune.'

'And if not, you'll give it up?' I ask.

'Of course not,' replies Patty, 'I'll go to another clairvoyant. So are you up for it?'

How can I refuse? Literally, how can I? She wouldn't let me; besides which, although like everyone else I do not believe in psychics, I'm curious as to what she'll have to say about the travel club. Like Patty, if she says anything bad I'll just dismiss her as a complete phoney.

On the way to visiting Cleo Castanello, the song 'Gypsies, Tramps & Thieves' is playing through my mind, so I have a very clear expectation as to what she'll look like: dark curly hair and lots of rings on her fingers. When she opens the door, she looks nothing like that well-worn cliché.

She hosts 'Clairvoyance Parties' where a dozen of us (all women) gather in her living room and a stunning young woman, who could be her daughter, serves us glasses of bubbly and canapés. It is a beautifully tasteful room of creams and golds, the type you see in *Homes & Gardens* but if you try to recreate it yourself, just looks beige.

Patty is immediately reassured.

'You don't earn décor like this if you're rubbish,' she whispers.

Cleo looks head to toe a top businesswoman, a younger Martha Stewart: blonde cropped hair, fabulous bone structure and dark intelligent eyes that look right through you. Everyone will tell you not to give anything away to psychics, but this woman could probably get any detail she wanted out of me.

The session starts with her explaining that like many others she has a gift; she doesn't know where it came from but from an early age she could just tell what was going to happen. The house, she says as she holds out her hands to her surroundings, is testament to that; she knew when the stock market would crash and got out just in time. An impressed murmur rumbles around the room and I decide to ask her about this week's lottery numbers.

One by one, we go off for our individual consultations in her conservatory. As each person comes out they are surrounded by others asking, 'What did she say? Was she any good?' Most people seemed impressed.

Eventually, Patty is called and as is always the case when it's someone you know, the consultation seems to last no time at all. I wait for Patty to reach me through the curious throng.

'She sees the colour red or orange playing a VERY important role in my future,' says Patty as if this is the most significant fact in the world now.

'Red or orange what?' I ask.

'She couldn't tell but she also sees my life full of music and laughter.'

I'm about to say that it all sounds a bit vague when my name is called.

Cleo examines my face for longer than is comfortable and then says, 'You've had a difficult time of late but you're starting to come through it.'

I nod and think that is probably a safe bet for many people who consult psychics and besides which my crow's feet would give it away immediately.

'I can see many good things coming your way' – she holds both my hands – 'but I'm afraid I can also see some sadness.'

'What do you mean?' I ask.

'It could be a misunderstanding or a difficult argument; even illness. It concerns a person that you're close to but don't always see eye to eye with.'

Mum springs to mind and a chill spreads through my body.

'There's also something back to the future about you; perhaps you'll rekindle a friendship or return to something you used to enjoy? Whatever you face, you come out of it stronger and there is so much happiness at the end of the year.'

The words 'sadness' and 'illness' outweigh everything else she says so I leave the conservatory numb and head straight for Patty. I drag her out of that house so that the bad news will stay there and not follow me home. Just to be sure that the jinx is thrown off the trail we divert to a wine bar and after an unladylike gulp of Shiraz I tell Patty what she said about getting bad news.

'I can't cope with any more sadness,' I tell her. 'Haven't I had enough?'

'She said it might just be an argument,' she tries to reassure me. 'I dye my hair bright red, you tell me it's awful and we have a blazing row about it; that way both of our fortunes come true.

'Or you start getting maudlin on my birthday over something you don't believe in anyway and I deck you one,' she adds.

'And how will I be happier after that?' Despite myself, I laugh at her efforts.

'Your nose breaks and we have to get it fixed; the surgeon turns out to be dark and swarthy. You gaze into each other's eyes before the anaesthetic, fall in love and when you wake up you both live happily ever after,' she says.

'Deck me now,' I laugh and the conversation naturally gets back to Patty's reading.

'There's a karaoke bar in town called the Red Door. Do you think that's what she meant?'

Open for Business

Our launch article appears in the *South Manchester Chronicle* this weekend and we get quite a few enquiries, so I spend today trying to turn them into bookings.

I've also been invited to go and speak at the local WI to talk about travelling safely and our women-only trips. The travel club seems to work better when it's explained in person, so I'll have to try to get as many opportunities as I can to talk about it.

Mum thinks I've gone mad as I also keep calling to check that she's OK and suggest trips out together; after my fifth call to her this morning, she blows:

'Will you stop mithering me? I'm busy,' she tells me.

I utter a wounded 'sorry' and she softens as much as she ever does.

'Are you poorly? Or has something happened? I thought you'd be busy with the new business.'

'I am, Mum. I just wanted to check that you're OK and you know that if you ever need me, I'm never too busy,' I say.

'I know that, girl. Now go and make tons of money.'

'So you can boast about me at the Caravan Club?' I ask.

'Oh I already do that,' she tells me. 'No, so you can fly me first class somewhere. I hear they give you lovely free toiletries on first class.'

Satisfied that she's not hiding some illness or dark secret, I decide to put the prediction behind me, except the part about rekindling old friendships. I haven't told anyone about that but I wonder if she was talking about Alan?

Warm and fuzzy from knowing Mum is OK, I decide that sometime this year, I'm going to buy her that first-class flight and she can nick as many of the freebies as she likes.

Towards the end of the day, just as I'm packing my leaflets ready to go to the WI, I notice Charlie standing open-mouthed staring at the door.

'Don't look now but a giant tomato just walked in,' he says.

I follow his line of vision to Patty dressed head to toe in red with swathes of orange scarves.

'What on earth…?' I venture.

'If a renowned clairvoyant has said that these are my lucky colours then I want to attract luck every minute of the day,' she explains.

Charlie and I just look at each other then nod, accepting this logical explanation.

'And you think the more red or orange you wear the more luck you get? Is that how it works?' asks Charlie, very bravely in my opinion.

Patty bristles a little but then chuckles at her reflection in the window.

'I might have overdone it a tad today, it's every red thing I have in the wardrobe.'

I explain that I'm off to do a talk and she offers to come with me for moral support. I'd never usually say no to any type of support but I'm concerned that she might scare off the customers in that get-up.

'Could you at least lose the scarves?' I ask.

She sighs at me but starts unravelling the yards of fabric adorning her outfit before declaring, 'Oh you people, you're just too conservative. Mind you, that lot was bloody warm.'

Somehow I was expecting to walk into a sedate crowd quietly chatting to each other. Instead the energy and noise erased any nerves I had and I felt instantly at home.

Throughout the night there is so much laughter and bonhomie. First of all, there's wine (Patty and I are signing up next week), then plans to do a midnight walk for breast cancer and finally, after a tasting of some home-made pastries, I'm on.

I'm well versed in this speech by now; the Mercury Travel Club is my baby so I know I speak with passion and I do believe that people will have a great time if they join up.

'For me,' I tell them, 'it's about having a brilliant time, making good friends locally and perhaps learning a little along the way.

'For example, it would be easy to run a champagne trip to the Champagne region but did you know champagne was drunk in 1966 at Formula 1 in Le Mans? It's a stunningly beautiful French town that has something for everyone. So that's where we go to celebrate everyone's favourite bubbly; it's not all about grapes and pressing, which can be quite dull if we're honest. For all of our trips, we've thought of something a little bit different and of course, when you get back, there'll be a little gift waiting for you to help keep the memory alive.'

There is an appreciative murmur (although I suspect that this group are nice to everyone who comes along – unless you're Tony Blair).

It's time for questions, which are generally quite easy to answer.

'How do we know that you're not going to go bankrupt?' asks one lady.

'My partner Charlie has run the agency safely for over ten years and of course we're ABTA covered,' I respond.

'And you can trust her; after all, she's a karaoke singer,' comes a voice from the back. 'What could possibly go wrong?'

It's meant to be funny I think, but most people are confused and it knocks me off my stride. I strain to see the speaker at the back of the room. It's Amanda.

In that second, it feels as if I'm on the school stage and I've wet myself in front of everyone. I feel the throbbing pulse in my neck spreading colour all across my face. I don't know what to do.

Cool as anything, Patty turns to her and holds out a decimated plate of flaky pastry.

'Here, try this,' she says. 'I hear you enjoy other women's leftovers.'

Ouch. I am so glad she came with me. Amanda skulks out and takes all the attention with her. I get off the scary stage and the chairwoman leads a round of applause for my talk.

'Well ladies, I'm certainly going to book up for this, it sounds fantastic,' she says.

I am pretty certain that the last thing a husband-stealer should do at a WI meeting is insult the ex-wife, so inadvertently Amanda did me a favour. I know I got a bit of a sympathy vote tonight but if it gets the business off the ground I'm happy to take it.

I feel victorious.

Empty Rooms

Come morning, I've been focusing on ideas for drumming up business, as my victory at the WI has inspired a hitherto unknown desire for world domination. This carries me through to lunchtime when a perky voice on the phone brings me back down to earth.

'I have some good news for you,' the voice promises, 'we have a firm offer on your house.'

An offer, above the asking price with no chain to worry about is every seller's dream, but this is it. Our family home will be gone. I haven't been back to it this year but it's always been there in the background: strong red brick waiting for us if we change our mind. I can't quite believe it will belong to someone else very soon.

The estate agent tells me she'll send the paperwork to both Alan and myself and suggests that I start arranging the clearance to 'ensure a quick sale'.

Briefly I consider dawdling for as long as possible to put the buyers off, but what good would that do?

It's over; it's actually over.

When Alan first told me about the affair, I felt as if I was falling from a great height even though I was sitting on the sofa. That nauseous sensation of free fall returns now and when I land, something I love and care for, a solid symbol of our family history, will be gone.

It takes me another couple of days but I eventually build the courage to face it; dressed in scrubs and armed with plastic bags I arrive at the house. My plan is to sort and throw out anything that won't be coming with me. I've managed to kid myself this will be just like any other spring clean (well I haven't, but that's what I keep saying and hoping I'll start believing it).

As I park in the drive I see Alan has been keeping the garden tidy; I wonder whether this is because of the sale or because he misses having a garden in his new flat. I hope it's the latter.

I've never attached a great deal of significance to 'things'. I know some people hold on to every painting their child has ever drawn or they press every rose they've ever been given, but I'm not that sort of a person. I could lose everything but the photographs and it wouldn't spoil the memories. This feels different; previously when I threw out an anniversary card or glitter-bombed advent calendar I felt reassured that another would take its place the following year. The constant was always the family home where they'd be displayed for that brief moment. No more.

I unlock the door and push against the weight of the junk mail still addressed to Mr and Mrs Hargreaves. Seeing the name doesn't faze me – it is junk after all.

It's the smell that breaks me; although fused with the mustiness of the empty house, it's unmistakably us. I stand in the hallway and breathe in the aroma of family: wellies and waxed jackets fighting with the plug-in air fresheners I scattered during the sale.

I walk into the living room where, even now, the sofas have retained the unmistakable dents where each of us sat. I sit down in my dent and pick up a cushion; I hold it close and wonder how we got to this. How it is that one minute, all of this is a safe, familiar haven and the next it's just another property to be cleared out as soon as possible? It feels like a death and I suppose it is the death of a marriage. *Sad* is such a tiny word but when you truly feel it, it's the biggest, blackest void you've ever known.

There are no photographs left on display, so this could be anyone's house, unless of course it's yours. Then you know you bothered keeping the really tatty footstool because it's the perfect height, and that the scratch in the floorboards was the result of the oversized Christmas tree Zoe begged for; she proudly brought all her friends round just to see it.

I brace myself and go upstairs. The emotions start pulsing through me with each step climbed, I'm getting so breathless I might as well be climbing Everest. The spare room and scene of the crime fills me with disgust and disbelief while our bedroom drives a surge of anger as I remember the irritating habits I used to put up with, the snoring and teeth grinding. I always used to say that snoring was a sign of a person you love sleeping peacefully and therefore I didn't mind it. No wonder he was sleeping peacefully, he was bloody exhausted. Bastard.

It isn't until I open the door to Zoe's room that the tears start; the second I walk in I'm back in the room of a little girl safe in her home with a mummy and daddy.

I know she's left home and I know that we're both still here for her, but she's right, it's not the same. Every event from now on – her wedding, the birth of her children, their birthdays – they'll all be a negotiation with new partners and *that woman* will be in *our* family photos. You can't just waltz in and steal someone's family.

I slump down on the bed and eventually I get so angry, the tears dry up. I feel like screaming but then hear the door open. At that moment, precisely the wrong people walk in.

'I shouldn't be here,' says Amanda. 'I wouldn't want another woman in my house, you shouldn't have asked me.'

I rush to the top of the stairs grabbing a slipper on my way.

'No you fucking shouldn't. Get out of this house – both of you,' I roar and throw the slipper full force at the door. It bounces off Alan's head, so I'm very relieved I didn't pick up the vase. It has the desired effect; they scarper.

It has the right effect on me too; I sit at the top of the stairs and calm down. This was my house, I made it a home with my efforts and those facts remain. Zoe would have left home anyway and perhaps we would have downsized. We're just not doing it together.

I may have rationalised what has happened but I can't take any more of this place. I stuff a couple of Zoe's teddy bears into a bag and walk out, knowing that as I lock the door, it is the last time I will visit this house.

I don't want anything, so Alan can take it or dump it, I don't care.

As I walk down the drive, Alan leaps out of his car where he's been waiting for me.

'I'm sorry Angie, I didn't think,' he says.

'You never bloody do, that's half your problem. And it's a bit late for apologies don't you think,' I spit out as I barge past him, getting into my car and slamming the door.

'Is it?' I'm sure I hear him say through the screeching of my reverse departure.

My mother has other plans and decides she'll sort out the house. I tell her I'm just going to leave it all behind and I might as well be saying that I'll be letting a free sample go untasted; she's horrified.

'You can't let her go rummaging through your valuables, taking what she fancies. She's done enough of that,' she says.

I can't imagine Amanda helping herself to anything but I couldn't bear the thought of either of them commenting on my life, a life they ruined for me.

'I'd rather the Cats Protection League took it all,' says Mum.

My mum hates cats (*always licking their bits in plain sight*) and wouldn't ordinarily contribute to the protection of any at all, so this is quite a statement from her. She's off this afternoon to claim her rightful bounty and from what I can gather she's taking an army of militant pensioners with her.

Good luck to them; I dread to think what the place will look like when they've finished.

My concern right now is making a success of the business that I've invested everything in. I give myself a target of having the Christmas trip completely sold out to help me focus.

I need to be speaking to more groups of people so I get out the list of the organisations I want to contact, but before I get the chance, the phone starts ringing with repercussions from my mother's clear-out.

'Your mother has thrown out all of my clothes and given all of my fishing gear to Help the Aged,' Alan wails.

I imagine I'll have the opposite problem when I see her; it's highly likely that she'll bring so much stuff back for me to keep '*just in case*'.

'In fairness to her,' I say, 'you never used it and if you haven't worn it in the past six months, you're not going to.'

'That's not the point, why did you even let her near the house?' he asks.

I take a deep breath, brace myself then tell him calmly.

'I can't go back, Alan, it holds too many memories. I also couldn't bear the idea of you both rummaging through our things mocking our time together. We weren't perfect but you won't be either in a few years. You'll buy tack because it's funny, you'll keep rubbish because it reminds you of something, and no one else will understand it. I didn't want our tat ridiculed, so I sent Mum in.'

'But my fishing gear?' he asks.

'Two things,' I reply. 'One, when did you last fish and two, do you honestly think the honourable Nigella is going to let you keep all that gear in a luxury apartment? Or maggots in the fridge? Do you?'

'That's true,' he laughs, and I can picture the warmth of his eyes as he does so.

'And you should thank Mum anyway,' I continue, 'because if you'd even tried to move all that stuff in, you'd have had your first row.'

'Oh that ship sailed some time ago,' he says. 'The florist made a lot of money that day.'

The first part both surprises and delights me; I ignore the second.

He always went to the supermarket for my flowers.

Ed

It's book-club night and I reapply my lipstick in the ladies before heading to the table to join them. I've been determined to keep coming no matter how busy I get; true I haven't read each book they've discussed, but I go along and nod intelligently. It's a moment of peace with a glass of wine included.

Each of us can make a suggestion of what we read next but I haven't volunteered anything yet because it's quite a revealing thing to do, recommending a book for others. Do you pick something safe like a classic or a Booker prizewinner or do you try to say something about yourself with an edgy contemporary author? Then you have to choose something that would appeal to male and female. I'll never forget the month that Caroline had to feign interest as the guys extolled the virtues of a zombie novel. She says she always picks something that no one will own so they have to buy it from her; I can learn much from her.

Ed is in the hot seat this month and he's picked a thriller, *Remember Me This Way*. This is definitely up my street; I adore trying to guess the twist (that inevitably happens) at the end.

'In some ways,' I say, 'I hate these books because I cannot put them down until I know the heroine is safe.'

'I know what you mean,' continues Ed. 'Did you think he was still alive, stalking her?'

'He had to be,' I reply.

Our passionate discourse about thrillers continues after the formal session. We discuss whether the twist made sense, whether the film versions were any good, which books should make it on to the screen but haven't, and who you'd want to investigate your murder if it happened, Dalgliesh or Scarpetta?

I haven't lost myself in a conversation like this for aeons and I'm surprised it's happening with Ed. I don't think I've even looked at him properly and try to do so now without being too obvious. The opportunity comes when he heads off to the bar to buy us a refill: taller than Alan with strong looking arms. He probably doesn't sit behind a desk any more. He wouldn't be my usual type; I'm a sucker for the pretty boys, the Pierce Brosnans or Richard Geres of the world. Ed is more of a Liam Neeson or Tommy Lee Jones. He's quiet and craggy with a hint of danger. OK, I made that last bit up but we are discussing thrillers and I'm trying to imagine how I'll describe him to Patty.

We don't really know anything about each other so move on from books.

'I'm doing the rounds at the moment, presenting the idea to societies and groups. That seems to work well for us; members tend to spur each other on and we get multiple bookings.'

'You should come and present to us,' he suggests.

I can't imagine what group he might be part of, perhaps university lecturers or the P D James Fan Club. I nod politely.

'We love a good party,' he adds.

This mild-mannered man then goes on to tell me he rides a Harley-Davidson and runs a club – they're called 'Chapters'. They're part of the golden generation who have private pensions to blow on fun and frivolity. Ed also does restorations and repairs; that would explain the arms, then.

Patty will explode.

'I tell you what,' he says, 'come out with us this weekend and meet a few of the gang.'

I hesitate and don't know how to start this next conversation. I twiddle nervously with my empty ring finger; he spots it.

'Don't worry,' he guesses. 'It's just a friendly invitation. I think I've forgotten how to date properly.'

He laughs and we both relax, I know exactly what he means.

So with nothing to lose and maybe some bookings to gain, I borrow a leather jacket from Josie.

'It doesn't matter how sunny it looks now,' she warns me, 'you'll be glad you have this when you're tearing up the motorway.'

I hope I look the part. I'm waiting for a motorbike to come roaring up the road and if this doesn't have the curtains twitching then nothing will.

It does. I climb on to the back of the bike and cling to Ed as if my life depends on it.

'*I'm on a motorbike,*' I squeal inwardly.

We ride into Cheshire with eight other members of The Chapter and after a wonderful tour of the countryside, stop at a dainty tea room in Tarporley.

'We have to call ahead,' says one of the bikers, 'or they have a fit when they see us drive up.'

I can believe that. I still find this whole scenario extremely funny; my image of the leather-clad biker (and I know I won't be alone in this) is of a rebel, a wild child with arm-to-arm tattoos. They rev up to some sleazy joint and neck tequilas or bourbon before having a fight with a pool cue over some woman. If they're really unlucky, a Terminator from the future will turn up and demand their boots and jacket before nicking said bike.

What they don't do is make sure that they have enough thermals on under the leathers, roll up to a tea shop and have a selection of scones. But that's exactly what they do.

'Could you pass the jam?' asks one.

I hand the glass preserve pot to the man on my left in the Motörhead T-shirt.

'You're bemused, I can tell,' says Ed. I nod.

'Most of us loved bikes when we were younger,' he explains, 'but you know how it is. You give them up for family estates in your twenties. Now the nest is empty and you go back to what you've always loved.'

I certainly understand that. So this group are reliving their youths while meeting new people, but of course they can't drink on a ride out so they visit the quaintest of English villages dressed like Arnold Schwarzenegger.

I swear I will never look at bikers in quite the same way.

So from wondering what on earth Mercury would have to offer this group of renegades, I'm reassured that I won't crash and burn when I present the travel club.

After a lovely day out, I wave goodbye and peel off the extremely sweaty outfit. A shower is definitely needed but it has barely warmed up when Patty calls. I wrap myself in a towel and lie on the bed to talk to her.

'So where have you been, Bo?' she probes.

All of a sudden, I feel a little coy. Despite the tameness of the group, there is no way I can tell her that I was out with a group of bikers without getting the third degree.

'Erm, just meeting some people who might be interested in the travel club,' I say and that's the truth after all.

'Some friends of Ed,' I add, going for nonchalant, but it doesn't work.

'Him from the book club?' she asks, 'that's moved on a bit hasn't it?'

'He's just a friend.'

'Good. I don't want you nabbing a man before I do,' warns Patty.

'That's hardly likely,' I say.

She rings off satisfied with my answer.

I had a bloody good laugh today and rolling up into towns riding pillion was quite exciting, better than just getting out of the passenger seat of a hatchback anyway. It would be nice to think things could stay like this; we'd be friends without any expectations of benefits. When I try to picture any relationship developing, I'm comfortable with the dinner and moonlight strolls but I can't envisage the bedroom scene at all. What do second-timers our age do? Would he undress me or would I disappear into the bathroom to slip into something more comfortable? And do I have to tell him what I like? What do people like these days?

I feel comfortable making that promise to Patty because when you play the scene through, I really don't want to go there.

I'm jolted from my thoughts by a noise in the front garden and a car door slamming. I sit very still for a few moments to make sure that I can't hear anything inside the house. I mentally run through arriving back home: did I lock the door? I'm sure I did, I always do.

It's times like this when you wish you still lived with a man; I would always have sent Alan to investigate noises in the night. Instead, I have to walk assertively down the stairs showing that I am mistress of my own abode and will take no crap from anyone. Sneaking down on tiptoes probably doesn't say that but it's all I can manage. If I were in a movie right now, a cat would jump out and screech. I pray that doesn't happen or I'm head over heels down these stairs, squashing it on the way.

I get to the (locked) front door without mishap and open it cautiously. The noise seems to have been caused by a beautifully planted terracotta pot, which was obviously very heavy to manoeuvre into place. I look up and down the street but there is no one in sight and no one sneaking a peek from any window. It appears I'm being stalked by Monty Don.

I kick the spilled soil into the garden and notice that Gnorman is holding something. Someone has attached a little plant stick and an empty seed packet to him so it looks as if he's carrying a little protest placard.

I bend down to pick it up; it's a packet of forget-me-nots.

It can't be – can it? Alan?

Cruising

Patty has taken up residence in the store today and we're in danger of her frightening off any customers with her scowl. She's also still wearing an item of red clothing each day, although thankfully it's a little more subtle now.

'I thought something might have happened by now,' she laments.

'I buy red Thai curry instead of green in case someone locks eyes with me at the supermarket and says, "Oh, my favourite too", I've switched to Bloody Marys because red wine looks too purple and I never leave the house without a strawberry condom. I just don't know what more I can do.'

It's not the most obvious list that springs to mind.

'Be patient, Patience,' I tell her, 'good things come…etc.'

'Yeah, right. Anyway, that's not why I'm here.' She goes into business mode. 'It's about the Granny-Okes.'

'Pats, I can't…'

'Don't worry, we don't need you singing but I wondered if you could do something else for me.'

Whatever it is, I know that I'll have to find a way of doing it, but in the end, it isn't too bad.

'Craig might be able to get us on the line-up of an eighties cruise if you put it in the travel club,' she says.

'We already sell this,' says Charlie when I show him the itinerary.

'But if there's a Mercury Travel Club offer, it might sell-out quicker,' I say.

'I wouldn't sweat that,' pipes up Josie, 'people are mad for this retro stuff.'

I know she's right; this is a simple seven-day tour of the Mediterranean. It has the tribute bands but also eighties movies and quizzes each night. I'm not sure what extra we can add for the Mercury members, it's pretty good now.

'What did you guys eat back then?' asks Josie.

I can't remember what my parents served at dinner parties, and when I started to go out for dinner with friends, it was mainly to Italian restaurants – I think lasagne was exotic then.

'Mateus Rosé,' exclaims Charlie, 'that was all the rage and everyone had a candle in the empty bottle.'

'Wasn't it totally, like, decadent with Thatcher and the City?' asks Josie. 'Lots of champagne everywhere?'

'Steak,' I remember, 'lots of steak in peppercorn sauces; nouvelle cuisine, Delia Smith, beef wellingtons and fondues.'

'And cocktails with Pernod or Malibu in. We thought we were being so sophisticated,' adds Charlie.

We grimace with such feeling it's obvious we both made that mistake in our youth.

Charlie is convinced that he can turn this into something special so I leave him to it.

I'm back on the road tonight with Ed's biker gang; it sounds far more exciting when I call my speeches at the WI and Harley Chapter my tour dates.

'Bo Peep on Tour' – maybe I should have a T-shirt printed? Although as I do sound more like a burlesque dancer than a travel agent, people might be disappointed when I arrive. I guess I could wear tassels.

Meetings are held upstairs at The Olde Oake and most of the group have walked here. I'm glad I've already met a few of the crowd as it means I can mingle politely rather than sit on the edge getting nervous. Ed is the president of this Chapter and he stands up to introduce me. I extol the virtues of the travel club, outline the calendar and offer to customise additional trips if there is enough interest.

'Perhaps a trip to Chicago where the first Harley showroom opened,' I say. (I throw this in to seem knowledgeable but as I only found it on the internet yesterday it's a good job no one pushes me further on it.)

Ed leads everyone in a round of applause at the end.

'That was great Angie, you've restored my reputation in choosing speakers,' he says.

'It wouldn't be hard to beat the flora and fauna of the Wetlands,' comes a voice from the back and everyone laughs.

Ed blushes and takes the ribbing with good humour.

I've heard it said that when some people smile, their faces change completely and so it is with Ed. Instead of craggy action man there stood a well-liked guy, comfortable in his own skin and happy to laugh at himself.

'Happy to help,' I say joining in the bonhomie and move a step closer to Ed.

I feel a twinge of something as he thanks me and pecks me on the cheek.

Baking Hot

It has been a stunningly warm June and not just 'British Hot' as Josie calls it laughingly but 'Aussie Global Warming Hot'. White legs and arms are turning pink everywhere you look and the world is a happier place, as it always is when the sun shines.

Across Chorlton, the pub gardens are blooming and cheeks are getting rosier as everyone enjoys a little alfresco tipple in the glorious sunshine.

So I can understand my mother's angst when she calls me and pleads, 'Please come and get her, my house is like Hades' Sauna.'

My daughter has taken up 'baking residence' in Mum's double oven and is spending every evening practising her recipes. Mum was very keen to begin with – after all multiple cakes were at stake – but the heatwave has made even the freebies unattractive.

When I arrive there is a type of science-fiction haze around the back door. It looks just like the special effects they used on *Star Trek* when they put up that cloaking shield thing; I didn't pay much attention when Alan was glued to it. Why is it that there are definitely 'men's programmes' and 'women's programmes' and they're pretty much universally consistent? I'm not sure a woman would invent a programme about spaceships, but I could be wrong.

Anyway, as I ponder, I walk into the haze and the heat hits me.

'Woah,' I say braving the inferno, 'how are you surviving this without protective clothing?'

My daughter looks up from her latest creation and adds it to a table laden with carbohydrates. If you'd been on the Atkins or Dukan diets recently, this place would be an absolute heaven or hell depending on your inclination to ditch it or stick to it.

'Where's Gran?' I ask.

I'm told she's upstairs, so go in search and find her sitting on the loo wearing her nightie and reading a magazine with a Chardonnay cooling in the sink.

I don't need to ask why: this is the coolest room in the house. I make myself comfy on the edge of the bath and take a slug from her glass.

'What are we going to do about her?' asks Mum, 'Amanda's a professional chef; all the others might be too, she's never going to win.'

It will break her heart to be beaten by Amanda, but I know my daughter and there is no way that she will back out now.

'We're going to have to help somehow.' I drain her glass and get up. 'Come on then before you take roots; you know Catherine the Great died on the loo don't you?'

Downstairs there lies every type of pastry known to woman-kind (as I imagine we can name more varieties than mankind). We all sit down to survey the bounty, some pieces looking more shipwrecked than others.

'I've tried everything and I just don't know what to go with,' sighs Zoe, although that much is obvious.

Mum starts sampling each one.

'OK then, let's get practical,' I say. 'What are the competition categories?'

Zoe digs out a flour-covered sheet which lists them: Pastry King or Queen, Lord of the Flans – you get the picture. I skim down the list and wonder which category Amanda will enter as it would be best if they weren't up against each other.

'How are your crumbles?' I ask looking at the Duchess of Desserts category.

'They're OK but I'm not going to win with an apple crumble, am I?' says Zoe.

'This one's nice,' chirps up Mum and we'll have to take her word for it as it's gone.

'And pray, what was it?' I ask.

'Key Lime Pie,' answers Zoe, 'I made it with a slug of margarita to give it a bit of a kick.'

'Maybe we should go for this one then,' I say pointing at the list.

'Tomorrow's Trendsetters; it sounds like quite a youthful category and you could probably make anything you like. Now, what's trendy? Those macaroon things?'

'So 2014,' Zoe shakes her head.

'Thank goodness for that,' mumbles Mum who, by the way, is still sitting in the background eating her way through the table.

'I couldn't understand all that fuss; they're only chewy biscuits in different colours.'

'How about taking your Lime Pie idea and making a cocktail cabinet of cakes? Like a Black Russian Chocolate Cake,' I suggest.

Zoe starts looking up cake trends online.

'Baking with spirits has been done,' she tells us. 'The next big thing is going to be baking with herbs according to this, like dark chocolate with basil. Maybe I could do a herb garden?'

'Sounds good,' I say, 'we've got the category but I still think we should give both ideas a go. Cocktails may be passé in professional circles but adding the word artisan might make them go down very well here. You research herb cakes and I'll do the boozy ones then we'll pitch our ideas to each other and see which one we think would win. We could ask Patty and Mum to be the judges.'

'They're going to pick the ones with the most alcohol in,' counsels Zoe, 'which is not necessarily what the judges will choose.'

'Then let's invite Charlie and Peter, too; Peter is very discerning. It'll be like *Dragons' Den*,' I say.

'Great, next Sunday, the Dragons' Doughnuts.' Zoe shakes my hand competitively; my daughter even wants to win this stage.

* * *

As the month ploughs on, the sweltering heat does nothing for bookings. 'Staycations' became popular during the recession when everyone decided to stay at home for their holidays. They would also justify it on environmental grounds at first, but their desire to save the planet was soon beaten down by the British weather and theme park prices. It's often cheaper to go abroad.

Nevertheless, when the long-range forecast is for more heat and potential drought, there is little incentive to book something just to get some sunshine. Our customers don't tend to travel during the school holidays or if they do, it's as a babysitting resource on their family package trips.

The Mercury Travel Club is about more than weather, so I spend the week going through our customer lists sending them details of short breaks and activities which might tempt them out of their summer hibernation. Our business plan forecasts bear no resemblance to reality at the moment.

Charlie is working on Patty's cruise trip.

'Some of these tributes are fabulous,' he says. 'In fact, I have no idea how she managed to wangle her way on to this line-up.'

I suspect having a friend who can get bums on seats has helped but I'm still impressed by the list of bands taking part. I reflect that if you're current, you take up residency in Vegas and if you're retro you live life on the ocean wave.

Charlie adds a little fantasy of his own to the trip: for Mercury Club members, we'll be hosting his little pool-side party à la Tom Cruise before showing the film *Cocktail*; living the dream.

We assemble the publicity shots into an email and send it to everyone we know. The response is pretty good with customers copying each other saying, 'Now this looks like fun.'

A group of four books up instantly and others ask for more information.

'I never thought I'd ever say these words,' I say to Charlie, 'but Patty might just save the day.'

We Have to Talk about Alan

As I open my door and leave for work, the terracotta planter reminds me that there is an issue I'm avoiding – my stalker.

It has to be Alan, who else can it be? A gardener who doesn't want me to forget them? He gave Gnorman a partner; he tidied up after the storm. I'm sure he must know where I live, after all.

Why is he messing with my emotions now? When the house sale is practically complete? When I've thrown out his fishing gear and insulted his new woman? When I'm finally starting to feel like a person in my own right and not just one half, the insignificant half, of a couple?

I don't know what to do. Patty would kill me if I took him back but there are other things to consider besides her needs. Zoe would have her family back together again; we'd hold on to our home; none of us would be living in rented boxes; and the investment in the Mercury Club would feel more secure if someone were earning an income. It would be like turning the clocks back (as Cleo predicted) but with a new, improved version. I'd put my foot down about having a life of my own and keep up all the new things I've done like the book club and the nights out with Patty; I'd probably have to stop the friendship with Ed, though.

It could work but am I sure that I want it to?

Or am I even considering this for a very different, very shallow reason?

You know the one I mean.

The sweet taste of victory when I look into Amanda's eyes as I saunter past with Alan.

'In the end, you and your cakes just weren't good enough. I won.'

Despite mentally practising the scenario many times over, I haven't acted on my suspicions. Like many others, I find the mantra 'if in doubt do nowt' to be fairly solid advice. To me it means, sleep on it and force the issue to start resolving itself. This is very important because the last thing I ever want Alan to be able to say is that I 'begged him to come back'.

I find that men have a knack at doing this; even in school I remember Martyn Jackson moping around until I asked him out. Then when he decided to move on to someone else he started moping again and I was the one who had to ask him if we'd split up.

Not this time. If this is him and he does want me back, then he has to do a bit more than leave the gnomes to do the talking. A lot more.

Anyway, I don't have time to worry about him. I'm very busy trying to persuade people to take a holiday; at least Patty's cruise is selling well if nothing else is. Come closing time I have to go online to find some innovative cake recipes, buy the ingredients and get ready to compete with my daughter on Sunday. Again I find myself wondering how on earth I managed to volunteer for this. I don't want to win even if it were a vague possibility.

The internet does me proud and I plan a Limoncello Drizzle Cake, a Chocolate Black Russian and a Gin & Tonic Cake. Yes, all of these delights actually exist. Who knew?

I must look like a complete health hazard as I whizz around the supermarket shelves adding only unusual spirits, sugar and butter to my basket. And then I remember that I need lemons, thank goodness for that; they must count as one of your five-a-day. I imagine I probably have enough gin in the house but perhaps if I have a little tipple first it'll help me to get into the swing of things. I best buy another bottle. After all, I mustn't run out of gin before I get to the cake.

* * *

The great Bo Peep bake-off
The clash of the cakes
The scrummage of scones
The battle of the buns
Mother v. daughter in a skirmish to decide soufflé supremacy

The billing is more impressive than the entrant – at least in my case.

'Why have you made three trifles?'

The room giggles at the innocence of Peter's question; he doesn't know about my childhood.

Zoe and I have set up our tableau in the dining room while our 'judges' enjoy a Pimm's in the garden.

We don't have to bake live at the competition, so we've created a display of the cakes we'd planned to make. It's true to say that my cakes have turned out like every other sponge I ever make – flat. However, I know that the skill in these competitions is in the presentation, so I have excelled here, or so I believe.

Using my full creative genius I have taken some very stylish cocktail glasses, broken up the sponge, added a bit of whipped cream for luck *et voilà*.

I scatter little umbrellas around, add glass charms and twizzle sticks then put a shaker in the background. In my mind, I have created an artful and innovative selection worthy of the Trendsetter category.

Following Peter's comments, however, I see my effort more clearly and indeed it does look more like three trifles let loose on a bar crawl.

Zoe on the other hand has surpassed herself. Her herb garden display is both rustic and contemporary with fresh green herbs and glowing nasturtiums surrounding four beautiful creations presented in little flower pots and trendy tin gardening mugs.

She's made Apricot and Basil Tart presented as a beautiful sunflower, Lemon and Thyme Cake, Chocolate and Chilli Mousse and some very sweet Rosemary Cookies. They look so delightful it seems a shame to eat them, but of course we have to and they taste as good as they look. I do not know how Zoe has either inherited or cultivated this skill.

'The question isn't "Can Zoe beat her Mum" because we all could.' My mother is giving me another vote of confidence.

'But are her herb recipes more likely to win than cocktail recipes?'

There follows a debate about whether cocktails have peaked or not. We decide that cocktails in jam jars have definitely peaked, alongside food served on slate. Peter sticks to the point and looks at the list of judges.

'You have an RHS winner as chair of the panel,' he declares, 'go with the herbs.'

This man has so much local insider knowledge that he could probably find a category I could win, perhaps the one with the local lush as chair. Or maybe that's a stretch too far.

Having decided the culinary direction, Patty tries to steer the conversation on to Ed.

'Have you seen *Knight Rider* recently?' she asks.

Everyone seems to stop mid-morsel and raise their eyebrows towards me; you'd think all my family and friends had suddenly had Botox injections. Given that I haven't even mentioned him today, I can only assume Patty has been divulging my private life to everyone while I slaved away.

'He's just a friend,' I protest, 'I'm trying to get business, nothing more.'

'Good.'

Zoe says so much with just the one word; I know she's hoping that I'll get back together with her dad, so now is not the time to tell them about the gnomes and my suspicions. In the cold light of day, it seems rather far-fetched.

There's a short awkward silence until Charlie gets Patty warmed up.

'So how are rehearsals going, Granny Lauper?' he asks.

'Would you believe, the girls wanted to discuss dropping Cyndi from the set list?' she replies.

And so this mid-summer eve will always be remembered for drinking cocktails at Mum's, eating cake and debating whether Cyndi or Madonna was the real Queen of Eighties Pop.

There are worse ways to spend the longest day of the year.

Put Necker Island on Hold

However, I can't think of worse ways to spend a Monday than looking through accounts; poorly performing accounts.

'With this heatwave and the downturn in bookings, we're not achieving our cash-flow targets,' explains Charlie. 'We need to cut costs somehow.'

Customers still aren't booking the big overseas trips and we're only taking initial deposits for the Mercury Travel Club weekends, so finances are quite tight at the moment.

'What are the options?' I ask.

Charlie starts counting them out but runs out of ideas by the fourth finger.

'We could cut trading hours, let Josie go, take pay cuts or ask customers to pay the full balance up front.'

We both know that three of the options will send panic amongst the customers and no one will book a holiday with a company they think is in trouble. I wonder how many times Charlie has been in this situation on his own and we haven't known about it; being the boss is tougher than it looks. I suggest the action I imagine he's taken before.

'I guess we have to shoulder the pay cuts ourselves, until things get better,' I say.

'Can you manage on less?' asks Charlie.

I have no idea but I know from reading the autobiographies of successful entrepreneurs that many go through hard times. I'm so busy romanticising this and thinking how good conquering a downturn will sound in my top businesswoman acceptance speech, I don't even think of the implications when I say, 'I'll find a way Charlie, how much less?'

'How about we only take the minimum until autumn?' he suggests.

I'm nodding while my mental calculator whirrs away; if the house sale goes through as planned, I'll be OK. I won't be able to buy anywhere else yet but I wasn't ready to put down roots anyway.

The most important thing is to hold our heads up high and act as if everything is going brilliantly; people are attracted to success. I need our local paper to run another feature on how well we're doing, but they're reluctant as they've only just done one. I have to give them something new.

'Patty,' I project as if she's miles away, not at the end of the phone, 'how do you fancy being the centre of attention?'

'Ha, ha very funny,' she replies.

My idea is to tell the *Chronicle* about her astounding success: '*From Karaoke to Cruise Ship*'; how a night out with the girls led to sharing the stage with a host of 1980s icons. They'd be able to feature pictures of the stars and mention that tickets are available from us. It's worth a try and she's up for it so agrees to call the editor as I've pestered him too much recently.

Ed calls. 'Hi there,' he says, 'I hope you don't mind me calling you.'

'Not if you're about to make lots of bookings for The Chapter,' I say.

He laughs so my cheerful veneer must be effective.

'Perhaps when this heatwave dies down. Right now we're making the most of the rare UK sunshine.'

Same as everyone else then – damn.

'I just wondered if you fancied getting some food after work?' he continues.

My entourage would warn me this is far too close to date territory, but I need cheering up and if I'm on minimum wage, I need someone else to start paying for my food.

'I'd love to,' I tell him.

We meet up for the early bird menu so both the time and the restaurant declares that we're just friends out for a meal rather than on a date. I'm slightly disappointed by this but it doesn't surprise me that Ed would want to take it slowly.

It's a warm and homely Italian place: not so child friendly that we can't hear ourselves chat over screaming crayon-wielders but not so couple-y that we're embarrassed by everyone except us holding hands and gazing into each other's eyes.

Alan and I used to play a game in restaurants; we'd eye up each couple and make up back stories for them.

'They met line-dancing; it was love at first sight and they haven't let go of each other's hands for six weeks. They even go to the loo together,' we said of one particularly nauseating couple.

'He met her at uni when they were both wild but now she's in corporate law and she chooses all his clothes for him. It'll be over by the end of the year.' Then we watched a real power-dresser straightening the lapels of her hangdog companion.

We found it quite entertaining and one night we watched a family having a blazing row in sign language. I've never seen such emotion silently expressed; it must be fantastic to be able to do that. Her parents obviously didn't like her boyfriend that's for sure.

I tell Ed about the game and he smiles.

'My ex and I used to play Punching Above Their Weight. We'd pick the most unlikely couple in the room and decide which one had won the lottery when it came to other halves.'

'Oh Lord,' I say, 'if everyone plays these games, it means someone is probably checking us out right now.'

'They'd definitely say that I'd won the lottery,' says Ed.

I groan at the cheesiness but am secretly pleased and in danger of blushing; I'm extremely grateful when the bruschetta arrives.

It's the first time he's mentioned an ex and I decide to make polite enquiries as casually as I can.

'So how did it end – with your ex?' I ask.

'I guess she decided she was punching above her weight. What about you?'

'Ditto,' I add.

So we've managed to get through that part with the minimum level of knowledge being offered or acquired by either of us. Men certainly don't talk the way women do.

Plates are cleared and pasta arrives, mine heaving with a creamy sauce. Although everyone thinks they can make a carbonara at home, there is NOTHING that beats this dish in a good Italian restaurant.

There is apparently a scientifically proven fact that the right combination of fat in a food can send signals to your brain cells and simulate an orgasm. This is true (you can google it), I have not made it up; it's why you become addicted to chocolate. I have a vision of a science lab where hundreds of women are sitting with stainless steel colanders on their heads. They're attached to a pleasure-measuring machine with jump leads and a scientist is feeding them pasta and cake. I wonder how I sign up for such experiments.

Enough fantasising. I tell you the Italians knew this way before anyone else and every mouthful of this sensational dish makes me want to break out into groans of delight. I restrain myself but the unadulterated joy must show on my face.

'It looks as if you're enjoying that. Do you cook?' asks Ed.

Coitus interruptus.

'No – in fact it's a running joke in my family. Let me show you something.'

I get out my phone and show him the pictures of the bake-off rehearsal.

'What is it?' A perfectly understandable question.

'They're cakes,' I declare pointing out the baked goods amongst the rest of the paraphernalia.

'My daughter is entering the Great Bake-Off competition so we were having a run-through.'

I explain the competition and the idea behind my creations. His glazed expression suggests that he's either deeply interested, deep in thought or deeply bored.

'Anyway, enough of my culinary disasters, shall we share the tiramisu?' I ask.

'A woman who offers out her dessert; what parallel universe have I been transported to?'

'Don't worry it'll only happen this once. The sharing that is, not the date.'

Damn. I've called it a date.

'Glad to hear it,' he smiles, and picks up the second spoon.

Artistic Differences

If I were a cartoon character, I'd be walking along the street with little cherubs fluttering around my head. Now that I think about it, how did they ever come to represent love? What on earth is romantic about fat children armed with bows and arrows? Nowadays, they'd be slapped with an ASBO and if you saw them in a family pub, you'd run a mile.

Anyway, enough with reality; I think I might be the tiniest bit smitten. After dinner we had a quick drink and then he walked me home. Not all the way home – I didn't want that awkward '*Do I invite him in or not?*' scenario – but to the end of the street where we progressed to a '*more than friends*' kiss. It didn't feel too awkward so I'm starting to imagine that falling in love at fifty might be just like falling in love at any age. Not that I'm falling in love, of course; I'm just very happy.

Patty is not.

'Bo, can you come round tonight and give us your objective opinion?' she pleads.

She rarely wants my opinion, so I know what she's actually asking is for me to tell the rest of the Granny-Okes that she is right and they are wrong.

They are having costume and set list disagreements ahead of the cruise gig. I'm curious about it so agree to arbitrate. Patty and the girls are struggling with the transition from small-time club singers to big-time stadium fillers, or at least you'd think they were with the angst that fills the room.

Kath and Sheila think things are good as they are; everyone enjoyed the last gig and that's the performance Craig hired them for.

All good points I think as I turn my head to Patty; this is like being the umpire at a tennis match. So far Patty is fifteen-love down.

'But every act has to progress,' she counters, 'otherwise people will get bored and stop coming to see them.'

Fifteen-all.

'On this cruise we can't just dress up like these people. Adam Ant might actually be there,' she adds.

Thirty-fifteen.

'That makes it even funnier,' says Kath. 'He could chase us off the stage or something.'

Thirty-all.

'These artists aren't props on a Granny-Oke gig,' says Patty. 'They take their music seriously and we have to if we want this to last.'

Forty-thirty.

'Let's build an identity of our own,' urges Patty, 'keep some of the things that work, like the Zimmer frames, but have a look that makes other people want to dress up like us.

'No one wants to be the starter act on these tours,' she continues, 'but we don't mind. We could be travelling the world if we want to. Come on let's go for this, please.'

I'm impressed and when I look back over at Sheila and Kath, they are too. The nodding heads tell me that this rally is over.

Game, set and match to Patty.

Grâce à Dieu

I'm sick to death of weathermen and their cheery smiles; everything is wonderful thanks to the glorious sunshine. Sales are up as everyone buys new clothes and barbecues, crime is down (because it's too hot to burgle someone? I couldn't make sense of that one either) and farmers are happy because the crops are abundant this year. It seems as if everyone is doing well from this apart from the poor old travel agent. Give it another week of heat and the whingeing will start; drought across the land, hose-pipe bans and fights breaking out on the tube because everyone's blood has hit boiling point.

The cruise is sold out, so I can't flog that any more. I need to fill spaces on the other events, in particular the trip to Monaco, which is rapidly approaching our 'lose your deposit' deadline. How on earth am I going to persuade people to leave this heat and sit somewhere hotter? I look up the temperature out of interest; typical, it's actually colder on the south coast of France than it is here.

That's it, the brain has waved. We sell this trip as an escape from the heat.

'You're gonna sell a holiday by telling people it'll be cold when they get there?' Josie is looking at me as if I'm mad.

'Not like that, but picture this,' I say. 'Cooling sea breezes, chilled wine on the terraces watching the sun go down, castle

161

visits during the heat of the day and air-conditioned bedrooms for a wonderful night's sleep.'

'I'd go for the air conditioning,' chimes in Charlie. 'I'm not sleeping a wink in this.'

'It's got to be worth trying, hasn't it?' I ask.

I don't have any other ideas at the moment but more than that, it's not the worst I've had.

'Let's give it all we've got,' Charlie agrees.

'I'll download some pictures: chilled wine, harbour walks, that kind of thing,' Josie fires up.

'Make sure it looks as if there's a gentle breeze blowing and try to find something that might say "refreshing night's sleep",' Charlie gets it.

All afternoon Josie emails, tweets and Facebooks mouth-watering images of exactly what you want to see in a heatwave.

I get on the phone to some of our loyal customers.

'Hi there, how are you enjoying this heat? I know a killer, isn't it? I was just saying to Charlie that it's actually cooler in the south of France – honestly…'

I should get a BAFTA, never mind an Entrepreneur's Award, as I deliver that line at least thirty times this afternoon and with the same amount of enthusiasm each call. Charlie collars everyone who walks into the store with the same line and by the end of the day we have a few definite bookings and even more promises to talk it over with the other half. As Charlie expected, the clincher turns out to be the air-conditioned bedrooms with someone to bring you chilled orange juice and fruit salad in the morning. We add these to Josie's social media posts then agree to stay open later so that people can pop in or call us when they've finished work or had the conversation.

We get some fresh orange juice in and invite people to have a chilled glass while they're booking. We really couldn't be trying any harder, so if there is a God in heaven, surely he will look down on these efforts and save our asses. I don't think he's busy with much else at the moment.

We get past our minimum sales number and close up. I walk home watching British café culture play out in the suburbs. I contemplate our complete lack of glamour compared to the vision I've just been selling; I wouldn't mind going to the south of France myself.

Here Lies Patty

Patty's complete level of focus on the upcoming cruise surprised me somewhat, so I thought I'd go and quiz her about it. She tells me to come round after her military fitness class in the park. I didn't think she even knew the word fitness but the fact that there's a suggestion of a burly bloke makes me believe that there may be another incentive for this sudden interest in exercise.

'No, I want to get fit,' she tells me as she pours us both a glass of mineral water – that's right, water. 'I can't perform every night if I'm not.'

'You're taking this very seriously all of a sudden,' I say.

'It floats my boat, if you'll pardon the pun,' she starts to explain.

'When Nige died, I didn't know what to do with myself, so I had a go at everything and I accepted everyone's invitations. People kept saying "You should do this" or "Come with us – you'll love it", so I did but I never found anything that I liked. Do you know what I mean?'

I nod; I know exactly what she means.

'But it's not as if I'm getting any younger,' she continues. 'The other day, I was perusing the lonely hearts as usual and I ended up reading the obituaries too.'

'You won't find much action there,' I say.

'And I thought, "What will they say about me?" *Here lies Patty*...wife? Not any more. Mother? Nope. It'd just be *Here lies Patty*. Not much to show for a life.'

Mine wouldn't say much more I think to myself.

'I'd tell everyone about the brilliant fun we had at the airline,' I say, 'if I outlive you, of course.'

'But that's the problem,' sighs Patty. 'I don't want the stories about me to be forty years old. I want brilliant fun now. It's taken me four years to accept that I am allowed a life of my own and I'm ready to live it,' she says.

'After all, everyone knows I was positively *born* to perform.' She smiles and the Patty I know and love is back in the room.

'If Craig is right and we could travel the world on this at least for a year or two, it has to be worth a go, doesn't it?' she asks.

'I'll miss you,' I say, 'but you're right, you have to try it.'

I fall quiet and she gives me a hug.

'Oh you'll be OK, Miss Travel Expert and Knight Rider Pillion. Do you think you'll ride him, sorry *with* him, for a while?' she asks.

'Subtle,' I reply. 'Nothing's happened if that's what you're asking, but I like him and he's one of the few uncomplicated things in my life at the moment, so as you say, why not?'

We clink our water glasses but don't bother drinking; if they'd been filled with wine, we'd have been on a refill by now.

* * *

The complications in my life return with a call from Alan.

'Have you heard from the estate agent?' he says. 'There's a delay in the sale, they've found damp or something in the survey.'

'We didn't have damp,' I tell him.

'I know that, it'll be a bloody tactic to reduce the price. Well I'm not having it; we should tell them they can't have the house for messing us about like this.'

My imagination runs wild and I wonder if Alan is trying to delay the sale, maybe even prevent it. After all, he needn't have called me personally about this. Play it cool, I tell myself.

'Can we sleep on it?' I ask. 'Wait to hear from them properly? I could do with the cash right now for the business.'

As soon as those words are out of my mouth I regret them, anticipating some, '*I told you so, biting off more than you could chew*' type comments. Instead, he's quite gentle.

'Cash flow is a killer, isn't it?' he says. 'I was wondering how you were getting on. It's always tough to start.'

He starts reminiscing about the early days of his business when we used to work out of the dining room but pretend we were in his offices to anyone who called; they were good times.

I feel as if I've had a little hug from him and I find myself wondering if I ever got the choice, which would I pick?

Old flame or new flicker?

Mum and Dad

If it's true that ultimately we all end up like our parents, I hope I end up like my dad. To the outside world he is the archetypal hen-pecked husband but behind that mild-mannered exterior there is a man who knows exactly how to manoeuvre my cake-snaffling mother. If he were in a political thriller, he'd be the Svengali who ensures the right people get to power. The Caravan Club is a case in point. They don't actually own a caravan.

They did own a motorhome for many years and we used to join them for lots of great family holidays while Zoe was growing up. When she reached the age where she preferred Barcelona to Bognor, they joined a club and began touring the UK with other abandoned grandparents. On one trip, they were pitched up in the grounds of a magnificent country house hotel and the weather was just appalling. Mum complained that she wouldn't get a wink of sleep with the rain battering down on the metal roof and while she was nattering with one of the other motor-homers, Dad, stealth-like, went off to ask about a room in the hotel. As everyone else got ready to leave the bar and trudge back through the mud to their vehicles, Dad revealed that they'd be staying indoors. Mum was delighted; I can just imagine the gloating: 'Oh he spoils me. I'd much rather be in the motorhome but I can't say no now, can I?'

Mum would never let him sell the motorhome as she enjoyed the trips out and meeting the other club members. However, over the course of the next couple of years, Dad pulled his hotel room trick a few times. Then he sold the big motorhome for a smaller version – which Mum thought was too cramped, so this led to even more nights in a hotel – and eventually Dad sold that one and bought an old Jaguar, which was ultimately what he wanted anyway. They're still members because Dad runs the weekly quiz team; Mum keeps telling people that they still love caravanning and 'when it's warm enough' they'll stop using the hotels.

Of course it's never warm enough unless it's too warm, but this is equally uncomfortable in a motorhome. Over the years, many of the other husbands have persuaded their wives down the same route so effectively it's now a caravan group that swapped its vans for classic cars. They all have a preference for life's luxuries and that's why it's worth my while being here tonight.

Mum has been desperate for me to do this talk. 'Now that you've been in the paper, people keep asking about you,' she tells me.

The local rag is international stardom in my mother's eyes. So I deliver my well-practised performance and have an anecdote for everyone I'm introduced to. I'm so happy to have done something for them.

I didn't want to come here first, I wanted to come along as a successful entrepreneur not one struggling to make ends meet and begging for business, but they don't know that yet. Mum holds court amidst the women who are telling her she 'must be very proud', while Dad does his Svengali bit and introduces me to the people who might make the bookings.

'I love the sound of New York,' one of the members tells me, 'but is there anything else interesting before then?'

I hadn't expected to be asked and stutter a bit before offering, 'There might be some extra availability on our Monaco trip.'

'Monaco,' my Mum has overheard. 'Oh how wonderful, royalty, yachts…'

'Casinos,' adds someone else.

'The Grand Prix Circuit,' adds another.

I could kick myself; why didn't I think? They're classic car enthusiasts for goodness' sake.

'Do you think you might have availability for us?' asks Dad seizing the moment.

'I'll check as soon as I get back, but I'll need you all to confirm immediately.'

They all promise to do so and I know that with these bookings, we're going to break even now, perhaps even make a tiny profit. The relief must show on my face.

'If you ever need a little bit of help in these first few months, you can come to us, you know that don't you?' Dad has his arm round me as I leave the meeting.

'I know that Dad, but some things you need to do yourself,' I say.

He nods and kisses me on the forehead. 'The women in this family, you're all stubborn to the core.'

With the Caravan Club bookings on top of our concerted efforts in the store, I don't have to go to make up the numbers, but I fancied this one from the start and in my magic wand list, I said that I wanted my new career to be fun. So I book myself on to the Monaco trip too.

Should I invite Ed? I imagine strolling arm in arm along the promenade each evening; we'd be wearing delicate chiffon (me) and crisp linen (him). As much as I'd love some company, it seems a bit presumptuous to ask a man to the south of

France – especially as I'd be asking him to buy himself a ticket and sleep in a room on his own. So now I visualise myself, still in chiffon, strolling on my own but not alone; I gaze wistfully over the Mediterranean and read Ed's text over again:

MISSING YOU, HURRY BACK X.

BEEP-BEEP

A real text drags me from the dream; and it actually is from Ed – spooky.

LOOKS LIKE A LOVELY NIGHT, FANCY TRIP TO THE COAST AND CHIPS ON PROM?

I don't think I'll wear chiffon for this one.

* * *

Living in Manchester, I miss the coast, but if you make the effort, it's less than an hour away. We've come to Crosby to see Antony Gormley's *Another Place*, hundreds of bronze figures that line the beach. They stare out to sea and seem to be walking out, looking out for distant lands. I love this installation and always imagine that one day, they'll run free. We leave them to it and head for a fish and chip shop.

'Thank you for bringing me to this exclusive restaurant,' I say.

'My pleasure, thank you for paying for this wonderful meal.' Ed scrunches up his chip wrapper and lobs it into the bin first shot; he's disproportionately pleased with this.

'Well you paid for the last one so it seems only fair. Anyway, I'm celebrating tonight. Our Monaco trip is sold out thanks to my parents and their Caravan Club.'

'I'll have to get my lot booking something before you've sold everything,' he says.

'Oh I'd always find a little something for you,' I smile.

We get up and walk until the sun starts setting; then without speaking we turn towards the sea. Together we watch that great glimmering globe melting into the horizon, already starting to wake someone up on the other side of the world. The evening turns chilly; it's the perfect moment for Ed to drape his jacket around me but he doesn't.

'Best get going,' he says, rubbing my arms as if I'm a school-child on a rugby pitch.

Men should watch more Richard Curtis – really they should.

Monaco

'It's an awkward time,' my mum is saying of our afternoon flight. 'Too late for lunch and too early for dinner here, then when we get over *there* it'll be too late for dinner all over again.'

'You don't have to eat dinner at the same time this week, you are on holiday,' I counter, wondering why I ever thought this might be a relaxing break.

'We can have supper when we get there,' placates Dad.

'Which would be what? A small portion of dinner? Then I'll be hungry all night and I just cannot sleep if my stomach's rumbling,' she moans.

'Then let's get you a packet of biscuits to keep in your handbag,' suggests Dad.

I'm surprised there isn't one in there already.

'Oh I've got one of those,' she says (*glad I still know my mum*), 'but it's not the same. You need a bit more than that after a long journey.'

I stupidly voice a question that floats into my head.

'Can you take biscuits through customs? Or any food for that matter?'

'Bill,' she panics, 'what if they confiscate them? What will I do then?'

Dad reassures Mum that biscuits aren't a threat to national security; they'll be fine.

172

He suggests going for an extra meal, 'like brunch but in the afternoon', and I say thanks but no thanks to joining them. I opt for a coffee and some quiet time watching the runways.

Airports have changed so much since my time; this place is enormous and so busy. Excited families and bored businessmen wait to take the same journey, each dreading sitting next to the other. I still get a buzz from just being here and watching the planes. I feel that wonderful sensation when you know you've left the ground and you're airborne, on your way. I used to watch nervous passengers with their eyes tightly closed, clinging to the arms of their seats during take-off, but for me it was the best part, I was flying, actually flying.

The airline crews sauntering through with their trolley bags fill me with envy. I know it's harder work now (and I have to say the uniforms look more threadbare) but it still seems glamorous and fun being part of that team and those captain stripes are incredibly sexy even now.

I'm always very polite to cabin crew, paying attention during the safety talks and asking for nothing awkward; I know what it's like looking after hundreds of people every day. For this reason, I anticipate Mum's request for an extra sandwich on the plane by giving her mine.

Eventually we land and step from the cool darkness of the airport world and re-enter the summer sun of the real world. I get everyone to our hotel and then I'm off-duty for the rest of the trip.

No matter how well you think you've dressed, in Monaco you'll always feel slightly shabby. The place loves to flaunt its wealth and this is particularly evident around Casino Square. The place just oozes the glamour and notoriety of the Rat Pack era; the cars are something else. You're either here to watch or be watched and if you want any visibility at all, you need a Ferrari or a Lamborghini or one of the ones I've never even heard of.

'Is that a Hennessey Venom GT?' asks one of my Mercurians.

My dad and his friends are in complete awe. 'It certainly is, one of the top ten most expensive cars in the world. Go on, name three of the others,' says Dad. This quiz team never stops.

Fortunately the owners of these cars like being gawped at. I order a glass of champagne and sit quietly on the terrace watching my charges enjoying themselves. I know we can make this club work and I know we can make people happy; we just have to be around long enough. If we get good reviews from this trip then we've a chance of making that happen.

I'm interrupted from my thoughts by an older gent and his expensive scent. He leans over me and asks me something in French. At first I think he's looking for a spare chair or something but then he tries again in English.

'You are looking for business tonight?' he says.

Completely misinterpreting the situation I'm about to say yes and ask him where he was looking to visit but my mother gets there first.

'You filthy beast, get away from my daughter,' she yells twirling her clutch bag around her head on the end of its little gold chain and launching it lasso style on the perpetrator. 'She's not some floozy, she's been brought up properly,' she adds.

I'm not sure who moves faster, my 'client' or the hotel staff, trying to restore calm. They can't get us out of there quickly enough. I feel the need to offer payment for my champagne but they wave it away while simultaneously seating a new group in my place as if the fracas hadn't just happened.

In a square full of beautiful people and even more beautiful cars, my mother has managed to make herself centre of attention and she's enjoying it.

'The cheek of it, my Angie doesn't look like…one of them women,' she says.

She pulls me close protectively while tightly wrapping my pashmina over my cleavage.

'He must have thought you were one of those high-class ones,' she rationalises.

'Gee thanks, Mum.'

'Let's go down to the harbour,' suggests Dad and we follow his calm lead.

There is so much to see in Monaco and by the final evening, when we hold our travel club extra of a night-drive around the F1 circuit followed by a champagne reception, people are already talking about having to take another trip together.

'We could all go back to Casino Square and earn a few euros to help pay for it,' becomes the standing joke of the trip.

My mother continues to be outraged that anyone could mistake me for a hooker, but I think she'll dine out on it for quite some time.

I'm glad Ed didn't come; if he had, I wouldn't have been on my own in a café, wouldn't have been propositioned and the group wouldn't have bonded as well. However, I don't want him to think I've forgotten him, so I include him in my jaunty text to Charlie:

GOING WELL, WONDERFUL PLACE BUT HAVE BEEN MISTAKEN FOR HIGH CLASS HOOKER! ALL HAVING FUN x'

I then delete 'hooker' and replace it with 'escort' – just in case he thinks I'm hanging around on street corners.

High class? comes the typically sardonic reply from Charlie.

That's one way to boost profit from Ed. No little 'x' at the end.

I really must give him that list of films to watch.

Bake-Off

'Bloody hilarious,' is Patty's reaction when I tell her about Monaco. 'I'd have found out how much he was paying before sending him packing,' she adds.

'You'd have got more than Angie.' We're all bug-eyed and open-mouthed after this comment from Mum.

'Well, she probably…knows how to do more things than you,' she explains.

Speechless doesn't begin to describe our incredulity, but Patty roars with laughter. 'Even better. My best friend's mum thinks I know how to turn tricks!'

Mum blushes. 'Well my Angela's never been that sort,' she fusses.

'Please Gran, stop digging,' begs Zoe, 'let's just get on with this.'

We're packing to go to the bake-off and probably hindering more than helping her.

'Let's decide cars first.' Zoe gets us organised

'I want to come with you,' bags Mum, linking arms with Zoe as a sign of possession.

It's a complete relief to me as I don't think I could cope with any further analysis of my sexual prowess, or lack of it.

'OK,' says Zoe, 'we'll take the table settings then you and Patty can take the cakes. You've got the air conditioning, that'll be better for them.'

She actually means there is more likelihood that they'll arrive in one piece without icing or edges nibbled.

'Now I want the table settings packed according to their final position and Gran, we'll need some extra plants and flowers just in case we have more space than we think. Abundant; think Mother Earth at her most plentiful, that's how we have to look.'

Mum salutes and takes her directions. We start packing the cakes which smell delicious. I hope they still smell like this when we get there.

'There's a spray you can buy,' Zoe tells us matter-of-factly. 'It smells of baking; restaurants and shops use it to get your mouth watering.'

'That can't be true,' I say.

'You think our corner shop kneads dough every morning for those baguettes? I'm telling you,' she replies.

'What a swizz. Are we using one?' asks Patty.

'We won't need to,' says Zoe, 'when the cakes warm up again in that room, the whole place will explode with aromas.'

An explosion of aromas sounds a whole lot better than simply getting out the Febreze 'Bun in the Oven' variety. How disappointing would it be to walk into someone's house and get a whiff of freshly baked goodies to discover it's a spray and the only thing on offer is a ginger nut?

'I should get some of that spray to use as perfume for any tricks with a mother fixation.'

Patty is still contemplating her alternative career.

'I could wear an apron and let them lick the spoon. People would pay a fortune in some circles,' she says.

'I told you she knew things,' my own mother adds quietly.

I just shake my head and ignore them both.

'Shall we get these loaded?' I ask.

There is something magical about an early-morning start before the world has woken up. A lie-in is a rare and wonderful thing, but to be up and laughing with the girls as the sun rises and warms us has to be a good omen. We pack meticulously, following every instruction we get, and finally we're on our way. Bake-off here we come.

'Do you think she'll win?' Patty slaps my wrist as I try to change from Absolute 80s radio to catch the news on the BBC.

'I've never been to anything like this so I have no idea,' I say. 'I'm not even sure that it's really about beating Amanda; it's about getting Alan to notice her.'

'Why do we still need our parents' approval at any age, eh?' asks Patty.

I shrug my shoulders and wonder whether I should call Alan and let him know how much his appearance would mean to our daughter. Better safe than sorry. I'll call him when we get there.

'So what's next after Monaco for the Mercury Club?'

'Your cruise, a wine tour and then finally the New York trip; plus of course selling the packages in between,' I reply.

'Is it all you thought it would be?' she asks.

'Tougher than I thought, but when you see people having a good time, I love it,' I tell her.

'Know what you mean,' she replies.

'And the Granny-Okes, how is that going without my star performance?'

Patty laughs, 'We'll be all right on the night, as they say.'

A tambourine beat starts up on the radio and Patty is ecstatic. 'Quick – turn this up.'

'Walk Like An Egyptian' fills the car.

'We've put this in the set,' she tells me.

Patty sings and I do the dance with all the '*Eh-os*' in all the right places.

We're still singing when we get there and will probably be whistling the chorus all day now.

'Our challenge,' conspires Patty, 'is to plant this song in someone else's head and hear it sung back to us by the end of the day.'

'You're on.'

We enter a huge auditorium swarming with activity; I've watched American beauty pageants on TV and they looked like this. There's obviously a circuit crowd who greet each other with bi-focal faces: the mouth is smiling hello while the eyes are snarling 'die bitch die'.

I'm sure there are good and bad pitches, but we have no idea what we've been handed. It's not tucked in the corner so it looks OK and the display area seems big enough.

'What do you want us to do?' I ask. 'Bring the cakes in?'

Zoe has eyed up her competition. 'Not yet,' she says, 'let's keep our powder dry for a while but get the display built.'

We do exactly as we're told until Zoe is satisfied and then with half an hour till judging we carry the cakes like precious newborns into the arena.

Only now does Zoe label her display and get out parchments with herb facts, her inspiration, and the recipes. She's designed this to ensure the judges have to spend a bit of time with her to read everything.

I leave her to it and call Alan.

'Are you at this bakery competition?' I ask.

'Of course I am,' he replies. 'Surely you're not?'

'Zoe's entered in the Trendsetters category; it would mean so much if you could come and see her.'

'Trendsetters? That's what Amanda's doing.'

Oh no, just what we were hoping to avoid.

'But she's a bloody professional cook, for God's sake,' I say. 'Get her to pull out, Alan; take your daughter's side for once.'

'Hold on for a minute, she's not competing; it's a showcase event. Even if she were, of course I'd support Zoe over anyone. What on earth do you take me for?'

I calm down as Alan promises to find Zoe and stay with her during the judging. I grab a programme and look up this show-case event, although I'm not sure I could stomach watching her. Mum on the other hand seems to have the stomach for anything and it is expanding by the minute.

'You're not supposed to eat the displays,' I tell her.

'You can after they've been judged,' she counters. 'They cut some of their cakes up. I hope Zoe doesn't.'

Patty reappears. 'The judges are with her now, fingers crossed everyone.'

'She doesn't need luck; here try this.' Mum forces a sample of scone on to us both. 'I think I'll buy some of these for your dad.'

'He's over there with Zoe, by the way,' says Patty.

I look over and see my lovely daughter surrounded by Dad, Alan, Charlie and Peter; it looks as if she's brought her own personal security. They're all smiles and the boys are working their charm on the female judges. After a few moments they walk away and I watch the team's shoulders drop with a collective sigh of relief. Everyone hugs and shakes hands and Dad pats Alan on the back with discernible disappointment. It's time to rejoin them.

'Well, what did they say?' I ask.

'They seemed to like it,' offers Zoe.

'You were brilliant. They absolutely loved it, trust me I know these people.' Alan plants a big affectionate kiss.

'And I wonder why that is,' murmurs Mum before waving an attendee off the stand.

'Shoo, these aren't samples you know,' she says. 'I don't know, the nerve of some people.'

Alan checks his watch and looks over at me. I nod and remind him that he has to get moving.

'Are we going to watch it?' asks Patty.

I look at Zoe for the decision.

'I have to Mum, the winners are announced immediately afterwards. It would look awful if I weren't in the room.'

'You go; I'll come in when they make the announcements, I promise.'

Mum and Patty go with Zoe while Charlie, Peter and I take an amble around the dwindling stalls.

'I was wondering whether we could turn this into some type of trip: Bake Baklava in the Baltics, maybe,' I offer, making conversation.

'Some of these people need Burn-Your-Butt-Off-Bootcamp rather than more baking,' says Charlie.

'Cookies and Kettlebells,' adds Peter.

'Bo, you have got to see this.' Patty has barged into our midst and drags me towards the exhibition stage.

Disco music spills out and there's a glitter ball on the ceiling; Patty plonks me on to a chair so that I can see Amanda and a male assistant both dressed in white shirts with tea towels over their arms. The wall behind them has optics lined up and the table in front has cocktail shakers, straws and little umbrellas on display.

She calls out to the audience and asks what she can get them. A pre-placed voice calls out 'gin and tonic'. She takes up the shaker, dances around with it for a few seconds, pops it into the fake oven and pulls out a gin and tonic cake. Using the same routine, she delivers a Limoncello Drizzle, a Black Russian Chocolate and a Malt Whisky Fruit Cake to great applause.

'That was my idea. They're even the same cakes,' I yell at Patty through the noise.

'I know, Alan must have told her about it,' she replies.

For the second time today I'm speechless, but I hardly have time to take this all in when the judges get onstage.

Blah, blah high standard; blah, blah exceptional new talent; blah, blah re-emergence of traditional skills like baking.

Just tell us the winner.

'And we're delighted to announce one of these new talents in our Trendsetter category…please give a round of applause to… Zoe Hargreaves,' they say.

My family holler and whoop for all they're worth; I am over-joyed until Zoe is joined onstage, first of all by Alan and then Amanda.

The miked-up judge murmurs in Amanda's ear, 'Chip off the old block', and Amanda has the audacity to nod affectionately.

I would have thrown something at her if at that precise mo-ment I hadn't heard someone in the crowd behind me whistling the chorus from 'Walk Like An Egyptian' and Patty tittering quietly to herself.

Meanwhile...

I'm having a coffee on the patio enjoying a rare moment where everything around me is calm and uncomplicated when I get a call from Charlie.

'It'll be a dinner party or a barbecue depending on the weather. I prefer dinner but his lordship likes to get out the tongs,' he says, inviting me round to his house.

I hope dinner, too. When you sit down there's less chance of a disaster with the ketchup bottle or any condiments for that matter. I tell Charlie this and he's horrified.

'Let me reassure you that if we're sitting down, there will be *NO* chance of a disaster with ketchup; what on earth do you take me for?'

I won't bring the circus with me; I'll invite Ed as my plus one and have a sophisticated adult evening. What a blissful thought.

Most of my dates with Ed have been on the back of a bike or casual affairs to ensure no one gets the wrong impression, but tonight, I want to dial it up a little: look fantastic and see where it goes. I might even go shopping and buy something to flash a bit of leg for a change; they've a slight tan so it won't be too traumatising.

With the day planned, I leap into action. I whip my T-shirt off, use it as a duster to flick over the house and then stuff it in the washing basket. Next it's a shower and presentable clothes (so that I'm given good service in the shops) and a bottle of wine plonked in the fridge just in case things do go well later.

Sorted. It's amazing how much you can get done in ten minutes if you try.

Today there will be no torture, no plucking or waxing just nurture and indulgence. I head for the nail bar to have a wonderful hand massage and manicure; my nails are painted Petticoat Lane Pink and my hands made so soft you would simply purr if I stroked your skin. Add a summery shift dress and nude slingbacks and I look like the type of dinner guest you would invite back. I won't be mistaken for a hooker tonight.

On the way down in the lift, a woman keeps taking sideways glances at me, which is annoying as I want to take sideways glances at myself and I can't if she's looking. I'm trying to work out whether my boobs could do with a bra that's a little more 'up and at 'em'.

'I thought it was you,' she eventually says with a broad smile, 'you came out with the The Chapter a few weeks back.'

Without the leather jacket and helmet most of them are unrecognisable, but I smile anyway and say, 'Yes, I remember now – we both look a bit different today.'

'I'm buying holiday clothes; we're off to the south of France next weekend. I can't wait,' she explains.

'Oh you'll love it, I was there last week. It's simply gorgeous,' I reply politely.

The lift reaches the ground floor and we head out.

'But I'm still taking a warm jacket,' she continues as we part company. 'I hear out there, it's colder than here.'

I wave a goodbye and smile thinking, 'I wonder who spread that vicious rumour.'

Ed picks me up and we head off to dinner; he's made the effort too and together we look like the catalogue models you see in Sunday supplements. They're a wee bit older than us but proud of their little laughter lines and salt 'n' pepper hair; they're fit and active, advertising vitamins or golfing shoes.

I was once told that no matter what age you're advertising to you should use a model ten years younger. So if you're advertising to sixty-year-olds, use a fifty-year-old model. No one wants to relate to someone their own age.

Armed with a bottle of wine that is appropriately expensive for an evening with sophisticated adults, we arrive to lots of hugs and kisses from our hosts. I'm dying to see if Peter has made any changes to the place.

'There's something,' I deduce as Charlie hands me a glass, 'but I can't work out what it is; it's subtle.'

The array of manuals and guide books are still there but…

'Got it. He's rearranged your books.' I go over to the shelves. 'They're not alphabetical or in size order. What is it?' I ask.

'They're in the order that we're going to do them,' he exclaims brushing his hand along the tomes. 'Scuba diving first to climbing Everest never. 'We've called it our compatibility shelf. If we can get past building a flat-pack table together then we're bonded for life.'

'And if you can't you might be bonded with glue anyway,' I jest.

'Brilliant idea,' pipes up Ed. 'I'd put something like "assisting a tyre change" as my compatibility challenge.'

'I'd have "surviving a weekend with my mother",' I add.

There's a sharp intake of breath as Charlie says, 'Oh, you're going to be single for a *VERY* long time girlfriend.'

Another couple arrive; they're friends of Peter's and members of the local Round Table. This is Charlie's magic wand dream: hosting a dinner party with the love of his life and becoming a pillar of the community. Is it really as simple as making a wish?

The evening goes well without any of the usual chaos that seems to infiltrate my life with alarming regularity. There's a brief recap of the baking competition where I gloat when Peter tells everyone that my daughter won and grimace as Charlie tells everyone, 'And then her arch enemy presents the exact same cakes Angie made in the trial run. They looked a lot better made by a pro but how did she know? Spooky.'

'It's not spooky at all, we have a toerag ex-husband in common,' I say.

Ed looks uncomfortable with talk of Alan so changes the subject and I'm relieved that he does. I'm happy to let them talk problem motorways and brake horsepower all night and have no part in it. I just relax listening to the hum of happy voices.

Later, Ed walks me home and I try to remember whether I left the box to the super-support knickers I'm wearing lying on the bathroom floor.

I open the door and send him through to the kitchen while I 'freshen up'; fortunately there is nothing incriminating lying around. I do a quick knicker change, swapping from all-night support into something that says, *'This is my normal underwear, I wear sexy but classy every day you lucky man.'*

It's amazing just how much a pair of smalls can say.

When I get back to the living room he has poured us each a glass and is sitting on the sofa. I join him, snuggling up against him, the sitting equivalent of spoons. He puts his arm around me and pulls me closer, I respond by lightly stroking his leg. It's far easier to be tactile in this position as you don't have to make eye contact.

He kisses the top of my head and then his lips move down to my ear lobes. I turn towards him so that we can get mouth to mouth. It's a long time since I felt a spark from just kissing, but I'm feeling it now as little fireworks go off throughout my body. I have no idea whether I'm supposed to initiate things or let him, but I raise my hand to his chest and let my fingertips caress the hairs under his shirt. He runs his hand down my side tickling me with delight as he does. His hand rests at my breasts and a full Catherine wheel starts to fizz away. I am desperately trying not to overthink this and go with the flow but at some point the flow will realise that I'm wearing a shift dress with a side zip and the sofa is no place to remove said item with any grace or allure at all. We have to commit, so I take a sip and say it:

'Shall we move this upstairs?'

He takes his own sip for courage and follows me as I lead him into the bedroom. We kiss further and then I take a step backwards and start undoing my zip, planning on my dress falling to the floor just as they do in movies.

I'm expecting a reciprocal unbuttoning of shirt but it doesn't happen, he's just staring at me. For a brief moment I'm convinced that he's simply taking in my mesmerising beauty but then he says the words no one wants to hear, particularly while nearly in your undies.

'Wait, there's something I have to tell you.'

Married? Dying? Transgender? Which will I put up with and which is a no-go? Panic rises and I stop the unzipping.

'It was me,' he continues. 'I gave Amanda your idea.'

'What?' Distance is now no object as I push past him and grab my bathrobe tying it over my dress like terry-towelling armour.

'Hear me out.' He raises both hands as if I'm about punch him and I just might.

'She's my cousin and I didn't know Alan was your ex; you've never mentioned him by name and even if you had, you've got different surnames. I didn't know,' he pleads.

My brain is riffling through its filing cabinet trying to work out whether this is true. Have I ever mentioned his name? Does it matter?

'When she said she needed a theme, I told her my friend's idea and that you weren't entering it. You weren't, you told me,' he continues. 'I promise I didn't mean to hurt you.'

I plonk myself down on the bed and he sits down beside me. It's funny but everyone says that they just want a man to be honest with them and here I am sitting with someone who has been more honest than my husband ever was and all I can think is that I wish he'd lied; I wish he'd never said all of that.

'I'm so sorry,' he whispers kissing me on top of the head.

I nod because I know that he is, but I'm not sure what to say.

'I need time to think,' I tell him and he gets up to leave.

I stay seated as I listen to his steps traipse down the stairs and then out of the door. I lie back and pull the duvet around me. Socks jumps up and snuggles into my feet as if telling me that I don't need anyone else.

I'm so numb I can't even cry myself to sleep tonight.

Dumped Again

'Oh Bo, I'm so sorry. I know you liked him.'

I'd called Ed earlier and thanked him for being honest but told him I needed distance from my ex and it wouldn't work because of that. He was soft and lovely and said he hoped we'd still be friends. He's such a nice guy, why on earth did he have to know Amanda?

My next call was to Patty for some kind words and comfort; she engulfs me and gives me one of her bear hugs.

I feel so stupid, as if the world is watching me make a fool of myself with one man after the other.

'Were you really going to…do the deed?' asks Patty.

I sit down and cup my stupid head in my stupid hands and think this question through. I thought he'd be safe; he'd be kind and he'd be as awkward as me the first time post split-up. I just wanted to show Alan that men still find me attractive, to get back on the bike or whatever the expression. Isn't that what people who've moved on do? I don't want to spend the rest of my life alone and I'm going to have to do it sometime – I thought last night would work and it very nearly did.

I don't say any of this, I just shrug.

'I suppose so.'

She hugs me tighter and I have to extricate myself before I'm crushed to death.

'So what's next?' she asks.

'Next,' I declare unconvincingly, 'I guess I get back to the original plan with no more distractions: build successful business and win back self-respect.'

I look at Patty now that I've stopped wallowing in my own self-pity and notice she's wearing a tracksuit. I didn't realise she knew such things were invented never mind owned one.

'What's all this for?' I say indicating the outfit.

'I've got a personal trainer coming round. I hope you don't mind but I told him to meet me here,' she tells me.

'Why have you got a trainer?' I ask. 'Is the military fitness not working?'

'I need to turbo charge things because the most amazing thing has happened,' she says pulling out a sheet of paper from her bag.

'Just look who's been added to the line-up.' She points out the focus of her excitement, but when I just look puzzled she pushes it closer to my face.

'Simply Red,' she declares, 'don't you see? The prophecy about red or orange playing an important role in my future; this has to be it. I'm going to win the heart of Mick Hucknall.'

'Given they're called Simplee Rouge, I don't think he'll be playing,' I point out.

'But there must be a lookalike,' she counters with logic.

'Anyway, I'm getting into shape, there's no telling who could be on that ship.'

Neither of us can think of any more eighties redheads so we leave it there; Patty is so sure the prediction will come true on this trip.

'Come training with me,' she suggests, 'get rid of all that frustration.'

It's not a bad idea so I change and when the trainer arrives, I set off jogging and jabbing like a woman scorned.

Oh hang on a minute, I am.

Later I pop in to see Caroline and tell her what's happened. She's friends with both of us and having had the experience of losing my married friends in the divorce, I don't want to go through that again with the people I've just met.

'I wondered why Ed was dropping out of the book club; he called this morning.'

I didn't want him to do that but at least it means that I can still go. I offer to take Dad or Zoe to make up the numbers again.

'How are you feeling?' she asks.

'Deflated, but I'm getting used to that,' I answer.

'I know it'll be little compensation right now but all your other key goals seem to be going really well,' she tells me.

I'd already reconciled this but hearing it voiced helps me to start wondering what on earth I'm fretting over. Sure I was in my best knickers at the time, but I'll laugh about that one day and it could have been worse: I could have still been wearing the Spanx.

Heading home, I'm starting to feel OK but could do with the boost of a little good news, just for me. It happens,

'Angie,' Alan shouts down the phone, 'can't talk now but just wanted to let you know that the house sale is back on – full price.'

And a little divine intervention to help me on my way would be nice.

Crashhh.

Overhead the August sky turns black and pebble sized rain-drops take everyone by surprise. It gets heavier and heavier sending people scurrying to the nearest doorway.

I stand still, laugh out loud and raise my beaming face to the sky.

'Why thank you.'

Lightning lends its force to the fury and uttered from the doorways I hear the words I've been longing to hear.

'*I guess the British summer's over, then.*'

Yeesssss. Time to start selling holidays again.

Business as Usual

The shop starts filling up instantly with people looking for late-availability trips.

We're unlikely to make up the money lost during the sunny months but at least the final part of the year should be rosy; the outlook is good – as they'd say on the weather reports while pinning a smiling sunshine on the board.

This extended staycationing has also made customers hungry for a little bit of excitement, so as well as selling the sunshine they ask for, we're also making great headway on the New York bookings. I can legitimately call our Mercury Travel Club members and tell them that Christmas is booking up quickly and ask them if they want to put a deposit down.

For the first month since starting the Mercury Travel Club we exceed our targets. Charlie and I have a very quick glass of fizz to celebrate, I buy myself a box of pralines from our local chocolatier and Socks gets a fresh salmon fillet.

It's the simple things in life that keep you sane.

The next day, and in fact every day of the next few weeks, we're flat out and fortunately for us, the instant surge in demand means that no one is discounting too heavily. It's perfect for us; one visit and we can get your holiday sorted much more quickly than many evenings spent hunting online. The more time people have, the longer they procrastinate, but if you need something for your family within the next fortnight then you want us to tell you you'll have a wonderful time, read a couple of customer reviews and just get it booked.

After the bookings we're busy with insurance, visas and currency; it's hectic and I love it. Customers come in tense with worry and leave with big summer-holiday smiles on their faces.

Then, rather strangely, it happens: the world becomes deserted, or at least my corner of it does.

When you have children, you don't realise this. For you, the summer holidays are chaos, confusion and cacophony as you try to balance your job with the childcare arrangements. Then you brave family-weary airports to whisk them all off somewhere far too sunny for two weeks where at least one of you will be badly burned and one will get diarrhoea. So somewhere in the world (usually Spain), the noise levels have risen in inverse proportion to the drop in the UK.

However, right here, right now in the last two weeks before school restarts, there is a bizarre tranquillity. Shops and restaurants are quiet, which I know isn't great for them, but this is the calm before the autumn and Christmas frenzies so they may be quite pleased to have the time to think; I know we are.

Charlie's thoughts aren't solely on the business though. 'Will you want to go on the eighties cruise with Patty?' he asks me.

I'd always presumed that I would be going, but of course someone has to look after the business.

'It would be nice,' I say trying to be blasé, 'but if you'd rather go, I've seen her onstage a hundred times.'

'I was thinking that I'd rather go with the wine tour. Well both of us; Peter's quite keen.'

Uh-huh. Why won't Charlie make eye contact when he says all of this? He's only dividing up the work and pleasure after all. Play it casually.

'No problem; it's far more you – South Africa, delicious wines, safari, gorgeous sunsets. Quite romantic,' I say.

'I know.'

This man is nervous. I need to find out what's going on.

'Is there something you're not telling me?' I ask.

'You're going to say that I'm mad,' he starts.

'We all are,' I say, 'come on spill.'

'I think he might be the one,' he says. 'I know it's only been a few months but I can't imagine being without him now.'

I can't either. Since the day they hooked up, they've been Charlie and Peter; Cheter as Josie calls them. I tell him this and he loves it.

'You do seem to just fit together,' I say.

'I think so, too, and I want our first holiday together to be something really special.'

'And you're telling me Patty belting out "Relax" won't do that? That's where I've been going wrong with my relationships? I wish you'd told me sooner,' I laugh.

He smiles and I let him pause thoughtfully before he speaks again.

'Here's the thing – he takes a very deep breath – 'I think I might propose.'

I look like a happy version of Edvard Munch's most famous painting.

'Oh my God, Charlie, I don't know what to say. That's amazing, incredible. Are you sure? Does Peter feel the same? I'm rambling now; tell me what you need me to say.'

'I guess those are the questions I've been asking myself,' he says. 'Am I sure? I think so. When we were laughing about the compatibility shelf, all I could think about was spending a lifetime doing all of those things with Peter. I know there'd be no hysterics – he'd help me through anything.'

'Wow, you are smitten.'

'And does he feel the same?' he continues. 'He comes home to me every night as if he's always done it and always will. There are two pairs of shoes kicked off in the hall now and it seems ridiculous but I love that.'

'It's not ridiculous at all,' I tell him. 'I used to love the three pairs of wellies stacked up on the garden step, a black pair, green pair and a little yellow pair with a bee face on the nose. I know what you mean, they say home.'

'So I'm as sure as I can be and I thought if we have one wonderfully romantic trip together, things might just happen naturally.'

'I hope they do Charlie,' I say, and I truly mean it.

I text Patty to let her know that I'll be coming with her on the cruise and then get on with planning our next travel initiatives; autumn means long haul and then winter sees the flight of the sun-bird. I need to develop a big Mercury Club adventure for the first quarter. I can't believe I'm planning next year already. I gaze across at Charlie as I work and wonder whether he'll be married by then.

What a year this is turning out to be.

Should I Stay or Should I Go?

The house sale completed today, exactly nine months after moving into my little starter home. I now have a huge sum of money waving at me from my bank account. I stare at the statement and wonder whether Alan and Amanda are doing the same, whether she's deciding how they're going to spend it.

This is it; my share of our savings has gone into the business, my salary pays the bills, so this is what I have to keep me safe for the future. The sense of responsibility has taken me by surprise. This set of numbers on a flimsy piece of paper feels like a test, what I do with it shows whether or not I can make it on my own.

The sensible move would be to buy a house: stop wasting money on rent, have something to leave Zoe, have the security of my own roof over my head and all the other good things that people like to say. I ring the estate agent who sold our house and make his day by asking him to send over some details for me to look at.

I'm underwhelmed when they arrive; everything looks so *small*.

'Why do you need big? Were you thinking of hosting the Philharmonic in your parlour?' asks Patty facetiously.

I give her my *ha-ha-not-funny* look.

'Up here, Bo Peep,' she taps me on the forehead, 'you still live in that big family home.'

She's right of course.

'But you don't, it's gone,' she continues. 'That millstone has been removed from your neck. No more shag piles and country kitchens, no more Victoriana bath suites; you can be all wet rooms and wooden floors now.'

'I like carpet,' I protest.

'You know what I'm saying. A big old house when you're on your own is just sad, I should know. You need something that says, *Go-getting world traveller. Too busy cruising to spend any time cleaning.*'

'And which of these says that?' I ask.

Patty flicks through the selection of houses that I've been sent and puts a few aside, but she's as uninspired as I am.

'Hmm, none of them. He's cast you in the role of old spinster with this lot. An older woman on her own; must want a garden and a downstairs loo. These houses look as if someone died in them.'

True enough, I have been sent more bungalows and ground-floor flats than I thought existed, and they're dowdy. If I'd been sent these in January, I might have settled for one of them. They match the cats and cardigans jibe Patty so cruelly made at the time and I'm no longer that person. She was right then and is right again, I need somewhere that reflects the new me.

'There are some new buildings in the Northern Quarter; they're calling it up and coming, which means it looks a bit rough but they say they're for young trendies. Artists, internet entrepreneurs – that kind of person. Might be the change you need. Why don't we go and take a look at them?' says Patty.

'Might as well,' I agree.

I get up and dump the details from the estate agent in the bin.

As we leave, Patty looks quizzically over at the front garden, which as ever is immaculate.

'You old rascal, have you had a man round and not told me?'

'Don't go there; that's a story for another day,' I tell her.

Mum calls and I explain where we're going.

'You're letting Patty choose you a new house? When was the last time she made a good decision?' My mum is less than pleased about being excluded from this next phase of my life. 'I'd pick something much better and I'd negotiate a better price. I'm a demon when it comes to getting something for nothing,' she adds.

I don't bother pointing out that getting an extra sample of rocky-road ice cream in the supermarket isn't the same as buying a house in a seller's market; it wouldn't be worth the subsequent debate.

'I know what we should do.' Her lightbulb glows from afar. 'I'll pick two houses for you to go and see then Patty can pick two and you decide which one you prefer. It'll be like that TV programme.'

At her insistence, I pass the phone over to Patty, and Mum lays down the gauntlet. They're both pretty fired up so I'll just let them get on with it – wading through estate-agent exaggerations was never my favourite way to pass the time anyway.

I give them my criterion, which essentially amounts to needing two bedrooms, and I give them an absolute limit on the amount I can spend; that's all they need and they're off.

* * *

The viewing weekend arrives and the rules are established: I view Patty's choices in the morning and Mum's after lunch. I have been given a scoring sheet and after supper in our local pub, I will reveal the scores I've given each house. Next weekend, I go back to view the top two and choose a place to live. Simple.

Patty asks us to meet her at the Mercury offices.

'This first house is walking distance from work, so nice and easy for you.'

She leads the way very professionally, as if the TV cameras are actually here.

I'm not allowed to see the paper details beforehand, but we soon get to an ordinary-looking semi-detached house on a street I've never visited. It seems a bit plain for Patty and I'm quite disappointed. We meet the estate agent at the house; she ushers us in and accepts Patty's suggestion that we look around on our own.

'Now I've picked this one because it's an easy transition for you,' explains Patty. 'There are *carpets* – as requested – and a familiar traditional layout but with a fabulous new kitchen. This is a smaller version of your old place but with a makeover.'

She's spot on, a normal house but immaculate and full of the sort of gizmos that I would never dare spend money on. It has an espresso machine and fancy pull-out taps – the things you end up never using but buy anyway.

I slip my feet out of my shoes and sink them into the lusciously deep carpet, bliss but still a surprising choice for Patty. I can see the cogs whirring in Mum's brain; she can't work out why she's put this in her top two either – there has to be a grand reveal at some point.

Patty opens a door to show us a small study with a chaise longue in the centre.

'You could work here. As you can see, this guy has it set up as a photography studio,' she says.

We head up the stairs to the designer bathroom and good-sized spare bedrooms; it's all very nice and I tell Patty this. When we're done with the other rooms she gathers us together outside the final door.

'And as we'll see, the main bedroom is quite something, too.'

She throws the door open and we gasp. Still open-mouthed we walk in, Mum and I glued to the photo canvases on every wall.

'It's a boudoir photo studio then,' I croak as my jaw unlocks.

The place is festooned with pictures of the couple in various stages of undress with a bizarre collection of props. I have to explain the concept to Mum.

'Couples have sexy photos taken of themselves to give as presents.'

'With a rose stuck up their backsides?' she asks.

I think it's supposed to be gently placed on her back as she lies supine on the sheepskin rug, but it does indeed look lodged in too far.

'And him looking like a Blackpool postcard?' Mum continues.

The attempted pose is a seductive recline on the aforementioned chaise longue with a whisky glass covering the target area. However, he's a skinny creature with the worst vest-shaped nuclear red sunburn you have ever seen and I'm sure that just at the ankle cross there's a hint of sock out of shot.

'You didn't bring us to see the house did you?' I ask.

Patty is bursting with morbid delight. 'Look in the wardrobe,' she says.

Ordinarily I'd refuse but well, you can't walk into this lot and not be curious, can you?

It doesn't disappoint: nurses' outfits, naughty traffic wardens, teachers' canes, handcuffs and feather boas of every colour.

'Who leaves their house like this for people to see?' I ask, thinking about the effort I made to depersonalise mine.

'Maybe they're hoping it'll bring in extra business,' suggests Patty. 'You know, people who quite fancy posing naked with three pizzas on their bits,' she adds referring to one of the worst portraits in this collection.

'Last time I'll ever look at a slice of pepperoni in quite the same way,' I grimace as we rejoin the estate agent. She must be getting used to people's reactions by now.

'Very entertaining,' says Mum when we get back outside, 'but you don't get a third go you know; that counted as one of your choices.'

'I don't need a third go, I'll win with this next one,' counters Patty confidently.

So it's a tram ride into the city centre for Patty's next choice and as promised she takes me to see a trendy 'Live-Work Space' in what used to be Ancoats. Mum clutches her handbag as if she's about to be mugged at any moment. If I buy here she's unlikely to visit so that's a point in its favour.

'So what's this Live-Work thing meant to be then?' asks my mum of the hipster guy showing us around.

'It recognises that we live more flexible lifestyles so the space is more freeform allowing you to create the environment that you need,' he replies without acknowledging or perhaps noticing the sarcasm in her question.

'So there's no walls,' mutters Mum under her breath.

It's a warehouse-style space with lots of exposed brick and huge windows; it feels like a New York loft apartment – the type they had in *Ghost* – and I have to say, it's quite exciting. I'd never thought that I would live anywhere like this. It makes me wish I had a creative bone in my body, and of course, a Patrick Swayze lookalike on hand to admire it.

'Let me get this right,' continues Mum, 'no walls and the bedroom is on that shelf up there?'

'The mezzanine level, yes,' replies the hipster.

'If you ever make curry you'll be smelling of it all night,' she tells me.

'I never cook, as you keep telling me,' I remind her.

'There's a balcony with great urban views.' Hipster opens the window and we step out into the sights and sounds of the city. Mum covers her ears and complains about the noise but I like it. I can imagine sitting here early evening, being part of the city yet apart. It reminds me of a tree house in a jungle.

'This is amazing,' I tell the two people who are not trying to put me off. 'It's different, it says new start, it's dynamic. There's a real buzz to this place.'

'Tell me something,' continues Mum, 'why do you youngsters never pull your trousers up properly?'

'Ignore her,' I tell the poor guy. 'I'm putting her in a home when we leave here. Tell me more.'

'Well, it's built with the latest technology,' the hipster adds. 'You control the temperature, lighting and entertainment from an app on your phone. You can warm the place up or cool it down when you're on your way back, get some mood lighting and sounds going for when you walk in. It's awesome.'

Mum senses victory. 'You're talking about a woman who can barely use the remote.'

With that she walks out, tongue firmly in cheek.

We have coffee in a bar overlooking the canal; this would be my local if I bought the loft apartment. Despite the dodgy rationale for seeing the first house, Patty has shown me two sides of myself – the comfortable but updated version and the potential future version. It's been a good morning although Mum still smells victory.

'We should have had a wager on this,' she says as we head off to see her choices.

In the afternoon, we drive into Cheshire and my first thought as we reach the small detached cottage with a huge garden is that she's picked a house for herself and Dad, not me.

Patty snorts, 'I'll take that wager now if it's still on offer.'

'Don't judge a book by its cover,' scowls Mum.

The interior is pretty and cottage-like, all beams and dried flowers; it's the sort of place that Alan and I might have downsized to and I guess that's what Mum was thinking. I make positive comments about it being lovely and well kept, but I know instantly this is not me. Not any more.

'One day,' Mum explains, 'you'll want peace, not the noise of the city. You'll meet someone new and spend evenings in the garden. Zoe will get married and she'll bring grandchildren home. They can't play on a balcony; if you buy that other place, you'll be moving again within a year, this house will last you for ever.'

I'm slightly shaken by the idea of for ever; I haven't allowed myself to think beyond the end of the year, never mind for ever. This may represent the path I was on but I'm astonished by how abhorrent it is to me now. I can't get out quick enough; Patty blows on her nails and polishes them in delight.

Although I'm not sure my blood pressure can take another of Mum's choices, I know she means well, so vow to be much nicer about the next place; fortunately it's very easy to do.

'Wow Mum – this is fantastic,' I say.

Even Patty is looking impressed at the converted apartment in a Georgian mansion. We're in Didsbury, far enough, but not too far away from my current life.

'It's a duplex,' boasts Mum and I know for sure she has just learned that word.

Patty looks out at the grounds just as a Silver Fox arrives in his convertible Mercedes sports car; she gives him a little wave. The whole place manages to ooze quiet success.

'To hell with you, I'm having this – where do I sign?' she says.

And I don't blame her. It's huge, all high ceilings and period features. The kitchen is just big enough to host a twenty-bottle wine cooler and a microwave plus there's a garden (Mum – there are *grounds*) that someone else looks after. This is the sort of place where Entrepreneur of the Year has her photograph taken but only when she's made it. I'd feel a complete fraud if I moved into this perfect place right now.

'Let's go for food.' I urge everyone out, just in case someone spots me and proclaims, '*She can't buy this place – we only have successful people here.*'

Over supper, I contemplate my reactions as Mum and Patty banter the merits of their choices; I promise that if I see any again, it will be the duplex and the loft apartment, thereby delivering a draw at Round One, which they both seem happy with.

However, I'm surprised at the relief I feel when I get back to Cross Road.

'I'm home,' I say to Gnora and Gnorman; their bulbous-nosed smiles are strangely welcoming.

As I open the door, Socks sneaks in and takes her place on the chair. Throwing down my things and sinking into the sofa, I compare what I have here to the luxury I've just left. Apples and pears; they were confident homes for people who know who they are.

I'm a work in progress, on my way to being Angie Shepherd, entrepreneur, but right now, still faking it.

This little house is helping me grow and I need it for a little while longer.

I take one last flick through the estate agents' details of the places we've just seen and giggle as I notice that they've omitted any pictures of the main bedroom in the first house.

I am going to dine out on stories about those boudoir photos for *years* to come.

Life on an Ocean Wave

'I'm Popeye the sailor man, I'm nabbing the cap-i-tan,' sings Patty as our taxi swings into Southampton docks.

'I don't think that's quite how it goes,' I tell her.

'Trust me it will,' she replies and we come face to bow with our glistening home for the next seven days. Even the knowledge that this is the trip Alan and Amanda booked can't dampen my mood.

'Wow, it's beautiful,' I say.

I'm in awe thinking how wonderful it must be to come to work on this every day, navigating blue skies and the ocean rather than grubby pavements and litter.

'Come on then, time to board the Love Boat.' Patty is still sporting red accessories with her new white linen cruise clothes. Her suitcase is enormous and I'd like to place a bet that over three-quarters of it is red or orange.

'Just as long as it doesn't turn out to be more *Titanic* than Love Boat,' I say, as everyone probably does.

It was the wrong thing for me to say as the Celine-like warbling starts and doesn't stop until we reach the gangway.

Sheila and Kath are already there with Craig; cruise employees have their own accommodation separate to paying guests. They're in twin rooms and Patty will be sharing with a magician's assistant.

'What if she cuts me in half in the middle of the night?' she asks.

'With luck she might make you disappear,' I mock and with that we go our separate ways, Patty to the staff quarters and me to the luxury cabins. Lying here, I contemplate that there are times when my job truly is the best in the world.

Tomorrow we're at sea all day and according to the entertainment plan, I could be downward dog at the dawn aerobics, eating hotdog at the poolside burger bar come lunchtime and then watching a Kate Bush tribute covering 'Hounds of Love' come evening. I wonder if whoever put this together spotted all of that and whether I have to wear Hush Puppies to go to any of it – boom boom.

Tonight, we have a Mateus meet-and-greet so Mercury Club members can spot each other. I get dressed just in time for the inevitable: Patty knocking on the door.

'She's tiny,' she says of her roommate. 'No wonder she fits in half a box.'

She whistles appreciatively as she looks around my cabin.

'Well I did pay for this,' I remind her, 'but it's huge so you could come and stay here if you like.'

I have no idea why I offered this and try not to let my relief show when she replies, 'Employees aren't allowed to fraternise with guests. Besides, I think I'm more likely to have an adventure below stairs.'

I have to agree with that but now I have guests to attend to.

*   *   *

The Mercurians are gathered in one of the lounges enjoying rosé wine. As I join them and mingle saying hello, I realise they all seem to know me or bits of me.

'You started this travel club didn't you?' they ask. 'You organised that scary book weekend.' Or, 'Your mother told us you were propositioned in France!'

I have a part to play here and they're all expecting a little bit of good-humoured chaos to take back with them.

Maybe that's what our motto should be: '*The chaos comes free*'. I'm sure Charlie and Josie would help me out with that.

After mingling, we go into dinner and I'm about to accept an offer to join some of my customers when I'm ushered to a table with other singles. When I explain what's happening, one of the customers tells me, 'You go and find yourself a nice man, you deserve it after all them losers.' This makes me think that France isn't the only thing my mother has told people about.

My instincts tell me that I'm not going to meet Mr Right at this singles table, although Mr Smarmy as throughout is certainly in attendance.

He's sandwiched himself between two widows but I daresay he'll move around the table over the course of the trip. I must develop a strategy for missing some of dinner, not only to avoid my turn being smarmed but with this amount of food every day, they'll be throwing me overboard and using me as a fender when we come into port.

I'm going to be a very professional host on this trip so will start with the quiz tonight. I let my Mercurians know and a few of us form a team heading off to display our collective knowledge. As we sit down I hear a familiar, 'Wait for us', behind me. I turn and am puzzled to see Alan and Amanda rushing towards the table.

How did they do that? We've already cast off.

'Sorry we didn't make dinner; we chose a romantic table à deux instead,' says Alan, 'I do like to treat my best girl well.'

Has he really just said this in front of me? I ignore him like the professional I am.

Amanda continues, 'Watching the ship leave port as the sun set with a glass of champagne, it was so romantic.'

I hope she lays on the buttercream icing as thickly as this.

'So can we join you? I've been swotting up number-one hits,' asks Alan.

We make space for them but this creates a huge team, so the quizmaster splits us up and thankfully I don't have to hear any more romantic drivel. This was the cruise they chose on winning that competition. Great.

I wonder whether this is my warrior journey: I must remain calm for one whole week at sea with my ex and Mr Smarmy and then I will become the sensei.

'In this year,' calls the quizmaster, 'the Berlin Wall fell, Robin Williams was telling people to "Seize the Day" and Richard Marx was "Right Here Waiting". What was that year?'

Alan and I instinctively look across at each other and I mouth, 'The year we met' – 1989. Alan hid that CD in my luggage when I left for one of my flights; no one had ever done anything as romantic and I practically gave up my job there and then vowing never to leave him again.

That incredible feeling of spontaneous internal combustion: love, fire and joy just bursting through every nerve ending you have. There is no feeling like it and reliving the memory I cannot help but smile at Alan before Amanda spots me looking at him and I have to pretend I was just gazing into the distance. I hope Zoe gets to feel that way one day; everyone should.

We didn't win but didn't disgrace ourselves either and while the others debate the questions they got wrong (1983 album covers proved to be our kryptonite), I sneak off to have a quiet night hoping that Patty might visit with tales from below deck.

When I wake up, it takes a moment to remember where I am. I see a shard of sunlight trying to push through the gap in the curtains, so I lift my head up to take in this strange room. Then the roll of the engines or the sea, I can't tell which, cuts through the memory haze and I lie back down for another few moments of peace. The second I leave this room, I'm on duty.

BANG, BANG, BANG.

Duty has come hammering on my door; well Ms P has and she slumps down on the spot that I've just made comfy. I sit on the bed beside her.

'She has a parrot,' she declares.

'Who does?'

'The magician's assistant, of course. Doves aren't original enough any more, it has to be an exotic bird.'

'What's the problem with that?' I ask.

'It's trained to talk, sort of a comedy magic act so when she covers the bird up for it to disappear, it shouts out, "I'm still here, I'm not gone yet."'

'That sounds quite funny,' I say still not seeing the problem.

'Not at 2 a.m. when you're trying to sleep so you cover up its bloody cage it's not,' explains Patty. 'Squawking "I'm not gone yet" all night. I tell you it very nearly was.'

I can picture it and laugh to myself.

'Do they allow animals in the cabins?' I ask.

'No, they're normally in a hold with costumes and props and things. She came back at 3 a.m. to take him down there, thank God.'

'Is she nice? I thought you might make a trip upstairs last night,' I say.

'Thought I'd best get to know the rest of the acts and yes, she's quiet but OK now that she's got rid of the menagerie.'

'So are the big tributes staying below stairs, too? Have you met anyone pretending to be famous?' I venture.

'No,' explains Patty. 'You'll notice they're headlining when we're in port. They get flown in for one night and then flown on to the next cruise ship. Just the early evening acts are staying on board.'

'Fancy breakfast?' She leaps up.

'Are you allowed to dine with me?' I ask with mock haughtiness.

'I'll doff my cap and you can say that I'm your personal food taster come slave,' she replies.

'Deal.'

So we head off for the first smorgasbord of the day.

Life on a cruise has a rhythm to it, which I guess we'll get used to over the week. If you're very keen, you can get up early to take a jog around the deck; this might help counter the enormous buffet breakfast you're about to consume but I can't see any of the crowd here donning trainers. I hear the same protestations every mealtime.

'I don't know what's got into me; I never eat this much at home. It must be the sea air.'

My mum would be having none of that rubbish. She'd be telling them, 'Your eyes are bigger than your belly', and although she might be right, she'd be decked for saying it. Thank goodness she's not here.

After breakfast, guests can just lie back and relax. On the days we're at sea, they organise activities in the afternoon like, 'Let's Get Physical' aerobics or giant board games; today we have Twister to help introduce everyone.

I must find an important business task for that hour of the day otherwise some helpful individual will think I'm not sitting alone by choice and drag me into the game.

On the three shore days we have, we'll dock at midday, visit the town on the itinerary and then be back for a sunset aperitif. We'll have early-evening entertainment like the magician or a movie and after dinner, the music starts.

Each night there are tribute acts followed by a disco. The Granny-Okes are the warm-up for each tribute except Michael Jacko-son who has the whole night dedicated to him, which seems about right for such a huge talent.

I think the main threat to life on this cruise won't be Man Overboard, it'll be Eighties Overdose.

Later, I retreat to a lounge trying to look busy with clipboard in hand until Twister is well underway and then as soon as it's safe, I can't resist a quick peek to see how it's going. Mr Smarmy is right in the middle of it all getting his left leg over as many times as he can. Still, he seems to be keeping some of the ladies entertained. I guess it's true, what happens on ship stays on ship.

I'm pondering the moment when Twister nudges over into sexual harassment just in case Smarmy moves on to one of my Mercurians when Alan appears at my side.

'Thinking of joining in?' he nods at the chaos.

'Only if they start hosing them all down with cold water,' I respond and then there's an awkward silence.

We're both staring forwards but I take a sneaky look at his profile and see the scar he got from a rowing accident one summer. We'd taken Zoe out on Lake Windermere and she spotted a plastic bottle floating on the water, near some cygnets. She wanted to get it out of their way so grabbed an oar to try to nudge it; of course Alan was holding the other end of the oar and when she made a grab for it, she accidentally whacked it into his face. She was so upset about that. I wonder if Amanda knows the history of his face.

'Where's Amanda?' I ask to make conversation.

'Oh, she's very excited.' He turns to face me. 'Julien Dubois, no I've never heard of him either, is our on-board celebrity chef. Big in the eighties, obviously, so she's gone to get herself introduced.'

I shrug, 'Fair enough. I'd be excited if Scott Baio walked through the door.'

'And if Tom Selleck climbed aboard, I'd be getting out the defibrillator for you,' adds Alan.

I smile. No one could interrupt *Magnum P.I.* in our house; it was my personal private pleasure. I can still remember my excitement when the music kicked off, it's playing in my head now just as Alan starts singing it.

'You read my mind. How are you keeping anyway?' I ask.

'I'm well, a bit sad to see the old place go but I guess we've both moved on.'

Thinks: *'Well you have.'*

Says: 'Yes, I suppose so.'

'Do you miss the garden?' I fish.

'Oh, I keep my hand in with a couple of little projects,' he smiles and before I get the chance to ask whether my gnomes are one of these projects, Amanda appears.

'I hear you've met one of your heroes,' I say.

She's gushing like a schoolgirl. Alan can't stop laughing at her enthusiasm and I can see how she must have made him feel when they got together.

But I'm sure that's not real love, is it? He used to do that look when one of our dotty neighbours admitted to putting deodorant on their hair and hairspray under their arms or some such; sort of like tousling a child's hair affectionately. Maybe I'm kidding myself.

It's surprising how quickly times goes when you're doing nothing; I think I even drifted off to sleep at some point in the afternoon. I woke up to the sight and sounds of the aqua aerobics class bobbing up and down to Billy Ocean. Surreal.

Before long it's time for the entertainment and cocktails; after Patty's description, I can't wait to see the magician, well mainly the parrot in truth, so I gather together some Mercurians and we take our seats in the lounge.

Patty was right about her size. She is teeny-tiny but even with that, I can't see how she can possibly contort herself into the suitcases and birdcages into which she manages to disappear.

The parrot is a hoot; the magician puts him into the cage that his assistant has just left and covers it with black velvet.

'And now,' he flourishes, 'this rare bird has completely vanished from this earth.'

'I 'aven't. I'm still 'ere,' squawks the parrot.

The magician taps on the cage with his wand.

'Now he has vanished from this earth – gone for ever.'

'Nawww, I'm still 'ere,' comes the voice from the cage.

The magician pulls off the cover and off course the bird is still there.

'Told you so,' the parrot says, delighting the audience.

In a split second, the magician flicks the cover back over the cage and then off again; it's so fast but the assistant is suddenly in the cage and the bird is gone. Everyone gasps.

Then the bird reappears from behind the curtains and perches on the magician's shoulder.

'I'm still 'ere,' he squawks to a final cheer from the audience.

Incredible. If this is the pre-dinner entertainment I hope Patty and the girls can live up to being part of the main act.

Dinner conversation revolves around whether the magician is really also a ventriloquist. For the Mercurians' continued entertainment I embellish the tale about Patty trying to get to sleep with the parrot in the room; I've learned my guests like to have something that none of the others know, and I'm here to please after all. Many of them already know the tale of the Granny-Okes but for those who don't, it still makes a great story.

The hour approaches, so I make sure everyone fills their glasses and tell them, 'My best friend is on next, let's do her proud.' We toast and head off for some fun.

I don't think I could be more nervous if I were up on the stage. The room is packed and that nervous anticipation when people have waited a millisecond too long starts to rise.

Then a doddery old woman in a raincoat and plastic headscarf gets up onstage and looks a bit confused. The audience throw glances at each other – *should someone tell her to get off?*

I relax knowing what's coming.

Another woman gets up with a Zimmer frame and then a third. The audience starts to get the act and laugh along. My whole body feels as if I'm filled with sherbet about to pop any moment.

'Anyone know the weather for the rest of the week?' asks Kathy.

And then it kicks off, 'It's Raining Men' as the opening track.

They throw off their coats and they're now all in matching outfits – surgical stockings under tutus plus black lace gloves with braces and cardigans; think Bananarama meets the Golden Girls. They've all got spiky eighties hair but with a lovely blue rinse.

They work the audience and tease the men as they go through their set. They're just brilliant and Patty, well, she is an absolute star. Talk about stage presence, I just want to stand on a chair and yell, 'I know that woman, we're best friends!'

She was meant to be there.

'I think she's found her destiny,' says the voice behind me.

It's Alan and as I'm no longer awkward when he makes these appearances. I just nod.

'Are you two going on shore tomorrow?' he asks.

I shake my head. 'Patty is rehearsing but I'm going.'

'Fancy company?' he asks.

'We might have to take some other Mercurians along,' I tell him.

'In case you throw me overboard?' he laughs and I give him an over-the-glasses-if-I'd-been-wearing-any glare.

The disco heats up as the Granny-Okes are replaced by an amazing Bronski Beat cover band. How we're going to keep this up for another four nights I don't know, but for now the whole floor is giving it everything they have. Even Alan is Dad-dancing, as Zoe would call it.

'I thought you'd learned some ballroom moves, must have misheard that,' I yell into his ears as we dance like teenagers.

In an instant he takes hold of my hand and twirls me around. It's intoxicating and not helped by the song that accompanies us.

'Never Can Say Goodbye'.

On-Shore Shenanigans

With the number of people sporting dark glasses at breakfast, we could have been shooting a film noir scene. It seems everyone remembers the words 'pace yourself' when it's too late. Only Amanda seems perky and that's because she's been up since dawn perfecting eggs Benedict with her new French buddy. I'm sure they were delicious, but like many others, I needed the full English to get me through the day.

I notice Mr Smarmy kissing the hand of a guest before guiding one of my Mercurians to a table à deux.

Hmm, I'm going to have to watch that situation. If she's come aboard for romance, fair enough, but I've an inkling he isn't the happily-ever-after type. I'm like a mother hen who's spotted the fox going after one of my chicks. Mum would have sorted him out.

When we were in Monaco, I watched people disembark from their glistening yachts and imagined the champagne lifestyle they led.

I feel like this now as we enter the port of La Rochelle; twin towers either side of the harbour seem to guide us in and we're soon admiring the medieval town.

We've opted for a trip to Cognac and it would be rude not to taste its namesake while we're there. As the coach pulls away, I watch the cruise staff getting on with their various jobs. I spot the magician having a heated conversation over a suitcase with a guy in a white van. I wonder if they have those elaborate costumes delivered over the course of the trip. The logistics of this seem more complicated than you'd think.

Amanda is coming on shore but she's heading off to the market with Julien, so I grab another Mercury couple and persuade them to join Alan and me on the excursion. The tour travels through the ancient town of Saintes before arriving at the Cognac house. The richness of aroma hits us the second we walk in. You could get drunk on this smell without tasting a drop; it's so warm and comforting. The tour is interesting and the ambience so relaxed that I have to remind myself not to copy the couple we're with and link arms on the way back to the boat.

'It felt natural,' I tell Patty when we get back.

'That man,' she wags her finger at me, 'doesn't just want to have his cake and eat it but he wants someone to be bloody baking it. Don't be the stand-in just because Amanda has found some French totty. *You're* the one who should be finding French totty and Lord knows there is plenty below stairs.'

'No thanks,' I say. 'I've made a big enough fool of myself this year. Are you ready for tonight?' I really want a change of subject now.

'Yes,' she says, 'a change of set list and a few new moves to keep people entertained. You coming?'

'Not tonight. You were brilliant,' I reassure her, 'everyone said so, but I need some sleep. I'm going to the movies where no one will notice if I nod off.'

'*Dirty Dancing*? You know that film by heart; just don't quote every line. They'll throw you out.'

'But no one puts baby in the corner,' I laugh.

* * *

I enjoy the peace of the cinema and the feelgood blanket of romance. I'm humming 'Time of my Life' wishing I could belt it out when I bump into Mr Smarmy and my Mercurian arm in arm.

'You look happy,' he says to me.

'The effect of a little nostalgia and romance,' I reply.

They gaze into each other's eyes.

'Oh we know that feeling,' says my Mercurian.

Mother hen mode re-emerges, so I ask about the evening and they gush about how wonderful it has been.

'The magician's assistant was stunning and the outfits were just dazzling. There must be huge wardrobes in those rooms.'

I know there aren't, so guess that they do meet their costume guy when they reach a port.

'Would you care to join us for a nightcap?' asks Mr Smarmy.

Although I am tempted to keep my eye on him for a little longer, the bigger temptation is a cosy bed and a night's sleep, so I say goodnight and watch them snuggle off together.

How do some people make relationships look so very simple?

*　*　*

Another day, another port; today we're in Bilbao. The guests now have their regular entourage and I watch the groups of new best friends head off together. Patty isn't working tonight so she's going to join me touring the famous art galleries of this town.

We're exhausted after just one, so head back to the port and watch the world go by from a little café. We sit admiring the explosion of work that takes place when the guests leave the boat. The magician is back with his costume van, food and drink is loaded and then a car with blacked-out windows pulls up. Patty grabs my arm.

'It's him,' she whispers as Michael Jackson steps out into the sunshine.

Obviously not *the* Michael Jackson but the best MJ tribute in the world according to his website, and from this entrance he's obviously permanently on duty. A purser arrives with a parasol to escort him on to the boat while his luggage is ferried behind him. I can't wait to see this act.

He has no warm-up act; tonight he is the star. I guess the real thing wouldn't need Patty & Co. to liven up the audience either.

When the hour comes, he's magnificent; there is no other word for it. The lighting, production, dancers and costumes, they simply leave you awestruck. Like many others in the audience, I spend the first half hour just staring at him trying to spot the differences (not that I ever saw the real MJ) and then with the opening bars of 'Thriller', I just let myself go and throw my arms around with very little rhythm at all.

After my spurt of energy, I retreat to the bar and he brings the tempo down with 'The Girl Is Mine'. Alan joins me quicker than you can say, '*These coincidences are becoming a little too frequent*', but Patty says it anyway then turns her back on him.

'Takes you back in time, all this, doesn't it?' he says, 'when we first met?'

I remember sneaking that first gentle peck before I boarded the plane. Crew aren't supposed to fraternise with customers but that made it even more delicious; forbidden fruits always are.

Patty turns back towards him in a fury that interrupts my daydream.

'Do you know what day it is?' she asks.

Alan looks blank but I dread what she's about to say.

'It's a year since I came round to your house to find the woman you're reminiscing with in tears because you'd walked out on her. So sod off with your rose-tinted memories.'

He does as he's told and I shake my head: 'I didn't need to be reminded of that.'

I'm sure she meant well but I don't want to relive it and anyway, he's making a real effort and I'm enjoying it rightly or wrongly.

Later that night I wonder whether I should call him and apologise for Patty's attack. Maybe I should invite him round for a '*no harm done*' drink. Patty would kill me for that.

Come morning, I invite Patty for a stroll around the deck; I'm going to tell her my suspicions about Alan just in case anything does happen. I don't want to lose her if he ever does come back.

'Oh, Bo, sweetheart,' she sighs, 'it doesn't amount to much evidence.'

'But the garden and the flowers; he booked this cruise guessing I'd be on it and he never leaves me alone,' I protest.

'I don't know how the garden is being done, true. Maybe the previous owner had a gardener and he's forgotten to cancel the contract so the guy keeps coming. This cruise? They won it and even you didn't know you were coming on it until a few weeks ago. His constant attention? He's a man, he's needy. His floozy has left him for a while and he needs someone to stroke his ego which you, my dear, are doing.'

I just stand deflated staring out at the horizon.

'When she's finished with her chef and comes back, his flirtations will be over. You know that; don't let him hurt you again,' she says.

'He won't,' I tell her. 'I've changed and I like the new me; I like the things I've done. In many ways, Alan's infidelity was the best and worst thing that ever happened to me, well, all of us. After all, you wouldn't be singing on a cruise ship without it.'

'True,' acknowledges Patty.

'But I don't want to be alone for the rest of my life and if Alan is hinting that he wants to come back, at least I have to know for sure,' I say.

'Even if nothing happens, I have to know that I turned it down for the right reasons. I don't want to wreck our family if I have the chance to reconcile it, just to prove a point.'

'I'll make you a promise,' says Patty. 'I'll withhold all judgement; I'll be nice to Alan and I'll watch from the sidelines. If I think he's making moves to come back, I will tell you. If, however, all I see is lovey-doveyness with Amanda, which is all I've seen so far, I'll tell you that too – honestly.'

'That's all I ask.' I hug her. 'Breakfast?'

'Thank goodness for that, I'm starving.'

Patty's first chance to observe comes sooner than either of us anticipates. Julien Dubois and Amanda are greeting everyone at breakfast. They've been working on pastries today and this morning a sensory overload is drawing us in like sirens to the rocks. Patty takes a glance around the room to find Alan; I'd already done that, he's working the tables taking congratulations for Amanda. He nods a hello when he spots us and to her credit, Patty gives him a polite wave.

It would be rude not to partake and like everyone else, with the first bite I am transported to butter and sugar heaven. Oh, how do two simple ingredients combine to create such bliss?

Maybe I don't need a man, maybe I just need an endless supply of Danish pastries.

I look around the room and it's as if someone has given all of the guests an aphrodisiac. Mr Smarmy and Ms Mercurian are taking turns to feed each other yum-yums and strawberries, mopping each other's chins (which I do find a bit unsavoury). I feel the need to escape before there is a brioche-incited orgy.

Anyway, I have to sort out the accessories for tonight's fancy dress. Naturally, it's an eighties movie theme and we Mercurians are going as the Ghostbusters complete with ghosts and Pillsbury Doughboy.

While the Mercurians are on shore visiting today's port, La Coruna, I've got to persuade the DJ to play the theme tune as we walk in so everyone will feel a little bit special. Then I have to see if I can get these water cannons to fire green silly string so that it looks like gunk.

A travel agent's work is never done.

I'm going as the goofy receptionist but using my lilac Granny-Oke wig; it's bizarre but I feel the need to get some use out of it.

I think about what Patty said and wonder if she's right, that my patio is being tended by a gardener who doesn't know his contract has been terminated. Like a wife who won't accept that hers has.

Costumes sorted, I'm going to have a few hours of sunshine before tonight. I might even get a little bit active and have a little swim. Alternatively, I could just lie back and watch the beach volleyball, although I can't imagine it will be anything like the *Top Gun* scene.

The Mercurians have returned and it seems that many of them bypassed the recommended colonnaded town square and headed straight for the beach instead. Now back on deck they're relaxing just as earnestly; bodies are stretched out in the sun, well-intentioned books have been abandoned and, everywhere, people watching from behind sunglasses is in full swing.

That's exactly what Patty is doing. Never one to do things by halves, from behind her magazine, she has Alan under surveillance. If the singing career doesn't work out, I'm sure she could find work as a private investigator, complete with a theme tune of her own. Damn, I now have *The Professionals* theme playing through my brain, which is a real nuisance as The Amateurs might be a better name for the operation.

As I'm getting dressed for the evening, Zoe calls me to ask how it's going.

'Have you seen Dad?' she asks.

'Yes and I haven't made him walk the plank yet,' I joke.

'Mum…'

'Sorry,' I say, 'he's being quite nice, to be honest.'

'Well that's a good sign, isn't it?' she asks.

Damned if I do, damned if I don't it would seem.

'Well, it would be a poor showing if we couldn't be civil,' I say, playing it down so as not to raise her hopes. I have to stop this conversation.

'Darling, I'm sorry but I have to go,' I tell her. 'I mean, I still have to get dressed, see a magic show with a talking parrot, have too much dinner and then get a group of people dressed up as Ghostbusters. I tell you, it's insanely busy.'

We laugh at the ludicrousness of my schedule.

Off to my first appointment with a magic act. I sit with the Mercurians and once more, we're all dazzled by the outfits. I tell them my theory about the portside costume exchanges and we debate whether they sparkle so much to distract you from the sleight of hand.

Tonight's show is all about audience participation.

One by one people are called up on to the stage; they have their valuables taken off them, put into a velvet bag, smashed with a hammer and then miraculously returned to them in one piece. I realise the magicians know what they're doing but I'm not sure I'd have the courage to hand over my valuables. What if I'm the one time the trick goes wrong? It has to happen sometime but fortunately not tonight.

More importantly the climax of the show runs smoothly too; the assistant gets into the familiar magician's box and we all know what happens next: she is sawn in half. The blade cuts through her knee-line and then her neckline. All the time, her bejewelled navel is on display. How do they do this?

Another swirl of the box and the assistant is back in one piece. A huge round of applause greets her. Although we've all seen this on TV, when it's happening right in front of you it is mind-boggling.

Next on my to-do list is the fancy dress, such a tough, tough gig. The Mercurians gather outside the ballroom and as arranged, I give a nod to the DJ, our theme tune cranks up and we burst into the room, proton packs at the ready, spraying silly string and yelling out 'Who you gonna call?'

A great team effort except for Alan and Amanda, who decided that they (for that read *she* probably) didn't want to spend the evening in a boiler suit, so they've come as Richard Gere and Julia Roberts from *Pretty Woman*. Patty would give me a 'told you so' look at this moment.

I wonder whether lifelong cruise devotees keep an array of fancy dress costumes as I watch my Mercurians partying with *Mannequins, Lost Boys* and, of course, *Seeking Susans*.

I did want to have a word with the team who turned up as the cast of *Grease* (two years short of our magical decade), but they don't win the group prize so I keep shtum. The winners are dressed as *Top Gun* characters and although our khaki boiler suit costumes aren't that different, they do have a guy who spends the whole evening with cardboard fighter plane wings attached to him and therefore can't reach the bar or buffet table.

All credit to him.

You forget how many classic movies there were: *Terminator*, *Godfather* and *James Bond*; both Bonds just wore tuxedos but Don Corleone distinguished himself from the secret service agent by carrying a hobby-horse head with him.

Come morning, I imagine there will be some very sore human heads. As I leave them to it, the cocktail bar is in high demand with guests consuming concoctions of every colour. I'm happy to back out early and win the lightweight of the evening award. We have two more shore visits and then we're home to start diets.

A diet to go on holiday and then another when we get back; no wonder the industry is worth billions. And while on holiday we don't see the irony in the three five-course meals we consume.

I get undressed and into bed. It's been a good trip and provided the next two days go smoothly, we should be able to mark this down as another success for Mercury Travel.

Emergency Services

As expected, there aren't many people at breakfast when I first head down. Mr Smarmy and Ms Mercurian are there and they wave me over. He's so charming that I have to say something.

'Can I be assured your intentions are honourable towards my valued guest,' I ask with a tone that I hope says light-hearted in a '*don't mess with me*' kind of way.

'Most certainly not,' he laughs and they clasp hands.

'Would you mind getting me some of that delicious-looking smoked salmon please, darling?' Ms Mercurian asks and he leaves the table to do her bidding.

When he's gone she leans in. 'Don't worry about me,' she whispers, 'I know what he is.'

'Oh, I wasn't worried,' I fake badly.

'Well there'd be good cause. He's already suggesting I invest my savings in his business in Cuba and that we live there together in a tropical paradise,' she laughs. 'He must have thought I was born yesterday. The only thing he hasn't suggested yet is that I wire some cash to Nigeria.'

'Why are you still with him, then?' I ask.

'If I'm not, then some poor innocent might be. At least I can handle him. Besides which, while he thinks I might be game, I get the most amazing attention,' she winks.

And on that note Mr Smarmy returns with her dish and a rose he's stolen from the flower display.

I raise my glass of orange to the wily old girl. Cheers indeed.

After this, I'm not really sure of the sequence of the rest of the morning, it all happens so fast. Sometimes you think you remember things but then you realise that you couldn't possibly have been in all of the places at once. You're putting together the memories of everyone there.

I remember hearing the rumblings of the ship getting ready to leave port. I start walking along the deck and a man barges past me demanding to see the captain.

'We've been burgled in our own cabin,' he protests as the crew try to calm him down.

I'm not overly concerned initially as I imagine they've just misplaced things after a few too many. I look over the railings and see that the magician's costume van is still parked there and that the gangway hasn't been raised yet.

'They must be getting more costumes,' I think to myself.

Then I'm aware of more noise inside the restaurant. I turn around and see that some of my guests have become embroiled in the fracas.

'Angie, you have to come and sort this out, they're not taking it seriously.'

Ms Mercurian grabs me by the arm and drags me into the restaurant where a number of people look very angry.

'What's happened?' I ask.

'There's been a robbery overnight,' she tells me, 'lots of people have had jewellery and money taken from their rooms. That man over there has lost a gold Rolex.'

I don't want to belittle what's going on but I have heard that more gold Rolexes have been lost and claimed for than were ever made in the first place.

'And that lady's missing a necklace; that man lost his phone.' As she points out the list of people who've had things stolen I realise I recognise them all.

They were all part of the magic trick last night and all of these things were on display, even the Rolex now I come to think of it. I have to get to the captain and separate him from the angry throng.

'Captain,' I say, 'I don't know whether this is relevant but everyone knew these people had those things in their cabins last night and they knew that they'd be at the party.'

Together we go to the magician's cabin and knock on the door. Nothing. The captain says he needs to check the register to find out where the assistant is staying.

'Oh I know that, come on,' I say.

We get to Patty's cabin and knock loudly.

'Hold on,' comes her voice, 'there's enough of me to go round.'

Patty opens the door in her robe, raises her eyebrows when she sees the captain and then sighs grumpily when she spots me behind him. We barge past her and see one tidy bed and one newly slept in. I pull open the wardrobes and drawers; only evidence of Patty remains.

'What on earth…?' she asks.

'The assistant, where is she?'

'Hasn't been here all night. I imagine she's bunking up with the man and his magic wand. Why?' she replies.

'Some of the guests have been robbed,' I tell her, 'and all of them were involved in the magic trick last night.'

'You think they might be the culprits?' asks Patty.

'It's starting to look like it,' I reply.

'Well they can't get off the boat, we're ready to leave,' says the captain as he picks up his radio.

'But the gangway is still lowered,' I tell him.

The captain finishes his conversation and darts off. I follow, as does Patty wearing only a robe and deck shoes.

We dash up the stairs and see the magician and his assistant starting down the gangway.

The captain speaks into his radio: 'Do not let anyone disembark until I get there.'

The magician overhears the instruction being given and looks up to see all of the guests hanging over the side yelling, 'Stop thieves!'

They grab their bags and start to make a run for it, causing a mass panic with guests tearing along the deck, trying to follow them. I have visions of the Mercurians falling into the sea and being crushed by their own cruise ship.

The crew do a valiant job of holding back the tide of angry customers, but the magician makes it to the end of the gangway just as it is a couple of feet off the ground. They throw their bags and cases over the barrier and the van screeches closer. The driver jumps out and starts loading the bags into the back. The magician leaps on shore and is legging it towards the van, but the assistant is afraid to try; he starts to leave without her.

'He's going to get away,' I exclaim.

Suddenly the dock is filled with the screeching of sirens and tyres as four police cars surround the van then drag out the driver and magician. The gangway is lowered and ship security takes the assistant on shore to be arrested.

A big cheer goes up from the dining deck and I realise we've all been yelling this on as if it were a spectator sport. Those who haven't had their phones stolen are sharing the videos they've taken; I expect we'll see this online at some point.

I follow the captain to meet the police. Patty starts to do the same but I nod down at her outfit and she rushes back to get changed.

It turns out that the magicians had quite an alternative act going on, genuinely making things disappear (I know, that pun will be used *so* many times over the next few days). They committed the robbery, using the act to establish who had jewellery worth stealing and then breaking into cabins when they knew people would be out at the fancy dress. They knew the guests would be partying hard so wouldn't miss their belongings until later in the morning.

They also had a laundering business going on; they picked up stolen goods from one country with their costumes and transported them to another, meeting a new courier at each port.

The captain and I convey this to the guests who have to identify their possessions now.

'I'm so sorry you've had to endure this,' I tell the Mercury Club. 'We'd never knowingly put you in any danger or send you on holiday with master criminals.'

I try to make light of it hoping that our reputation hasn't been destroyed; I needn't have worried.

'Are you kidding?' exclaims one guest. 'This is the most exciting holiday I've ever had.'

Sadly for the beautiful harbour town, the delights of its market square and cafés are only a backdrop to the constant retelling of this morning's tale, which even made it back home.

INTERNET SENSATION AGAIN :) texts Charlie.

He also reports that sales have started increasing again as the news and the videos have started spreading. Bizarre to think that we all now need to be part of something outrageous to have a good time; sunsets and sights are no longer enough. I'm not sure how I keep this up. Do I have to get people eaten by lions on the South Africa trip?

Stormy Waters

Patty is making hay. First of all, as the former roommate of the master thief, she is deemed to have some insight into the minds of these international criminals and now moves from table to table accepting a free drink then exaggerating this newly found knowledge.

Second, the ship needs another pre-dinner act for our last two evenings, so she's agreed to host a karaoke competition as Granny-P; she's already stoking up interest as she works the crowd.

I leave her to it; after this morning, dealing with the police and then ensuring all of my guests have all of their belongings back, I just want to have a few moments of peace. I need to find a quiet space on the boat so run up the stairs to the sky deck, which I know will be deserted at this time of day. My guests think I'm some sort of mastermind giving them adventures they usually see in films; it truly is insane that my disasters are other people's entertainment.

As I get closer to the deck, the horizon opens up and with a quick glance behind me I run the last few steps hollering like no one is watching.

'You look like you needed that.'

Bugger. Alan.

'Just a bit,' I say. 'Anyway, what are you doing up here? All the excitement is down there.'

Looking over the railings on to the sun deck, we can see golden parasols opening to form a honey-coloured hive and we know that underneath them the bustle and buzz of gossip will still be in full flight.

'You've done well. I wanted to tell you that,' he says without looking at me, and as I can't think of an answer I say nothing.

'I was a real shit but you've come out smelling of roses.'

'That's what you do with shit, isn't it? Fertilise roses,' I reply.

'I taught you something then,' he laughs.

It's now or never, I'm going for it.

'Do you know where I live now?' I start.

'Of course I do,' he replies.

'And have you ever visited my house?' I continue.

'Yes, but you weren't in,' he tells me.

This is it.

'I need to ask you something and I need you to promise not to make fun of me.'

'Promise,' he crosses his heart.

'Have you ever bought me a gnome?' I ask.

He bursts out laughing and I feel so stupid.

'You promised.'

'I'm sorry but that was the last question I was expecting. Why on earth would I do that?'

What seemed feasible and logical now seems ridiculous and my only consolation is that no one else can hear this conversation.

'You don't think I want to get back together do you?' he asks.

'Well, you did follow me on to this cruise.' Embarrassment starts to turn angry.

'I won it.'

'And you've been overly friendly.'

'To show that we're both adults getting on with life, nothing more,' he says.

'It's more than that,' I protest getting more and more heated, 'half the time it's bordered on flirting.'

'Flirting? I have no idea what you're talking about,' he replies. 'Would you rather I insulted you every time I saw you?'

Him being reasonable and calm is just infuriating me every time he opens his mouth.

'You know what you're doing?' I feel bloody stupid now. 'Trying to hedge your bets with both women.'

'You have one hell of an imagination,' he says getting up. 'I'm going now.'

'Oh, drop dead will you,' I tell him.

I know it's not the most articulate insult I could have thrown, but I've just humiliated myself and I need him to go. He does so, hurling more comments about my vivid imagination.

I want to howl, just like a werewolf. Howl and howl and howl. I've seen dogs do it when they're left alone or feel extreme angst and I need that release. However, I can't guarantee Alan is out of earshot and hearing me cry like a banshee won't help my sanity case.

Nor will alcohol; I head back downstairs and straight for the gym. I find the punch bag instead. I pound it with everything I have and then more. This lasts about thirty seconds – they're much tougher than they seem in films. The gym instructor looks me in the eye and suggests that I spar with him.

'No thanks,' I murmur, 'I'm just letting off steam.'

He hits me with a little jab.

'I said no,' I tell him astonished.

'You need this, I can tell,' he counters and jabs me again.

I punch him back but he blocks and gets me round the side.

I try again and make contact. He holds his hands up to his face and tells me to go for it. I punch and punch and punch until I've beaten a smile back on my face.

I have sweated that complete humiliation out of my system by the time we're finished.

'You were right,' I beam taking off the gloves, 'I did need that.'

* * *

Getting ready tonight I look in the mirror and know that I'm glowing red with exercise rather than anger and embarrassment. I give myself a talking to.

'OK girl, no more. You've done so much this year and now you need to get this into your head. IT IS OVER.'

I'm going to tell Patty what happened so that she can keep me on the straight and narrow from here on in. I head off to her cabin where she's getting dressed for her new role as karaoke compère and spill the gory details.

'Go on,' I tell her, 'say it.'

'Told you so,' she obliges then gives me a little hug.

'But you probably had to hear it from him before you would believe it,' she adds, 'and at least this time your angst wasn't broadcast on the internet.'

'Do you think I'll ever learn?' I ask.

'Think of this year as getting a diploma in breaking up,' she says. 'You've just graduated with honours.'

'That's a more positive spin.'

'But you've passed the exam now, so stop retaking it.' She hammers me on the skull to drive it in.

The Kids Wanna Rock

Granny-P is ready to face her audience; the lyrics for 'Material Girl' start up on the karaoke screen and as the music begins, she jumps up onstage urging the audience to give her a round of applause: 'Come on boys and girls, like the advert says, I'm worth it.'

She starts singing along, camping it up as much as possible, and as you can imagine that's to quite a high standard.

'She's like a woman doing a man doing drag,' whispers someone on my table.

Patty finishes the song and then starts her act.

'Where's the daft bunch who turned up to an eighties costume party as the cast from *Grease*?'

A cheer goes up from a table on the left.

'Did you learn nothing in history? Nineteen seventy-eight, I was a mere babe when it first came out,' she scolds.

Scornful heckling rises.

'Mind you, I'm still a babe now,' she continues.

Wolf whistles from the audience; this woman can work a room. She finds the couple who came dressed as Danny and Sandy and cajoles them on to the stage.

'Your punishment for not knowing your seventies from your eighties is that you can go first. The good news is that you get to pick who goes second. Music, maestro.'

She's chosen 'You're the One That I Want' for them to sing and the night kicks off. This crowd love nominating each other, so the night flows well until Patty closes her first act of the evening.

'That was bloody awful,' she says, 'but points for trying. If you want to see it done properly, we Granny-Okes are up next, so fill your boots and come back cheering.'

We've sailed into our final destination, St Peter Port, tonight and we'll spend our final day visiting Guernsey tomorrow before getting back to Southampton. So there's an end-of-trip buzz about the evening and everyone is in the mood to party. Tonight we have an evening of soft rock with a Bryan Adams tribute headlining; Alan is going to love that, 'Summer of '69' was his 'once more around the block' song. I think everyone has one, the song you drive once more round the block for and you won't get out of the car until the track finishes.

Tonight isn't fancy dress but a few of the guys have dressed up and are sporting 1980s rock-star wigs; they're reliving the days they had long hair and are having the time of their lives. You can tell when someone is having a nice time and when someone is having a *brilliant* time. I wonder how long it is since any of these guys got the chance to let it all hang out to rock music? Their kids would die of embarrassment if they could see them now.

Patty's set is quite short tonight and of course she ends with Bon Jovi and the Zimmer-frame air guitar, which Sheila brandishes to wild applause and cheering. In a triumph of rock-star frenzy, she throws the Zimmer frame into the audience and there's an unreal scramble for it. I have a moment of terror when I think Patty is going to attempt to crowd surf but to my great relief she doesn't, although the thought flickered across her face; I saw it.

Mind you, if she had, this crowd might well have caught her. In a couple of days, their lives will be back to washing the car and cutting the grass, but tonight they're partying as if they never had to grow up.

The star act comes on to the stage and Alan, with the be-wigged guys at the front, goes wild: head-banging, jumping up and down, barging into each other. I fail to see how this drunken performance is any different to my karaoke session. If I'd put this online and called them Grandad Rockers or something he'd have no right to question my sanity. Maybe there are always double standards when it comes to men and women.

I spot Alan right up at the front pumping his fist in the air; he always adored Bryan Adams and Bruce Springsteen. I look but can't see Amanda anywhere.

The heat in this room is now overwhelming and I need to get away from these sweat-soaked walls for a minute or two. I step out on to the deck and at the first blast of cool night air, I sigh with pleasure.

'Bliss,' I say to no one in particular as I look out on to the night lights of Guernsey.

'Only improved with a chilled glass of Pinot.' Patty sneaks up and hands me a glass of just-what-I-needed.

'Could you do this every week?' she asks.

'I don't think so; I think I'm a landlubber or whatever they're called. What about you?'

'I wasn't sure,' she says, 'but Ang, they've asked me to stay on and do the karaoke act for a few weeks, until they replace the magician. Do you think I should?'

'Do you have enough knickers with you?' I ask.

'They're upgrading me to a room with a sink and washing line,' she boasts.

'Then I think you're sorted,' I say and click glasses. 'Just do it, life is too short for regrets.'

She looks quite relieved, although I can't imagine she was waiting for me to give her permission.

'Shall we go and watch your ex make an ex-hibition of himself,' she asks.

'Yes and let's take a video of him to post online.' Which of course I won't do.

We head back into the ballroom and struggle through the wall of heat just as the crowd are screaming for an encore. There's Alan, wearing a freshly acquired wig that sits skew-whiff on his head. He looks exhausted with a face like a shiny red portside buoy.

Bryan comes back on and they go wild, they're all chanting for the classic they haven't heard yet.

'Summer, Summer, Summer,' bay the crowd.

The chords strike up and there's a huge cheer. The crowd start leaping up and down and bellowing the lyrics; they all know 'Summer of '69'.

I take a picture of the band and crowd and then tour the room taking photos of the Mercurians enjoying the night, lots of happy faces to go into our next newsletter. I turn back to the crowd to get a close-up of Alan but can't see him; he's not in his spot at the front.

I skim the crowd and then spot him trying to get away from the masses. He must have had too much excitement for one night. No staying power, I muse.

I watch him and then realise he's struggling; he's holding his chest and trying to steady himself grabbing at people as he walks past. All they see is a sweaty drunk bloke and they brush him off. Then it happens, he falls to his knees clutching his chest while his face is paralysed with agony.

I dive in slow-motion speed to get to him, pushing the crowd aside as I go. No one seems to appreciate what's happening here and I feel as if I'm in some awful nightmare. A room of people partying and someone dying in their midst yet they haven't even noticed.

'Get help, get a doctor,' I scream but no one can hear me over the din.

I have Alan's head in my lap and the people directly around me start to see that we're in trouble. A Mexican wave of concern works its way around the room and then from the stage Patty's voice. She's been watching me and when I ran for Alan, she ran for the mike.

'Get a doctor now, there's a man having a heart attack,' she calls out.

The band stop and the crew get the crowd out of the room. The ship's doctor reaches us and places Alan in recovery position, then gives him oxygen. They transport him to the medical bay and I move to follow.

'Are you his wife?' asks the doctor.

'Yes…' I start to say.

Amanda comes rushing into the scene.

'Alan, oh my word, what's happened? Darling, can you hear me?'

'I mean no,' I sigh, 'this lady is.'

I watch as they wheel him out on the stretcher with Amanda clutching his hand.

Patty puts her arm around me.

'I told him to drop dead,' I despair recalling my last words.

'Well he hasn't and he won't. He'll be fine now thanks to you,' she says. 'And well done with Amanda, I know that was hard.'

He's still one of my guests and I have to be sure he's looked after, so go to find out the options from the doctor and captain. Being so close to the mainland, the best option for him is to be flown to Southampton General. I explain this to Amanda and she agrees to it; I wonder whether I'd have insisted if she hadn't agreed.

I would have no right to. I sit with them both while we wait for the helicopter to arrive and I witness the tenderness and affection between them. It's taken a near-death experience for me to accept that they're the couple now.

The coastguard crew are masterful; the backdrop of the night sky, the flashing lights of the helicopter and everyone knowing exactly what to do. I have permission to stay with the couple until they're safely on their way and Patty stands with me.

The ship's doctor supervises the move and then comes back to stand with us as the rescue team take flight.

'You got to him in time,' he reassures us, 'he'll be fine now.'

I turn to thank him for his help and am struck by what I see. Patty and the doctor standing side by side, not noticing each other as they both watch the helicopter.

As a couple, they're bathed in the flashing lights of the landing area, the flashing red and orange lights which seem to focus their beam only on these two.

I discreetly take a picture of them.

'Oh Patty,' I think, 'Cleo Castanello was right after all. And to think, you're about to be stuck on a ship with this man for a few more weeks.'

'Shall we go inside,' says the doctor, guiding Patty.

If only she could see it too.

Land Ahoy

I opt to take a morning boat to Southampton rather than wait for the cruise ship to get there later and as soon as I land, I'm relieved to be back on terra firma.

I go straight to the hospital and sit in the waiting room alongside weary-looking relatives bearing carrier bags of food. It seems the sick these days would rather have chocolate and Coke rather than grapes and flowers. I wonder whether I should have brought anything. I can't think what would be appropriate for your ex – especially one who's had a heart scare.

Visiting starts in twenty minutes and I've had a call from Zoe to say her flight from Manchester has landed and she'll be with us soon. Amanda has been out a couple of times to tell me that he's stable; it feels extremely odd hearing news from someone else but I need to be civil for Zoe's sake.

At that moment, my daughter bursts through the door as if she's appearing in *ER* and gives me a big hug. The clock hits the appointed hour and the whole waiting room disperses down the various corridors. We find Alan in a private room hooked up to monitors and machines. Zoe rushes to him in tears.

'Oh Dad, what were you doing?' she asks.

Amanda stands aside; it's as if there's a new hierarchy being established. I might be behind Amanda but Zoe is definitely in front of her when it comes to Alan's affections.

'Reliving my youth,' answers Alan, his pale face showing genuine joy at the sight of his daughter. 'You'd have been ashamed of me.'

Zoe takes both of us by the hand.

'You two need to stop doing this,' she smiles. 'I can't cope with my unruly parents.'

She looks to Amanda. 'If you keep him under control, I'll sort her out – deal?'

'Deal,' we all say.

At that point a nurse walks in and hands Alan the *Southampton Gazette*.

'Look at that, I'm more famous than you now,' he says.

Alan spreads the paper out to show a front-page headline of a dramatic rescue at sea. It's a fantastic photograph of his stretcher being hoisted into the helicopter against the landing lights and the shadowy silhouettes of the crew.

'I don't want either of you famous, I want you alive and well,' scolds Zoe, still more grown up than either of us.

Visiting time is nearly over, so I ask Amanda if I can have a word with Alan. She leads Zoe out of the room.

'I'm sorry,' I tell him, 'I didn't want my last words to you to be "drop dead".'

He takes hold of my hand. 'Thanks to you, they weren't your last words and my last words won't be abusive either. I think you've been brilliant this year.'

'Do you think we could be friends?' he adds taking me by surprise.

'I'm not sure yet,' I say honestly, 'but we can always try.'

We peck on the cheek and I say my goodbyes.

I need to get back to Mercury Travel as Charlie will shortly be off on the wine tour. With assurances that they'll keep me updated, I head for the train station. I must sleep for most of the journey as I remember none of it; my rolling head jerks me awake when we reach Piccadilly and then I get a taxi home. Despite all of this sleep, the god Morpheus blesses me for another nine hours when I finally put head to pillow in my own bed.

Heaven is indeed a place on earth.

Flat dry land feels strange after the trip and the office even stranger, familiar yet new. We're busy from the moment we open the doors thanks to a local follow-up article about Alan's rescue.

In this interview he tells them about the cruise and how he was having the time of his life. There he is in his hospital bed holding up a T-shirt which says, 'Old Guys Still Rock', loving the attention. He's mentions Mercury Travel and praises our handling of things; he couldn't have given us a better advertisement. Our website traffic is through the roof and with the flux of customers it's created, I have to reacquaint myself with the job quicker than I'd anticipated on my first day back. I have to do without my usual hour of coffee and gossip.

'Are you sure you can cope?' asks Charlie.

'Josie is going to come in full-time and I'll just work longer hours, answer the online queries at night. You never know it may die down in a couple of days.'

'I hope not,' he says reading my mind too.

This level of busy is exactly what I need for the next few weeks while both Charlie and Patty are away. The contrast of the busy cruise liner I've just left and the quiet starter home I go back to will be even starker without them.

Yes, busy is good.

We make hay while we're all here to man the pumps and convert huge numbers of enquiries to sales; many people are asking about next year and we haven't got that calendar planned yet.

As well as customer enquiries, we have emails from venues and tours that would like to be part of the Mercury Travel Club. That's another task for the next few weeks, to take all of these ideas and have a draft calendar ready for Charlie and me to review together.

Busy is very good.

Later, a local journalist comes in following up on the story; he's heard about the magician too and wants to make this a wider piece about high jinks on the high seas. I have Zoe's voice ringing in my head, '*I don't want either of you to be famous*', and quite frankly, I don't want to be either. Instead, I suggest the names of some customers that he can talk to. As anticipated, the customers embellish the details, provide personal photographs and enjoy their fifteen minutes of fame. They call to reassure me that they've said nice things and to make sure they're on our mailing list. It seems everyone wants a little piece of Mercury chaos in their lives.

Busy is exhausting.

Mum calls while my dinner is rotating in the microwave. I dread it pinging during our conversation, confirming all of her comments about my cooking, but sod's law, it does.

'I was just telling Moira that businesswomen like you just don't have time to cook,' she says. 'I bet that Mary Portas doesn't cook when she's finished sorting out people's shops.'

'Moira?' I interrupt ignoring the flattering Portas comparison.

'She hands out the samples in the supermarket. They had their new fancy range out yesterday and I was telling her that it would be perfect for a businesswoman like you but I would have to try them out first. I showed her your picture in the paper.'

Mum is even dining out on Alan's heart attack.

'We both agreed that you're a real hero. Moira said she wouldn't rescue her ex if he were choking on one of her ready meals.'

'She sounds lovely. Anyway, how's Dad?' I ask.

'She wants to know how you are,' she yells at him and there follows a mini row with him telling her not to shout and her saying she's not. The usual exchange; I wait until they remember I'm still here.

'He says he's very proud of you,' Mum says, 'we both are.'

The power of the media and as Mum calls them 'proper newspapers not internet things'. They can be folded up, stuffed into handbags and then handed out to shop assistants, hairdressers and a host of people who didn't want them in the first instance. And in the hands of my mother they can be used for bartering and scrounging.

'The man in the pub gave Dad a free pint when I showed him your article.'

'That's very generous,' I say.

'Well, I said I might be able to get him a discount off one of your holidays,' she confesses.

By the time I've finished paying for all of Mum's freebies I'll be bankrupt.

No Such Thing as Bad Publicity

The article in the local paper takes the wind out of my sails; instead of the heroic rescue angle, it suggests the travel club might be a danger to people's health.

'The owners refused to comment,' I read out to Josie, 'but the questions remain, did they put their customers within arm's reach of known international criminals? Did they persuade customers to party like youngsters with no thought of the consequences? The answer to both these questions seems to be a resounding "guilty as charged".'

'That's garbage, no one will believe that,' says Josie.

The article then goes on to ridicule the photographs that the customers have given to the journalist and promises more online.

I can't stop myself and we head to the website where the main picture is a clip from the only Granny-Oke gig I did.

We're doing 'Should I Stay or Should I Go' and the subline is, '*we recommend they go – now*'. We get off the website.

It gets worse, I start to feel as if I'm on *Ice Road Truckers* with a forty-tonne articulated lorry skidding towards a crevasse – the local radio station announces that it has an interview with the journalist and a phone-in about 'growing old disgracefully'.

I don't know whether I should warn people that their trust has been abused. I feel as if I've let Charlie down and am just glad he's mid-air by now. I hold my head in my hands and cannot bear to answer the phone when it rings. Josie picks it up, nods a few times, and then with the receiver held in the crook of her neck, she taps out a website address and turns her screen to me.

I go over and look at what she's showing me. The response is unbelievable.

'Condescending prick,' sums up the outpouring from people furious about the article.

'So Jagger has to stop touring? Attenborough stop travelling the world?' asks one contributor.

'What have you ever done with your life?' asks another.

'This man is a complete liar. We had a brilliant time on that cruise and told him so. How do we report him?' says one Mercurian.

The site is on fire, so by the time the radio interview starts, there are people outside the station protesting over the reporting, the ageism and the closure of the local swimming pool, although I'm not sure how they managed to justify riding this wave.

I'm already finding the coverage completely unbelievable when we get a call from *Ladies At Lunch*, a national TV programme. They want me to talk about reliving my youth and making a business helping others to do the same.

I have difficulty saying no to anyone, many women do and we end up promising away every ounce of our spare time and energy, but I really don't want to do this. Would Charlie give away this much free publicity? What if I'm rubbish on TV and it ends up being a disaster? How could it when we're not doing anything wrong? Why on earth did I think I could run a business in the first place?

ARGH – WHY DON'T THEY ALL JUST GO AWAY?

I'm beating myself up when Alan calls me to reassure me that he didn't badmouth the travel club in any of his interviews, he'd never do that.

'Thank you,' I say. 'Now do you fancy saying that on national TV?'

And that's how my ex-husband became a national advocate of the Mercury Travel Club. He was fabulous.

'So give me a list of the things you'd like me to give up,' he says to one interviewer and then, 'What date exactly do you plan to stop enjoying yourself?' to another.

He tells everyone how the team from Mercury saved his life, getting to him before anyone else noticed that he'd fallen in the crowd. It was a good move: having the guy who went on holiday and had a heart attack while enjoying himself was a far more powerful advertisement than I could ever have been. The show was overwhelmed with tweets supporting him as well as a few saucy ones asking for his number. He loved every minute.

Later we even get an apology from the journalist bowing to 'people power' and some free Christmas advertising as recompense. There's a surge of protest bookings; customers telling everyone that they're not too old to live life to the full and wanting us to help them.

Mercury Travel Club has a lot to live up to.

'Don't get trampled by a stampede of wildebeest,' I tell Charlie when he calls to say they all arrived safely.

'Oh I don't know,' he replies, 'at this rate we'd just be keeping up the reputation we're building. Come to Mercury and live life on the edge. You know what we say, the chaos comes free.'

'I think a reputation for injuring our customers might work against us,' I say.

'Don't worry I'll bring everyone back, in one piece, with no scandal, no airlifts and no diamond smugglers. Just good wine, majestic wildlife and African skies as you promised.'

'Sounds perfect,' I reply. I wish I'd gone on that trip.

I settle into a few days of quiet but solid work, making the most of the past few days but trying not to stoke it any further. I leave the phone on answer-machine mode, calling customers back immediately but ignoring any journalist requests. After a fortnight the news is old and I stop getting calls. I let my guard down and as sure as a dog will always find a bone, one of them gets through to me.

'Ms Shepherd? I'm Sarah from *Business Today*.'

'Sorry, wrong person,' I panic, 'we're not doing any more interviews.'

'Oh, I didn't want an interview,' she says, 'it's about the Entrepreneur of the Year awards, could I speak to Ms Shepherd?'

I ascertain that she's not giving me an award; she just wants me to sponsor them.

'Sponsor them? What do you mean? I want to win one, when are they?' I ask.

'The closing date is tomorrow and we already have so many entries, I doubt you'll have time to do yourselves justice whereas sponsoring the evening...' she continues.

I'm not listening any more. Whatever can be said about me – and there are many things, I know – no one can say that I shirk from a challenge. Deadline, schmeadline.

I get her to send me the details and keep hitting refresh until they come through. This is how I'll make it up to Charlie. I'll work all night to put in an outstanding entry for the Mercury Travel Club and ensure our spot on the stage next month. I flick to the bottom of the email to find out who's hosting, hoping to discover that we'll be photographed with Mr Necker Island himself. I feel slight disappointment when I spot that it's the business editor and not my hero handing out the gongs on the night. Oh well, I'll get to him one day.

That evening I puzzle over the application. Having never done one before, I have no idea what to write. If only Peter were here, he'd know. I think about calling him but I want to do this on my own. The questions are very open:

Q. 'Tell us why you should win this award'
A. Because I have very low self-worth and need to prove that I have a talent for something.

Q. 'How have you contributed to the local economy?'
A. Bought lots of new clothes and given many of the local community a bloody good laugh – usually at my expense.

Q. 'How will you promote this award if you win it?'
A. I'll give the trophy to my mum, who'll keep it in her handbag and show it to everyone at the hairdressers.

Q. 'Give examples of when you have provided excellent service'
A. I once left a customer with a lothario conman because she was flattered by the attention.

Despite these answers being the truth, I don't think they're quite what they're looking for. I remember Peter saying that our business plan was pretty good so I dig that out and start drafting some sensible answers. It takes all evening but before the midnight hour, I have something I think Charlie would happy with too. I press the send button with scornful satisfaction: 'Who won't make the deadline – eh?'

These awards are what I've been waiting for all year and I'd forgotten all about them. If we hadn't achieved such notoriety, the paper wouldn't have thought to contact us, so I guess old Oscar Wilde was right – there are worse things than being talked about.

Busy, Busy, Busy

You don't realise how much you miss your annoying best friends until they're not there, well, annoying you.

The only thing I've been able to do is focus on the business, which I suppose is just as well.

Bookings have continued to flow in and cruise companies are now giving us fabulous discounts to hand on to people. We're still working bloody hard to get people on holiday but at least now we have something extra to offer them.

Charlie returns to us in one piece with no injuries or major catastrophes to report.

'That's a bit dull,' I laugh. 'How will we keep up our notoriety without a disaster or two?'

'Well, this is doing the rounds of social media,' he says.

He flicks up a beautiful picture of a very handsome couple enjoying themselves against a backdrop of lovely acacia trees, or it would have been a beautiful picture if a huge baboon hadn't photobombed them with his big blue bottom.

'That's ace,' shrieks Josie, 'it has to go on our end-of-year round-up.'

We've been working on that end-of-year booklet together, gathering photographs of all the things we've done this year. I'd planned it as publicity for next year's holidays, but I imagine that when we sit down and look through it, we'll be astonished at just how much we've done, and it's obviously not over yet.

We'll also be surprised by how much we've moved on. I mean to say, Patty is an entertainer on a cruise ship, Josie has been happily dating Matt since the wine tasting and Charlie? Hmm, I wonder why he hasn't mentioned the Peter aspect of his trip at all. I'll ask him when we close up.

'This is the draft itinerary for next year's travel club,' I show him.

I've added a few more adventurous activities like hot-air ballooning and by popular request have extended the musical cruise trips through the decades.

'The January and February trips are selling well already,' I say.

'I'm not going on that rock and roll trip,' warns Charlie. 'All that jitterbugging and jiving is another heart attack waiting to happen.'

'No, I didn't think that would be you,' I say. 'I had you down either for a bit of Rat Pack or The Divas of Vegas.'

'A fortnight of Bette and Mariah?' he says. 'Pack my linen suit now, I'm already on the boulevard.'

'We need some longer long-haul trips in this. Our customers have the time now,' suggests Charlie.

'And road trips too – like driving Route 66 or Highway 101. We'll organise everything and all you have to do is turn up and drive away in your Cadillac.'

'Brilliant idea, very *Thelma and Louise*,' I say jotting it down. I'd love to do that.

'I met so many people ticking off bucket lists,' he continues, 'sad in a way but inspiring too; at least they're going for it while they can.'

'Talking of which,' I say jumping on the opportunity, 'did you go for it? With Peter?'

'We had a wonderful time,' he replies, 'glorious.'

That doesn't answer my question and I have to probe further.

'But what happened to "he's the one"?' I ask. 'I half-expected you to come back sporting matching ethically-sourced diamond rings.'

'I crumbled,' he sighs. 'I just couldn't do it. There we were in the most glorious setting overlooking the sea, waves crashing into the cliffs, the night air filled with the scent of jasmine and I looked across at him and thought to myself, this is just perfect.'

'And?'

'What if he'd said no and I managed to ruin the most wonderful moment of my life? No it was safest to keep schtum,' he replies.

'Oh you big soft coward,' I tease.

'I know, but if it's meant to be, there'll be another moment,' he laments.

I consider myself their fairy godmother as I got them together through the book-club weekend and I wonder if there's anything I can do to create that moment for them.

'Whatever you're plotting, stop it,' says Charlie, spotting the cogs whirring.

I exclaim innocence.

'I want the moment to happen naturally,' he says.

I promise not to interfere; after all, if I were any good at romance, wouldn't I have created a successful love life for myself?

*　*　*

The whole country is now well settled into post-holiday work mode, getting on with the routine until the next big event, which is only ten weeks away: Christmas. Like everyone else, every day I battle the weather to get into the shop, I do as much business as I possibly can and then do battle again to prepare a warming ready meal for me and a delicious tin of cat food for Socks. Autumn brings its own sense of peace I always think; because it gets dark earlier, you don't feel obliged to live outdoors for hours on end. You're expected to curl up at home and who am I to disappoint?

The scare of the hot summer is a constant reminder of the need to get next year's bookings under the belt. I was terrified that the business would go under and having survived one storm, I'm not about to let this ship sink now.

We produce a mid-year review with photographs and quotes reminding people what a fabulous time they had. I also use this to design an advert for the paper with the free space they gave us. We send calendars to our best customers printed with a Mercury Travel Club suggestion each month and we get a radio station talking to us about the bucket list trips that people take; Charlie's doing that interview.

All in all we're giving it everything we have and customers are calling in. Charlie was right about people wanting to get away for longer. Snowbird trips, where customers go away for the whole of the winter, are our top sellers. Our first Mercury Club adventure is a dog-sled holiday to Lapland. Josie has been nominated to go on that one and is taking Matt; as much as I'd love to see the Northern Lights, I'd like it to happen somewhere warmer. Being Aussie she's curious to try minus twenty-five-degree weather and three feet of snow. Glad someone is.

In the midst of all this activity, I get a call from the Entrepreneur of the Year awards telling us that we've been shortlisted.

'That's brilliant news,' I say. 'What do we have to do now?'

'Customer feedback is important to any business, so for the next stage,' says the caller, 'we'd like to hear what your customers think of you. Can you arrange that?'

I tell her that I can, I know lots of people who'll endorse us. I put down the phone and tell the others the news.

We dance around the shop and start singing 'We Are the Champions' at the top of our voices. I hope we're singing it again for real in a few weeks' time.

I Blame Noah

Although his recommendation alongside the dramatic rescue pictures would be hard for anyone to beat, I can't ring Alan as he's entering these awards too. Maybe I should just check that he still is before completely dismissing the idea.

I don't get as far as asking him.

'So glad you called,' he yells down the line as if we're the best of friends.

'I wanted to invite you to a bit of a gathering at my place. Charlie too, and of course any plus-ones but not your mum if you can avoid it. After the last time she was here…'

I imagine that was Amanda's instruction and giggle to my-self. I can't think of a reason to decline quickly enough, so end up accepting. I wish my partner in crime was at home. If she weren't gallivanting around on a cruise ship…

a) I'd have a plus one
b) I'd have something better to do in the first place and could have refused easily

However…

c) She'd be so curious as to why he'd invited me to a party we'd have to go anyway.

I don't want to turn up alone, so call Zoe to see if she wants to go together.

'I'm taking someone, Mum,' she practically blushes down the line.

Blimey, everyone is going in two by two: Charlie is with Peter and Josie is with Matt. So I call Caroline. Fortunately, she is curious to meet the evil home-breaker I've told her about so agrees to come along. You can bet he'll be on the charm offensive the whole night.

Of course, I need to look stunning and yet casual at the same time. I need to look successful and desirable yet unattainable.

'… and it can't look as if I've made any effort,' I tell the personal shopper helping me achieve this impossible yet much-sought-after standard. I've come to the conclusion that only the fabulously wealthy ever achieve it.

Amanda has gone for the same effect and we greet eachother in matching 'simple yet flattering' silk blouses with one piece of statement jewellery. We glance knowingly at each other.

I half expect the room to stop and stare at me when I walk in, all whispering, 'What's she doing here?' but they don't. I'm introduced to a couple of people as the woman who saved Alan's life rather than his ex-wife, which I guess makes it easier on everyone and explains my invitation. I look round at their lifestyle: the apartment is tasteful, the seafood canapés delicious and the wine chilled; just what I expected. Perhaps I should sneak a photo or two for Patty.

Zoe walks in and I'm surprised to see the man she's with is considerably older than her. She looks so happy, unlike Alan who cannot hide the glower when he's introduced.

'Classic Father Figure substitution,' says Caroline as she watches the scene and reads everyone's mind.

I nudge my way through the room to give her a big hug and shake his hand warmly. James heads up a local firm of architects and they've been dating for a couple of months now. They want to talk to me about booking somewhere nice for his fortieth birthday next year. It's a good job Patty isn't here: a forty-year-old is her definition of a toy boy.

There are a few people here I know, couples who knew Alan through work and sided with him on the divorce. We talk about the new business, exchange other pleasantries and promise to keep in touch now that '*the dust has settled*'. Yeah, right, you weren't there when I needed you; there'll be no mates-rates for you.

I'm not watching where I'm going and manage to headbutt a very solid torso. I know who it is before I even look up.

'Ed, how are you?' We air kiss.

'I heard you'd been invited,' he says. 'Do you two get on now?'

'Well, I didn't kill him when I got the chance.'

I laugh but it sounds far more sinister than I'd intended, so I remind him about the whole heart-attack episode. It dawns on him that I'm kidding.

'I'd probably put Sherlock Holmes on that case,' he smiles, referring to our joint love of detective novels.

'I'd never get away with it, then,' I laugh.

Despite his innocent faux pas and our disastrous night together, he's a nice guy. I'm about to ask to come back to the book club when Alan gets everyone's attention by clinking his glass.

'Everyone, could I have your attention for a moment,' he says.

The guests turn towards him.

'I wanted to have this little party to celebrate life. As many of you know, hell I think the whole country knows, I had a little heart incident this summer.'

A ripple starts around the room. Boy is he milking this.

'And it made me realise how lucky I am, a beautiful daughter, great friends.' He points his glass at me and I nod in response.

'And a wonderful partner,' he continues. 'Scares like that make you realise that you may not see tomorrow so make the most of today.'

He pulls Amanda towards him and kisses her passionately; OK so I'm at the back of the room but I am here. This feels weird.

'In fact, that's exactly what I'm going to do right now.'

Oh no; surely not – in front of me?

He gets down on one knee and grabbing a napkin ring holds it up to Amanda. Everyone gasps, Charlie and Peter move to either side of me and hold me between them.

'Darling, will you marry me?' asks Alan.

I don't hear the response as my knees give way and the guys rush me out to the balcony.

'He didn't warn you that he was going to do that?' asks Charlie and I shake my head, which is still attached to my body so didn't explode with incredulity after all.

'It was obviously an impulsive move,' says Peter. 'People don't think these things through enough. That's why there's so much divorce.'

He checks himself.

'Sorry Angie, I just meant that I think you have to be sure,' he continues and I can see Charlie's relief at not having acted on impulse on the trip.

We head back into the lounge where Alan is standing between Amanda and Zoe for photographs while James stands to the side. It's one of those new family photographs that I dreaded seeing at the beginning. This will adorn the shelves of their house and will eventually be joined by a wedding photograph and, Lord help us, surely not a christening one? Is Amanda young enough?

'Earth calling Mars.' Charlie is waving his hand in front of my face, trying to change the subject. 'James – what do we think?'

I shake myself from the daydream. Technically, Zoe and Amanda could have babies at the same time. Alan would celebrate his sixtieth with a four-year-old in tow, rather him than me.

'I need to go home,' I say.

I make my goodbyes, relieved to see that Caroline is talking to Ed so I'm not abandoning her. Charlie and Peter leave with me.

'He seems nice,' I answer getting back to the conversation as soon as we're in fresh air. 'A lot older than her, but seems nice. I just hope that there isn't an older wife left behind at his house and that Zoe isn't a trophy girlfriend.'

'How ironic would that be,' adds Charlie and then mouths 'sorry'.

'Don't worry,' says Peter, 'there's no wife at home, I know him. He's a workaholic, never had time for relationships before. In fact, I'm surprised to see him prised away from his drawing board now.'

'That'll suit Zoe,' I reply, 'but how on earth did they meet?'

'A networking event,' continues Peter, 'and if you two want to win that award, it wouldn't do you any harm to go to one.'

Maybe so, but my next social engagement will be with my daughter to find out everything I can about the man who seems to be making her smile again. I took a picture of them both on my phone as we left the party and if I want to find out *everything* then I'll need an accomplice. I'm sure that my mother will be only too delighted to turn Chief Inquisitor once again.

Happy Families

'Men my age are still living at home with their mothers,' explains Zoe.

Sensible boys I think to myself.

'They've got uni debts, nowhere to live and someone still does their washing. They just haven't grown up, it's awful,' she continues.

'And they've got them beards now,' adds Mum helpfully.

We're in the bar of Zoe's hotel; being the grandmother of the manager is still suiting her very well; she heads off to say hello to the staff and no doubt blag some snacks.

'How long have you known him?' I ask, hoping the generic question brings out the answers to everything else I want to know.

'About three months,' she answers and I realise that was around the time of the heatwave and my obsession with the business.

'We held a network event for local businesses.'

Peter was right.

'And he came to that?' I ask.

'No,' explained Zoe, 'he'd already been commissioned to do some design work for the hotel so was working on it. He was sitting in a quiet part of the lounge trying to avoid everyone and we bumped into each other when I tried to do the same; two loners together.'

She smiles reminiscing.

'And,' I prompt.

'We just talked about his designs, the hotel and about you.'

I let her continue.

'I told him you'd been thrown lemons after the divorce but had made exceptionally good lemonade with them. I told him I was proud of you,' she says.

I've never heard her say this before and it melts my heart. I take her hands and thank her.

'But stop changing the subject,' I prod. 'I want to know all about this man.'

'That conservatory thing is nice.' Mum returns from her wanderings.

'The atrium,' corrects Zoe. 'James designed that; he's very talented.'

'Is he rich?' asks Mum, getting to the point.

'Gran, you can't ask questions like that,' exclaims Zoe.

Mum shrugs an '*I just did*'.

'He's successful, yes,' concedes Zoe, 'because he's very good at what he does.'

'He's a lot older than you, though. Does he have any kids or other skeletons locked in the closet?'

Go for it, Mum.

'Yes, he's thirty-nine and no, he doesn't have any children or ex-wives or ex-husbands. As far as I know, he's not an axe-murderer and his gran is still alive so he hasn't bumped her off either,' says Zoe.

'In fact,' she continues, 'his gran thought I might be a gold-digger preying on her wonderful grandson. Now she's met me she thinks I'm the best thing since sliced white. Is there anything else, Gran?'

'Gold-digger? My granddaughter? I'll show her what's what,' splutters Mum.

'Well she can't wait to meet you now, I've told her you know all the best cake shops.' Zoe plays Mum like the old wind instrument she is.

My daughter is having fun. She's laughing and smiling like any other twenty-year-old, making fun of her gran and her eyes are shining at last. After everything Alan and I have put her through this year it's a joy to see her like this.

'I have one question,' I say. 'Does he love you?'

Zoe blushes.

'I know it's very early but I think he does, Mum, I really think he does.'

It's possible to burst with pride; it's possible to cry with joy and to crush someone you love in a hug of sheer happiness. I know this because I do all three at that moment.

'Then that's all that matters,' I say wiping my tears from her shoulder.

Pressing the Flesh

Manchester Town Hall is a testament to Victorian pride, vision and skill. It's also a metaphor for life if you think about it, as I have a tendency to do.

The council needed a building to house some people and a few filing cabinets, so they could have built something plain and ordinary. Instead, they created this neo-gothic masterpiece oozing beauty and strength to tell the world they were a force to be reckoned with. You can either be splendid and noticed or ordinary and overlooked, it seems to say.

It's a frosty November evening but the weather seems to complement the architecture. As we stroll through the cloisters admiring the stained-glass windows and world-renowned carvings, I give Charlie a little pinch.

'Can you believe we're here?' I whisper.

He nods. 'I can. We've come a long way this year.'

Rather than consuming us with fear of being ousted as fakes, this place does inspire a sense of belonging. The building was created by ordinary people doing their best and it's now filled with local businesses trading their wares, making a living and building their legacies. The jobs they do might be a little different but the intoxicating buzz of enterprise remains the same, I imagine.

There are a lot of people patting each other on the back asserting a type of camaraderie and belonging. The scene isn't very different to what I expected except there are more women than I'd thought; every group of four or so men seems to have a woman holding her own at the centre. Of course they've made far more of an effort to dress up; whereas some of the male entrepreneurs think badly pressed shirts or poorly fitting suits are just fine, there isn't a woman here who hasn't agonised over what she's wearing. We may be making millions for the economy but we still care what others think.

It's all very well standing on the sideline critiquing the crowd, but at least they've had the guts to socialise and I need to do the same. If I'd come along a few months ago when sales were very slow, I wouldn't have had the courage to talk to people. Everyone will tell you 'yeah, business is good', but I'm no good at faking it, so I'm relieved that I can say those words with conviction now.

I make Charlie promise that he'll stick by my side.

'I don't know how to mingle,' I tell him.

'Let's just walk up to other people who look lost and introduce ourselves,' he suggests.

And so it starts. 'Hello there, we're from Mercury Travel and it's our first time here. What about you?'

The lost people are very glad to have someone make the first move and soon we've created a newcomers sub-set who busily introduce themselves to each other.

I meet the owner of the hairdressing salons responsible for my original transformation. He tells me that I look fantastic, although in fairness, he has to say that if the person responsible for it was trained by him. I also meet a specialist baker who tells me that her cakes are far superior to Amanda's and a marketing guru who assures me she can grow my business exponentially.

I express interest in what they have to say and am awarded with business cards. The currency here seems to be business cards: the more you manage to give away, the more successful you're likely to be, or something like that. I've collected many but given away few.

Charlie calls me over to meet a guy who runs a law firm and is interested in us pitching for his company's annual overseas conference, so I finally get to hand someone a business card. In the background, I hear a Spanish accent and make a beeline for the speaker. They run a language and cultural centre, perfect for another business-card giveaway. This is quite easy now that I've picked up momentum. I make my way into one of the cliques and adopt the persona of Patty. I have a little flirt, tell them who I am and give away half a dozen cards. If I've got the laws of networking correct, we should be multi-millionaires by next year.

No one here seems to have entered the business awards – or at least no one confesses to it. They all tell me that awards are 'too much work' or 'not worth anything in the real world'. It could be that they did enter but weren't shortlisted or it could be that they're not as needy as I am. I disagree with them.

'I don't know,' I say, 'if I were an actress, I'd want an Oscar. If I were an athlete, I'd want a gold medal.'

There are a couple who agree with me but more who tell me that the local entrepreneur awards are hardly the Olympics. I don't care, I've always loved a gong; from getting my first badge at Brownies to Zoe's bronze for swimming, I'm proud of them all. I think I even put my MOT certificate on the fridge door once. Well, passing that was quite an achievement with my old banger.

The keynote speaker moves to the podium and the room settles to listen to him. The speech begins with some statistics about the growth of enterprise within the region since the recession and the need to stick together to sustain that growth.

Most businesses fail within three years he tells us, and there are knowing nods around the room.

Stepping back and looking at the crowd, I'm struck by their age. It hadn't hit me before this but most of these people look like me. The speaker later tells us that over two million businesses in the UK are run by the over-fifties while at the other end of the spectrum, running your own business is also one of the top career choices of the under-twenty-fives. Both age groups face age discrimination at work, are at higher risk of redundancy and quite frankly don't see why they should answer to anyone else.

The speaker ends by encouraging everyone to speak to someone new, to make a commitment to helping that person in some way. I guess I could have my hair done again.

I approach some of the younger people and having spoken to them, I can picture them living in one of those loft apartments – they belong there. They're more confident than the oldies and talk with the passion and conviction I hear from Zoe all the time; it's not bluster, it's conviction. I wonder when we lose that self-belief. Perhaps some people aren't born with huge reserves, but I doubt that.

The businesses oldies and youngsters have quite different approaches. We oldies are more traditional and we swap cards with 'Managing Director' or 'Partner' written on them. Our counterparts hand us cards hailing such professions as 'Ink Artist', 'Skate Beast' or 'Pooch Pack Leader'.

The owner of 'Heels on Wheels' introduces herself; she runs a mobile pedicure business, which I imagine is quite useful for people. I always fear that I'm going to ruin any work done by shoving my huge feet back into my trainers after I've made the rare visit to have them beautified. There's the added bonus that no one else can either stare at or be horrified by the unkempt nails and bunions. Patty always tells me that I have feet like a Hobbit – still, what are friends for?

'How can I help your business?' I ask and she asks me to email my customers just prior to going on holiday and in return she'll give them a discount and recommend Mercury to her customers.

We shake hands on the deal, then say goodbye and I step out into the fresh air to wait for Charlie. I recognise one of my fellow networkers and wish him a good evening.

'I liked what you said about the business awards,' he says, 'and I wish you luck, they should go to people who care.'

I thank him and imagine my desperation to win must be written all over my face.

Charlie sneaks up on me and links arms.

'Look at you Miss "I don't know how to mingle",' he says. 'Who was he?'

'I don't know,' I reply, 'but he seemed very nice.'

Welcome Back

There are times in your life when you welcome the peace and quiet of your own industry and then there are times when you crave something a little more salacious.

After several weeks being sensible Ms Shepherd, I long for my partner in crime and the re-emergence of Bo Peep.

'Ta-dah! Did you miss me?' Patty bursts into the shop scaring several customers, but I rush up to greet her.

'How on earth did you do that? I was just thinking about you,' I say hugging her to death.

Life at sea is suiting her; she looks tanned and relaxed and, well, taller. It's one of those strange facts of life that when people are doing exactly what they should be doing, they grow a couple of inches, or at least they seem to.

'You look fabulous,' I tell her as she does a twirl for me.

'I always did,' she replies. She hasn't become more modest then.

'Tonight, my place, bring wine and I will tell you all,' she promises blowing kisses to Charlie and vanishing as quickly as she appeared.

Only the puff of smoke and swirl of the cape were missing.

Buoyed by the evening of gossip that lies ahead, I get on with the business of selling holidays. I make an appointment with Heels on Wheels for myself and Josie, just to make sure that we're happy to recommend them, and make sure that everything is in place for the New York trip next week. It doesn't seem two minutes ago that we were in our BIN session inventing this trip. The Big Apple around Christmas is a bucket list trip for many people. Buoyed by the movie scenes of people skating in Central Park and *Miracle on 34th Street*, it holds an allure that other cities just can't match. I'm probably looking forward to spending time with Patty more than anything; I miss her more than I'd ever confess.

The business day over, I stop at the off-licence and get two bottles of wine, having never known a Patty and me session stopping at one. I wonder if the doctor did turn out to be the one prophesied by mystical Cleo.

Patty greets me with a bottle of perfume in hand.

'Come in, Bo,' she says, 'I'm fumigating the house.'

'With Chanel?' I ask.

'Whatever I spray into the air will ultimately land on me,' she explains. 'I'd rather not smell of pine forest.'

'Good point,' I reply sniffing at my jacket, which should smell of Ocean Breeze if her theory is correct. It doesn't.

'The house smelled unloved and unlived in,' she explains. 'The neighbour kept a look out and dealt with the mail, but it's not the same as being here every day.'

'I never thought…' I feel guilty now. 'I could have popped by, but the time has flown – or at least it had until this week when I realised I was dying for you to come back. It is so good to see you again. How was it? Come on spill.'

She makes me wait while she pours a glass of wine and makes herself comfortable.

'Brilliant, there's just no other word for it.'

She pauses as if reflecting on the memories.

'I know how you feel now when you're arranging all of the holidays and looking at new opportunities to build the business. You've found the thing you're good at.'

'I think I have,' I say.

'And although loads of people would say this is a ridiculous thing to be good at, I'm starting to think that my calling is to make people laugh,' adds Patty.

'Joan Rivers did rather well from it,' I say.

'I was compère every evening pre-dinner,' she starts explaining. 'I hosted the karaoke competition then one night I had an idea to turn it into a version of *Popstars*. I told the audience that my fellow Granny-Okes had to go in for hip replacements and that I was looking for new band members. I got the singers to audition for a place in my supergroup and the audience voted for who they wanted to see in the finale.'

'Sounds great fun,' I say.

'It was, we had some good singers but also some atrocious ones who just liked dressing up. The audience loved it and kept voting them in.'

We're through the first glass so I top us up and get the olives out to make sure we get one of our prescribed five-a-day. I presume olives count.

'I dressed the winners up in Granny-Oke wigs and cardigans and we closed with "Like A Virgin". That seemed to work best with the non-singers, although every night I had to pretend I hadn't seen a septuagenarian thrusting away in a purple wig before. Men don't half love dressing up.'

She takes another glug.

'I tell you, they loved me. Do you realise that some people thought I was a man in drag?'

I shrug, not confessing that I'd heard it too.

'Quite a compliment I suppose; men in drag always have better legs.' Patty examines her own as she says this.

'Home must feel quite sedate after all that excitement,' I say.

'Every entertainer needs a period of resting after a major gig. Oh you'll love this. One of the tribute band members was telling me that Brighton is so full of lovelies that "resting" is an official employment status on the benefit-office forms; you couldn't make it up.'

'Anything else to report? Anything relevant to a certain psychic's premonitions?' I hint and Patty springs to life.

'Of course, I'm sorry, I forgot to ask, how's Alan?'

'He's fine, engaged to Amanda now. He did me the courtesy of dropping down on one knee, without warning, in front of all my friends – old and new.'

'He always was considerate.'

'But what has that got to do with the psychic?' I ask.

'A row with someone that you don't get on with – your ex,' says Patty. 'A dark moment – it was night-time – and an illness, the heart attack. It was all there. Now he's recovered she was right about it ending well too, provided you're well and truly over him that is.'

'I am,' I say reconciling all she's said.

'Engaged, eh? So what else has happened?' asks Patty.

'Zoe has a man. He's forty so I've warned her to keep him away from you.'

She flicks her head back dramatically.

'No need to worry,' she declares, 'I am now spoken for.'

I fill both our glasses and get the next bottle out.

'Now we're getting there. Spill,' I instruct.

'Well, I was a bit nervous when you all left and I was the last Granny standing,' she says. 'I'd planned to keep a low profile: do yoga, eat healthily and preserve the voice like a professional.'

'I can't imagine that happening,' I say. 'Go on.'

'Simplee Rouge didn't work out as I'd hoped,' she continues.

'I was trying to get into it but they weren't very good and the one who played Mick had no charisma. I was convinced that Cleo had it all wrong. Then on the third week, we got the line-up through and there he was, Rock Astley. After everything Cleo said, I was sure that this had to be it and I couldn't very well let my destiny pass me by.'

'Something tells me this doesn't end well,' I say.

'Oh it does, but not how I expected. I got all dressed up and went to the gig. I went up to the balcony and was watching quietly from the back, being all nonchalant.'

'Again – that's hard to imagine. So what happened?'

'I only knew one of his songs and he played that at the end, "Never Gonna Give You Up"; you know it. I got quite into it and started dancing along with some of his fans, the Rick-Rollers, they're called.

'In the chorus we had a little dance routine. We reach to the sky, then to the ground and finally do a big twirl.'

She gets up to demonstrate these moves.

'Simple enough, but it was quite good fun and then when he finished the Rollers made a rush for the bar where he was signing autographs.'

'Keep going,' I say wondering where on earth this is going.

'Well, all of my crimson scarves had wound themselves around the railings when I was twirling, hadn't they? When I ran with the crowd, I damn near garrotted myself and when I yanked them free I didn't know my own strength and went flying down the steps backwards. They all just ran past me. I tell you, never rely on a Rick-Roller for help when you're ill; they certainly do "give you up" and at the very first sign of trouble. I ended up in the sick bay.'

'Finally we get there,' I murmur. I urge her to continue.

'I had a sprained wrist and bruised coccyx. I was under the doctor all week after that, literally,' she taunts.

'I knew it,' I exclaim, 'I knew you'd get the doctor.'

'Oh Bo, he's just wonderful. What he doesn't know about a woman's body…'

'He should probably do some training for,' I suggest.

'So Cleo might have been right for you, but she was way out for me,' says Patty.

'I don't know,' I say, 'listening to redhead Rock Astley, killing yourself with red scarves – without them you wouldn't have met him.'

'It's a bit vague, I might have worn a blue scarf that night.'

'No chance, you haven't worn any other colour for months. Besides which, there was this.' I pull out my phone and show her the shot of them both bathed in red light.

'I knew you'd end up with him as soon as I saw that,' I say.

Patty gazes at the picture then hands me back the phone.

'And you still let me sit through two weeks of gingers wailing?' she laughs. 'Thanks a bunch.'

It is so good to have her back.

'What's next then?' I ask. 'Is he on leave now?'

'Yes, he's divorced but has kids and grandkids that he's gone to visit. I needed time to think anyway,' replies Patty. 'I mean, I haven't been with a man for over four years – although naturally I haven't been short of offers.'

'Naturally,' I reply.

'And there's something else I have to think about…' She pauses and then says, 'Bo, they've offered me a residency for the season.'

I am delighted for her but sad for me.

'For how long?' I ask.

'The winter season around the Caribbean, so January to March; it's the perfect time to get away from here and Dr Lurve would be on the same rota,' she explains.

'You really call him that?'

She nods and we giggle.

'It's a nineties cruise though, so I'll have to learn some new material,' she adds.

'You can still do Madonna,' I say.

'Ooh yes, a bit of "Vogue",' Patty replies, doing the hand movements, 'and I thought maybe some Britney.'

I imagine only Charlie would get away with the appropriate reaction to the idea of Patty in a school uniform so I say nothing.

'So it's new man, New York, New Year and new set list,' she continues.

'I'll miss you so much,' is all I can say.

'Who wouldn't?' She tilts her head sympathetically and I throw an olive at her, getting a direct hit.

New York, New York

I'm packed and ready for our final trip of the year. As I close the lid on my case, I reflect on the amazing roller-coaster year I've had and I'm glad I managed to hold on and enjoy the ride. I've heard people say that when they were made redundant or when their husbands walked out, '*It was the best thing that ever happened to me.*' I don't know how anyone can say that about the initial pain but it does change things and I'd never be packing my bag for this trip if it hadn't happened. I wonder what adventure is coming next; my phone rings and I find out more quickly than I'd wanted.

'I'm sorry, there's nothing I can do.'

The estate agent is telling me that my landlord is giving me notice. He'd like me to vacate the house.

'Can he do that? Just ask me to leave? Why?' I ask.

She apologises profusely but tells me that my landlord's son is getting married and he wants to let them live in my house (well, technically his) while they save for a deposit on their own place. She promises to send some details of other houses that are available.

It's not unreasonable; I'd probably do the same for Zoe. It's just inconvenient for me.

'When I said that I wanted to enjoy the ride,' I tell the heavens, 'I didn't mean it had to get bumpy again right now. Could I not just have a few months of calm?'

The doorbell rings and it's Patty dragging her luggage; she's spending the night here so we can get an early cab together tomorrow.

'I'm going to be homeless,' I tell her recounting the call I've just had.

'So what will you do?'

'I don't know,' I say. 'I really don't want to just move from place to place. I suppose I could take a room in Zoe's hotel or maybe stay with Mum and Dad.'

'Will I have to spit out any chewing gum when I visit you like I used to?'

I smile and nod; that's still one of the rules in Mum's house. She loathes chewing gum.

'There is another option.' Patty is suddenly very animated.

'Stay at mine,' she says. 'Seriously, it would be perfect. You'd have your own place, you could chew as much gum as you like and it would save me hiring a house-sitter while I'm away.'

'Your place is huge for one person. I'd rattle around in it.'

'Get a lodger, preferably one who likes cocktails of course,' she says raising her glass to me.

'I can just see the advert: "*Wanted – Lodger for B&B plus G&T*".'

'I'd reply to that one,' she adds.

'I know and who'd want to live with you?' I joke.

'Go on, Bo,' Patty continues. 'It would be three months living somewhere that you know while you find something else. It would help me out too; I'd feel safer if I knew you were staying in my house.'

'Are you sure?' I ask.

'Definitely, and I'd let you bring men home. I bet your mum won't,' she says.

The thought of returning to the curfew of my teenage days has us both giggling away.

'OK, you're on,' I tell her.

Cheered by having that dilemma resolved, we decide to go out and start the holiday early.

'I was thinking earlier about how much has changed this year,' I tell Patty as we sit down to eat.

As an act of patriotism prior to the trip, Patty has brought me to a contemporary British restaurant. We toast with a sloe-gin cocktail.

'You can say that again, you're the owner of a renowned travel business – you,' she says.

'What about you, you're a cruise-ship entertainer.'

'The talent was always there,' she says, 'it was just hidden.'

'Very deeply,' we laugh.

I read the trendy British menu, which includes some delicious-sounding game dishes, and I know I should be more adventurous but sometimes you just want fish and chips. We order the same, fish and chips and gin. Beat that New York.

The following day, we settle into our seats and belt up as instructed, next stop the Big Apple.

The New York trip was always the pinnacle of our Mercury Travel Club calendar. Patty and I booked ages ago and Josie is also with us as a reward for having held the fort so often this year. The business is going well and even Ed has been in to book some travel for his Chapter now that we're friends again.

Charlie and I sat down to plan the future recently. To thank Josie for all she's contributed this year, we promoted her to assistant manager and told her she was coming on this trip for free. She was delighted, especially as we also gave her an end-of-year bonus so that she could hit the shops out there. It felt marvellous to be able to make someone so happy.

Although being on the trips ourselves has been wonderful, and in many ways has created the reputation we're enjoying, we both know it's not sustainable. This is my last trip away for some time. I'm going to stay office-based much of next year to stabilise the business and Charlie is only going on one trip, one of Patty's Caribbean cruises. I've talked up her act so much he's dying to see it for himself. I won't tell him about the Britney number; I'll let that be a wonderful surprise for him.

As neither of us will be on many of the other trips, we've developed an idea called 'Guest Hosts': one of the customers agrees to take on the role of unofficial host making sure that newcomers or even shyer guests are included and looked after. We don't know if it will work yet, so I've asked my dad to host the first trip and we'll see how it goes. I'm going to surprise them by booking those first-class flight tickets I promised as their reward.

They've been inspired to embrace their retirement, so they're no longer just the quizmasters of the Caravan Club – they're actually planning on doing more travelling.

'We'll get Jamie's parents to come along too,' Mum tells me. 'I've already told her when all the best food tasting takes place.'

Mum sharing her food? Miracles do happen after all.

I manage to snooze for much of the six-hour flight, so I'm fairly well rested when we arrive. I've opted to bring everyone to the Meatpacking District, which I'm assured is the new trendy place to come. As we drive through streets of, well, meatpacking warehouses, I hope that they're right; my genteel clients are looking rather wary at the moment.

It's freezing cold and we're all exhausted from the flight. I had an email on the way out saying that we've been diverted to another hotel because ours has suffered water and frost damage.

We're now in The Standard overlooking the Hudson River. The reviews look good, so I have my fingers crossed.

When we get there, the hotel team put my mind at rest, greeting us with the effusive smiles and excellent service that Americans are known for. They've put us all on the same floor and I'm told the lounge is also on that floor so that we can all get together with ease after our sightseeing, a thoughtful touch.

My hotel room is stylish and spacious. I often wonder what Americans think of British hotels, especially London hotels with their poky little rooms. They must look shockingly awful.

I've barely taken in my surroundings when someone knocks on the door. I open it to Josie and Patty, behind them the guests are exploring each other's bedrooms.

'Have you seen the bathroom?' exclaims Josie. 'It's deadly.'

They push past me and show me what they're talking about: the bathrooms have floor-to-ceiling glass windows on the edge of the building. You sit on the loo taking in the full view of New York.

'Can anyone see in?' I ask the first question anyone would.

'I don't think so, it must be privacy glass or something,' guesses Josie. 'You can see out but no one can see in.'

It's fabulous and explains the Mercurian tour of bedrooms that's taking place. Concern over not being in Times Square has been eradicated by the stylish en-suite and everyone now looks ready for an adventure.

There are so many things we could be doing in New York but I've opted to show people food and films: the best eating experiences and famous movie locations. It gives everyone something to take back home.

We do *Breakfast at Tiffany's*, *The Seven Year Itch*, *Sex and the City*, *Ghostbusters* and *Harry Met Sally* amongst others. You wouldn't have thought standing over the same grate as Marilyn Monroe would be that inspiring but bizarrely it is. Not as exciting as being in the deli where *the* best fake orgasm scene ever was filmed, though. I try to restrain Patty on the coach back but she's already initiated a sound-a-like competition that everyone is enjoying. The winner sounds more like Eeyore but he has everyone in stitches.

The food is something else. Our tour takes in everything from the best hot dog in Greenwich Village, the best pretzel on the East Side, waffles with sausage in Brooklyn, ice cream in Little Italy and so it goes on. Food and culture in one big mouthful; that's New York I guess.

Our evening cocktail lesson is back in the hotel. The coach pulls up to the entrance and suddenly there's a shriek from the back:

'Oh my God, you can see through the glass.'

She's pointing up at the designer bathrooms which we'd assumed had privacy glass and we're watching some poor guy zipping his pants up. There are shocked screams and laughter alongside some guilty photographs.

'I am definitely giving people something to look at tonight,' laughs Patty.

'Oh pleeeaase don't,' I beg, envisaging the entire tour being arrested for indecent exposure.

I promise everyone I'll try and get us moved to rooms with more modest internal bathrooms; I'll use our very Britishness as the excuse. The group protest vociferously.

'We love it,' they exclaim. 'We're never going to stay somewhere like this again.'

I don't know how I could have missed this detail about the hotel – it wasn't on page one of the reviews. I search further and see that it's just our floor, the one beside the lounge. I'd have rejected this as our alternative hotel if I'd known, but as it stands, once more our little club manages to hit the slight notoriety button that is making us famous. They probably think we manage this on purpose.

Getting ready for tonight's masterclass, I order extra towels and hang them across the bathroom windows. The concierge tells me that everyone else has done the same thing. Perhaps people are more modest than they like to profess.

Our mixologist for the night is gorgeous and if my tongue weren't already hanging out for the manhattans, it would be for him. Dark wavy hair, soft brown eyes and a savvy New York smile. He's wearing an open-collared white shirt and waistcoat, but even under two layers of clothing you can see a very muscular frame. He might just be reviving my mojo.

We hang on every word as he takes us through the steps of making the city's signature cocktail. I feel the spirits warming me up but I'm sure some parts of my anatomy were already getting quite heated.

'You realise you're staring at him,' says Patty, reminding me there are other people in the room.

'And?' I huff.

'And his rather attractive girlfriend over there is very amused,' she says pointing at an equally stunning woman waiting by the bar.

I glimpse myself in the mirror and see a very happy-looking fifty-three-year-old. I burst out laughing.

'Well you never know, he might have had a mother complex.'

'Grandmother don't you mean.' Patty gets a punch for that one.

The cocktail class over and the guests nicely chilled, conversation turns to what we should do next; we're in New York and it's early. I'd left this night free in case they wanted to go their own ways, but they're keen to stick together. Josie asks the guests if there's anything in particular they'd like to do.

'It's unanimous,' she tells me.

'What is?' I ask.

'They all want to see you two do a karaoke,' she says.

Patty gives me one of her looks.

'Go on Bo, we won't be together again for ages, let's do a swansong.'

I sigh my defeat and we're directed to an amazing bar, which has every song you could ever imagine in every language on the planet. That's true multiculturalism for you, 'Material Girl' in Swahili.

Unlike the UK, which warms up when everyone has had a few drinks, this crowd are giving it their all and they're so good, almost as if they expect an agent to walk in at any moment. I watch Patty sizing up the room; we don't want to go out on a whimper.

Our guests take their seats. I doubt any of them have been to a karaoke bar for several years, if at all. This is just part of their adventure and we have to make it safe but memorable.

Josie spots an Australian flag and goes bounding over to the table to introduce herself. After a few minutes she comes back beaming.

'We've got ourselves our very own Commonwealth Games,' she declares.

The tables thrash out the rules: one male solo, one female and one all-in. The other team nominates the song and the winner is decided through the biggest round of applause.

'We'll need a compere for that.' Patty jumps up to assume her position as centre of attention.

I sit back and watch the chaos unfold. Some Canadians in the bar insist on being part of the competition and then some Japanese tourists decide they're part of the Commonwealth, too.

'See the beast that you've created,' says Patty while one of our male guests murders, 'I Should Be So Lucky'.

'Me? I think Josie had something to do with it,' I say checking my watch.

'You're not thinking of going?' asks Patty. 'We haven't sung anything yet.'

'No,' I say, 'I was just thinking that it'll be six o'clock in the UK. It'll be over.'

'What will?' she asks.

'Alan's wedding,' I tell her. 'He married Amanda today.'

Patty puts her arm around me.

'Oh Bo, you didn't say. Are you OK?'

'I am,' I say, and I'm telling the truth. I now have a rather dysfunctional extended family but I want them all to be happy in life.

'Did Zoe go?' asks Patty.

I shake my head, 'She was in Paris for James's fortieth birthday.'

I was secretly pleased to learn that the dates clashed and although it may seem petty, I'm glad she won't be in his photographs. She wasn't in mine after all.

Onstage, the very cruel Mercurians have given the Japanese team, 'Supercalifragilisticexpialidocious' from *Mary Poppins* for the group song.

Cruel but hilarious, everyone is wiping tears of laughter from their eyes as they get offstage. They get a huge round of applause, so it might yet backfire.

Patty gives me a big hug and then jumps back onstage to resume her compère post.

'That was both the best and worst thing I have ever seen,' she declares to the crowd. 'And if they don't win, there is no justice in this world.'

The crowd cheers and the Japanese team are so excited you'd think this were the real Commonwealth Games.

'Now you may not know this,' continues Patty, 'but in the UK, I'm a bit of a star.'

Whistles from Josie.

'And although the star quality was always present, it was hidden deep within,' she mock flirts with a table of men. 'One woman helped me unlock that talent and I want to sing this one for her, join in if you recognise it. Little Bo Peep – this is for you.'

The unmistakable intro to the theme tune from *Friends* kicks off and the whole room jumps up onstage. An international entourage led by my best friend, telling me 'I'll be there for you.'

The tears stream down my cheeks for the whole three minutes, fourteen seconds of the song.

So proud of them all, I blow Patty a big kiss. Life doesn't get better than this.

Come morning, I'm still basking in the love of last night and float down to Central Park with the Mercurians.

'You should move here,' says Patty hugging herself against the cold. 'It's the only place on the planet you could wear every cardigan you own at the same time.'

'Very funny,' I reply, not mentioning that I've swapped one layer of cardigan for a discreet thermal vest.

We sit in a café sipping hot chocolate as Josie and some of the Mercurians ice-skate while others take a horse-and-carriage tour around the park. It's all very romantic and memorable in a rather different way to last night.

'Thank you for last night,' I say, 'it was really very special.'

Patty links arms with me and the extra warmth is wonderful.

'We've had one hell of a ride this year, haven't we?' she says and I nod in agreement.

'Would you rather none of this had happened? You hadn't got divorced?'

'Can I pick the good bits and have none of the pain?' I ask.

We agree that I can.

'It might have been nice to have found someone to go home to. Everyone seems to have paired up this year, even you with Dr Lurve.'

Patty rubs her hands together lustily.

'Zoe has James, Josie has Matt and Charlie has Peter,' I say.

'To have and to hold,' says Patty.

'What do you mean?' I ask.

'I'm sworn to secrecy,' Patty tells me.

I just raise my eyebrows in a 'tell me now' kind of way.

'You have to promise not to tell Josie, and I mean it this time,' she says.

I cross my heart.

'Peter has been making secret plans for the cruise this January. He's getting the captain to marry them when they reach Barbados,' confides Patty.

'Oh my word, Charlie is going to love that. I'm gutted I won't be there,' I say.

'No one will be,' she reassures, 'just the two of them on the beach at sunset. It'll be so *An Officer and a Gentleman*.'

'How wonderful, I'll arrange a party for them when they get back,' I say.

'Then they'll know I told you.'

'As if Charlie isn't going to call the second the ceremony is over,' I reason and of course he will.

'Besides which,' I continue, 'I like to think I've played a role in this and in fact all the romances this year. One divorce has led to four relationships.'

We clink our hot chocolate glasses.

'And for that,' says Patty, 'I shall be forever grateful.'

I get up. 'Come on, it's the last day, let's give this skating lark a try.'

We open the door and the cold New York air blasts us. Patty rushes back to her seat and huddles down.

'I said grateful, not stupid.'

I shake my head at her cowardice and totter over the ice for yet another new activity this year.

And the Award Goes to…

Safely back from New York, I read the reviews for the trip and once again the customers seem delighted; many have already booked up for another travel club holiday. As we all sit working our way through the bookings for next year, I have to stop myself staring at Charlie and grinning; I get a frisson of excitement every time I think about the surprise wedding. To keep the conversation on anything but weddings, I tell him that he has Patty doing nineties tunes to look forward to.

'OMG – do you think she'll do the Spice Girls?' he asks, hitting on yet another car crash waiting to happen.

'Well I think she's bloody scary,' says Josie.

'Nah,' – Charlie is really thinking this through – 'it would have to be Ginger – the Union Jack dress and everything. If she did Posh, it would just be a bird in a black dress scowling.'

'She could do Baby,' adds Josie, 'with those bunches in her hair.'

'*All ready to plait them for Britney,*' I think to myself.

I leave them contemplating Patty's outfits and head off early to get ready for tonight's award ceremony. I couldn't sleep last night practising my acceptance speech over and over again. I'm not even sure if they let you give a speech but I have one ready just in case. A lack of sleep is not conducive to looking one's best and when I glance in the bathroom mirror one of those wrinkly Shar-Pei dogs seems to be staring back at me. There will be photographers at this event and the pictures will be circulated widely; I wonder if I have time for a facial? I pull the loose skin back towards my ears. Oh dear, I definitely have to find the time. I ring the mobile beautician and ask if by any chance she does more than feet. Fortunately she does and agrees to come round in an hour or so.

My dress is ready and hanging there waiting for its moment on the stage; it is beautiful but just looking at it makes me nervous. Should I have chosen a cocktail dress instead? Full-length is a bit of a gamble when it comes to walking up steps. This is ridiculous, I have to stop dwelling on tonight until, well, tonight.

Of course I can't stop thinking about it at all. In my fantasy life, I've won the award and glided graciously on to the stage like a BAFTA-winning actress. I've then come back to my modest starter home and the first thing I do is place the trophy with pride at the centre of the mantelpiece. *Entrepreneur Magazine* and maybe even *Hello* then come round to do a profile and comment on the modest circumstances for someone going places. Hmm – so how does the fantasy work now? I guess being homeless is even more modest, but Patty's house isn't that modest so it ruins the story; where am I going to showcase the trophy now? Where will the magazine shoot be? Is this an omen that we're not going to win? I suppose we could keep it in the office.

Before I have the chance to worry any more, the beautician arrives complete with her folding massage table and a CD of whale music; that and the aromatherapy oils soon do their thing and I start to relax. One thing at a time. I'll move into Patty's but then I have to find my own place – I'm ready now. Meanwhile, focus solely on lying back and relaxing while this wonderful therapist works her magic and gives you back the skin of a twenty-year-old.

If only.

I hear someone snoring gently and eventually realise that it's me. I don't know how long I've been out but the deeply nurturing moisturiser has done its job and although I couldn't pass for forty let alone twenty, I look rested and I'm ready for a fabulous night.

A beep of the horn tells me the cab has arrived and I take one final look at myself before heading down. My new burgundy gown has a fitted full-length skirt and a velvet bodice making the most of my figure. The scooped neck with discreet beading and three-quarter-length sleeves take the attention away from all my worst parts and I feel as if I've already won. We head first of all to my parents' house – my dad is my date for tonight; I booked six places and hoped that by now, I'd have a plus-one. Dad comes to the door in his rented tuxedo and looks as if he's going to burst with pride. Mum insists on taking picture after picture and I'm so pleased that I don't have a date. I'd much rather be giving my folks this little adventure.

The cab pulls up at the five-star hotel hosting tonight's awards and I take a deep breath as Dad holds out his arm and we head in. I couldn't be more nervous if there were a red carpet and paparazzi in tow. Checking the events board, I make my way to the champagne reception and the excited chatter of people telling each other that tonight is just a bit of fun. I spot Charlie and Peter across the room and head straight towards them. Someone grabs my arm and I turn to see Josie with Matt.

'This is awesome,' she whispers and I have to agree.

Matt has interpreted the dress code rather liberally. Wearing jeans and a purple paisley shirt with bootlace tie he stands out in the crowd; everyone passing gives us a quick stare.

'I like your black tie,' I say.

'No point blending in I always think,' he replies.

No sooner have the words left his mouth than a newspaper photographer comes up to take a picture of him and Josie.

Splendid and noticed or ordinary and overlooked I reflect.

I hear them talk about the unique proposition we're developing and the great fun we have on our trips. The journalist loves some of the anecdotes and in the midst of all the formal conversations in the hall, my crowd are laughing and sparkling.

I've been to events like this before, whether it's Rotary Club or charity fundraisers and know there's a set format. First of all the meal is served and it's always something in a jus. My challenges during eating are:

1. Not to spill anything down the dress
and
2. Not to eat too many bread rolls so that my stomach doesn't bloat when I get up to accept the award.

I doubt the men in the room are pondering such trials and tribulations. There's entertainment between the main course and dessert and tonight we have a comedian who has been on TV. He's been given enough information about some of the audience to tailor his material and manages to keep everyone's attention throughout his set. I've been to these events when the entertainment has been awful and the audience have just kept talking. It's rather rude, but this is probably the one night off these business owners have and they're as keen to catch up with each other as they are to listen to someone else. It's a tough gig entertaining this lot.

Throughout the evening, as the wine flows, the noise levels rise and rise. The comedian gets a standing ovation, which I think is as much due to the amount of alcohol now flowing through the room as it is to do with his talent. A couple of people grab him as he comes offstage to take selfies with him. I bet all celebrities wish they could go back to the day when all people wanted were autographs.

The chair of the judging panel climbs on to the stage to start the awards presentation. I grab hold of both Josie and Charlie's hands.

'Here we go,' I say.

A bottle of champagne arrives at our table and my heart misses a beat. For a second, I think this means that we've won, but it's from Peter who pours us each a glass and offers a toast:

'Whatever happens tonight,' he says, 'you guys have been incredible. You had an idea and you made it happen. You've had fun and you're heading for even more.

'You're already winners,' he continues. 'To the Mercury Travel Club.'

We all clink glasses and toast our year; it's a lovely gesture but I still want the real thing.

The prize-giving seems incredibly drawn out; one by one the categories are announced. There's a short video about each nominee and then a local dignitary gets up onstage to open the envelope. I can see the pile of envelopes sitting on a table by the stage and am sorely tempted to run up and rip each one open to see if we've won. Instead, I clap politely for every nominee and every award winner until my hands are raw. I've entered us in three categories and the first of these is now being read out.

I can't quite hear the other nominations or the videos because of the blood pounding through my brain. My body is like the Edgar Allan Poe story where the heart beats so loudly, it drives someone insane.

The envelope is being opened and Charlie grabs me. I can't look but I can hear and it isn't our name I hear being called out. I'm devastated but can't let it show. I applaud the winning company wondering what they've done that makes them better than us.

'We'll get the next one,' reassures Charlie.

We have to endure two further awards before our next category is announced. I'm less nervous now, my fear has turned into determination; we're going to get this one I tell myself.

The envelope opens and I stare at the speaker defying him to pick us this time. He doesn't and yet another business walks up to the stage with huge smiles on their faces, accepting the trophy and lifting it to the ceiling as if it were the World Cup.

'They're just saving the best until last,' chirps Charlie in real danger of being clobbered.

There is a quick break in proceedings before the main award of the night. We all try to stay upbeat and go to congratulate the winners. I last a few moments before needing a bit of fresh air; I step outside to join the smokers.

Those who recognise me commiserate but tell me, 'there's always next time'. I resist punching them in the face.

It's soon time to go back in for the final award, Entrepreneur of the Year. I want this too much and I keep telling myself that it doesn't matter, but of course, it does. I don't have a home, I don't have a man – at least give me this I beg the powers that be.

We're back at our table and the compère waffles on about how wonderful this evening has been, how high the standards were and how difficult it was to judge. Yada, yada – just get on with it please.

He reads out the nominations for the final award.

'Sticky PR' – there's polite applause.

'Bikes and Beyond' – a couple of whoops and more applause follows.

'Tech-Start Support' – there's hardly any noise; they're either unpopular or very small.

'Mercury Travel Club' – we raise the roof with our cheering and then to my horror I hear the final nominee.

'Hargreaves Security.'

Of course, I knew he was entering but didn't think we'd be in the same category.

There is now one thing I want more than to win, I want to beat Alan.

I hold my breath as the envelope is opened.

'You've got to beat that waste of space,' says Dad reading my mind.

'In second place, highly commended,' starts the judge then delays for dramatic effect. 'Sticky PR.'

There's a cheer and the table gets up to take a bow and accept a bottle of champagne. We can still both win and we can still both lose. I have a horrible feeling about this.

'But the winner of this year's Entrepreneur of the Year is a company who have taken an idea and turned it into a business.'

I think we've all done that – it could be us, I suppose.

'They've capitalised on market trends,' continues the judge.

That sounds more like us than Alan, I think.

'And it's true to say, they're really going places now.'

That's an obvious travel joke, it has to be us. I'm clinging to Charlie's hand and don't take my eyes off the judge.

'Ladies and gentlemen, the winner is…Bikes and Beyond.'

There's an enormous roar of applause around the room and the team get up to accept their award. My crushing disappointment is tempered with relief that although we're going home empty-handed, so too is Alan.

Peter orders another bottle of champagne to toast our nominations but I don't feel like celebrating. What am I going to put on the mantelpiece now? The mantelpiece I don't have.

The compère calms the crowd and asks us to welcome one of our sponsors, the President of Virgin Enterprises. I'm not paying much attention until Charlie nudges me.

'Isn't that the guy you were talking to?' he asks.

I look up and see the man I met at the networking event, the one who told me he was pleased to hear I valued these awards; a fat lot of good that did me.

'I've heard it said,' he begins, 'that these awards don't matter and of course compared to cash-flow and profits they don't. They do, however, let you know that you're doing something right, that someone appreciates you even if it is just your local business community.

'The other people who let you know whether you're doing something right, or wrong for that matter,' he continues, 'are your customers. They have so much choice today and being a small enterprise, you're unlikely to be the cheapest – so let's face it, you have to be the best.'

Nods and here-heres around the room. I just wish he'd let us all go home.

'There is a business here tonight, a very new business, that has been delighting customers since it began. Let's hear from those customers.'

He plays a video which shows members of the public extolling the virtues of someone. The praise is exceptional and it isn't until a few people have spoken that it starts to dawn on us.

'I think they're talking about you lot,' murmurs Dad.

I can't quite grasp what is going on, but the video ends and the president is handed another trophy.

'You can't nominate yourself for this award; it's decided solely through customer endorsement, and this year, there was one phenomenal winner,' he says.

'Mercury Travel Club, please join me onstage to accept this award – the People's Champion.'

I'm screaming and crying and laughing all at the same time. All three of us get up onstage and shake hands with the president. We take turns to hold the award and lift it up, posing for the photographers and just taking in the moment. From the stage I can see Dad standing and cheering, hugging Matt and Peter and wiping the tears from his eyes. I blow him a kiss and try to take it all in; I want to remember everything.

This is the most perfect moment of my life and it simply could not get any better.

'And now let's hear from someone else who likes what you've done,' announces the president.

We look up to the video screen and there he is – my hero Richard Branson. I gasp and probably hold my breath throughout his speech. He tells us what a great job we've done and how we must keep on innovating.

It may just be a video but I know he's talking directly to me.

'Can I take it home?' I ask the others.

'Going on the mantelpiece?' asks Charlie.

'No – I'm going to cuddle it all night,' I confess, snuggling it to my bosom.

Happy New Year

I'm still living on that cloud as I sit here looking around my little house; I think back to when I arrived feeling wounded and sorry for myself. I was wrong though. This wasn't a 'finishing off' home at all, I've done more here than I could ever imagine.

Now on to my next phase, life as Patty's house-sitter. The removal van gets here first thing tomorrow and although it won't be a big operation, the experts will make a far better job of it than I ever could. I haven't added much to the house since I got here, a few cushions and bookshelves. I wrap up my odd assortment of wine glasses. I've always envied people with full matching sets of crystal glasses and wondered how on earth they managed to keep them complete. They can't use them for nights in with the girls, that's for sure.

I walk from room to room, which doesn't take long as there are only five. I check that everything is packed and the rooms are immaculate. The young couple moving in deserve a beautiful shiny start to their new life together and finding an old pair of my knickers down the back of the radiator would not be the best introduction to their new home.

Satisfied that everything is gleaming, I head out to the pub for this year's final book-club meeting; no books just a leisurely dinner to celebrate friendship.

My new friends Caroline and Ed, with Peter of course; I didn't know any of them this time last year and here I am laughing and celebrating a fun year together. Between courses, Peter gets up.

'I've written a poem,' he says.

Whoops of appreciation all round.

'An ode to our book club,' he continues, 'so fill your glasses and I'll start.'

Ed heads to the bar. I notice Caroline watching him and she spots me doing it.

'He's a nice guy,' she says.

'He is,' I tell her, 'and you'd be great together.'

Caroline smiles affectionately then shuffles to one side letting Ed sit down beside her when he gets back.

Peter stands up and clears his throat. 'My friends,' he starts:

Since we first met, near a year has passed,
And thanks to you all, it has been a blast.
A haunted castle was one of our dates,
And there, in a dress, I found my soul-mate.
We've seen young Ed come out of his shell,
Now all the women seem under his spell.
But it's Caroline who has the magic wand,
And with just one wave, your purpose is found.
Angie, your journey, well what can I say?
Around you there truly is ne'er a dull day.
I hope we're all here toasting in another year's time;
To good books, good friends and bloody good wine.

And that really is all you need in life, I think, through my cosy-fire and red-wine induced euphoria. I get home and spotting Gnorman and Gnora on the step, I take them in to be safely packed away. Once inside, it doesn't take long for the calm satisfaction of a year well lived to lull me to sleep, dreamless, deep and restorative sleep.

The refuse truck making its pre-New Year collection wakes me up. It takes a moment or two and then I remember the day's proceedings. Efficiently I get washed and dressed, packing up my remaining belongings and storing them all together. A final clean and one by one, I close each door for the final time.

The removal van does road-space battle with the refuse truck but somehow they manage to manoeuvre around each other and complete their tasks for today. Everyone wants to finish work and get the party started.

I leave the new people a bottle of champagne to welcome them to their new home, pack my bag and with a final glance, throw it in the car. This is it – off to Patty's.

I wind down the car windows rather than scraping the ice and put it into reverse.

'Here goes.'

Taking off the brake, I roll backwards and as soon as I do I hear a screech of pain. I lunge forward and get out to see what I've done. It's Socks; she'd been sleeping behind my wheel and I've think I've run her over. She's not moving but is meowing in pain. I pick her up gently.

'What a silly place to sleep,' I tell her and lay her on a jumper in the back seat.

We drive to the vet and wait with a genuine menagerie to be seen. He examines Socks and tells me that I've run over her tail and that she'll have to have an X-ray to check on the damage.

'Is she insured?' the vet asks, stroking Socks.

I can imagine that this man has many a pet-owning lady swooning. He looks like an Athena poster, strong arms nurturing a soft kitty. He just needs to turn sepia tone for the full effect.

'Er, I don't know; she's not mine. She just sort of adopted me,' I tell him.

'Let's see if she's microchipped then.'

He runs a scanner over her neck.

'Yes she is, she's registered to a Jenny Ashcroft. Do you know her?' he asks.

I shake my head.

'The registered address is 95 Cross Road and there's a phone number here,' he tells me.

'No, I won't phone,' I say. 'I'd rather go round and tell them in person.'

I'm about to ask whether Socks will be OK but one look at her nestling in Athena-Man's arms and I know that I probably wouldn't move from there either.

'Don't hurry back,' she seems to be purring.

The day I wanted to run smoothly and efficiently is not going according to plan. I pull back into Cross Road and find number 95. It's right at the other end of the street so I don't feel as guilty for not having met these people.

I park and walk up the immaculately kept garden practising my apology. I ring the bell and take a step back so that I'm not directly face-to-face when they answer. For some reason, I've always found this impolite and slightly confrontational.

The door opens and I turn around to face a rather good-looking man who looks surprised but then smiles as if he knows me.

'Oh hello, it's good to finally meet you. Come in,' he says holding out his hand.

Puzzled I shake hands. I wasn't expecting this and my pre-rehearsed speech didn't factor in a friendly introduction. I enter his living room and sit down as he invites.

'Coffee?' he asks and then adds, 'I'm Michael, by the way.'

Why is he offering a person he's never even met before a coffee? I shake my head and murmur, 'Angie,' in response.

'No, no thanks,' I add as he disappears into the kitchen to retrieve his own coffee. 'Look, I'm really sorry but I have some bad news for you.'

I have to tell him soon before he does anything else nice.

At this he sits down.

'I am so sorry, but your cat was sleeping under my wheel when I reversed out,' I say slowly, hoping that he'll reach the inevitable conclusion without me saying it.

He does and his expression saddens. He must think it's worse than it is.

'Don't worry,' I add, 'she seems fine and she's at the vet's but is going to need an X-ray. I can drive you there if you like?'

Looking relieved he gets his coat and we head off.

Socks is still recovering but the vet shows us her X-ray and confirms that the end section of her tail has been fractured. He says it will heal with a bit of rest and we can take her home in a couple of hours.

We both relax a little as we head back out into the winter sunshine.

'I know that it doesn't compensate for running over your cat,' I say, 'but can I take you for lunch while we wait?'

'Don't you have to be somewhere?' he asks and I shake my head.

'Then yes,' he says, 'I'd like that.'

We drive to a bistro pub on the canal. It's setting up for to-night's festivities, so we grab a table outside next to one of the patio heaters. It's early afternoon and the sun is already starting to set behind the buildings; there's an end-of-year peace about the place. We both take warming bowls of soup served with great doorsteps of bread, comfort food to ease the stress of the morning.

We talk about the beauty of winter, the simple wonder of soup, the redevelopment of the wharf, in fact everything and nothing until the time comes to go back to the vet's. Conversation flows easily and I wonder how a couple I could have been friends with lived on the same street as me and yet our paths never crossed. It's been a nice day, running over the cat notwithstanding.

We drag a reluctant Socks from the arms of her hero and drive her home. She snuggles into her basket and I turn to leave.

'Thank you for a lovely lunch,' I say as I reach the door. 'I am really sorry about Socks but it looks as if she'll be fine.'

'Socks?' he asks.

'The cat,' I explain, 'I called her Socks because of her white feet.

'Ah,' he says, 'her real name is Grace, after Grace Kelly, my wife said they looked like white gloves. Jenny thought she looked very elegant.'

'I'm sorry, I did see that on the microchip registration. She's your wife's cat, isn't she?'

'Was,' he says. 'My wife died.'

Oh Lord, I nearly killed the cat that is the only living mem-ory of his dearly departed wife. I would have truly been on my way to hell.

'I'm so sorry,' I say.

'Thank you,' he says. 'It was a year ago today that we buried her. When you turned up and said you had bad news, well I thought, not today of all days.'

A year ago today? I cast my mind back and remember driving in for my fresh start but watching a hearse leaving the close. I remember a sallow face in the car behind.

'I moved in a year ago today, that was you,' I think aloud.

'I remember,' he said. 'I was thinking how strange it was that life was going on for some people. Jenny's death released her from a lot of pain but I felt so guilty for even thinking that.'

'That New Year's Eve was just awful,' I agree and sit down again.

We sit silently for a moment, both of us remembering that night.

'These big celebrations are horrible if you're on your own,' he says eventually and we both nod.

'Grace really missed her until you came along,' he continues. 'I saw that she came to see you and you didn't seem to mind.'

'I enjoyed her company,' I reply. 'She helped me through a lot. I feel awful I didn't meet you sooner,' I confess, 'but I'm moving out today.'

'Yes, I saw the removal van doing a dance with the rubbish truck earlier,' says Michael. 'Grace was lucky that you ran her over and not them.'

We both laugh.

'I hope you're taking Nobby and Nessy,' he adds.

'Who?' I ask.

'The gnomes. I thought the one you had needed a partner, so I bought him a little girlfriend,' he tells me.

'That was you?' I'm astonished.

'I also tidied up the garden a bit,' he says. 'I could see that it wasn't your thing but I did leave some instructions when I planted the forget-me-nots.'

'I saw them.' I am gobsmacked.

'Well, you were looking after the cat,' Michael continues, 'feeding her and everything. I felt that I should do something for you.'

'Why didn't you say anything?' I ask.

'I felt stupid. There gets to a point when frankly rocking up and introducing yourself as the guy who's been secretly doing your garden seems weird, so I just stopped,' he confesses.

I burst out laughing and tell him that I thought I was being stalked.

'By a phantom lawn mower,' he joins in. 'I am sorry, I didn't mean to frighten you.'

He has a gentle smile which lights up his face and very blue eyes.

'You didn't,' I lie. My phone buzzes with a text from Patty, I have to go. I stand up.

'It would have been good to meet you sooner,' I say.

'Yes,' he replies, shaking my hand for longer than he needs to. 'It would.'

'Do you have plans for this New Year,' I ask. 'Will you be having a toast to Jenny?'

He shakes his head. 'She wouldn't want me to spend every New Year thinking about her death. I celebrate her life and I do that once, on her birthday.'

'So I guess tonight,' he continues, 'it's pizza and TV.'

I pause briefly then go for it.

'Well,' I say coyly, 'if it doesn't seem inappropriate, would you like to come to a party with me?'

Epilogue

Spring has sprung and the Mercury Travel Club team is still going strong. Our second BIN night resulted in Josie leading a 'Learn to Flamenco' trip; her own personal attempt was a sight to behold. After Matt posted it online, she can never again mock my Granny-Oke days.

Mum and Dad have started a new killer quiz team with James's grandparents and are cleaning up wherever they compete. They call themselves 'Three Centuries and Counting' – that should keep them going for a while.

As a consequence, Zoe and James have had to stay together for the sake of their grandparents. Mum has threatened that James will get custody of her should they ever split up. It's just as well they're still very much in love.

Cheter came back from their cruise gushing as much about Patty's nineties tribute (her MC Hammer brought the house down) as their wedding. They're now working their way through the compatibility shelf as newly-weds; last month they learned how to cook authentic Thai and next month they're going back to the Caribbean to try swimming with dolphins.

Patty's relationship with Dr Lurve has blossomed at sea – so her frequent, gory texts expound. I honestly didn't need to know that she pretends to be unconscious so that he can give mouth-to-mouth, but I do now. I can't wait to have her back.

And as for me, I've bought a luxury duplex in that mansion block after all. I'll move out of Patty's when she gets back and will of course be taking the gnomes with me. Michael and I have seen a lot of each other, but I hope when I have a place of my own, I'll be seeing even more.

I have absolutely no idea what Alan is up to.

Acknowledgements

My thanks and much love to:

Mam and Dad for teaching me to read and beginning a life-long love of books.

Jason for your support and cajoling – I got there in the end!

Chris and Victoria for the music and banter.

Clare for proving Bucks Fizz wrong and John for being John.

Julie, Hazel, Janet, Jonesy, Clare, Debbie, Verity, Trish, Pauline and Julia for being my guinea pigs and for your kind words.

Clare, Heather and Anna from RedDoor Publishing for making it happen.

And finally, the musicians and song-writers who give us all one helluva good time whatever our age!

A Letter from the Author

Thank you for buying *The Mercury Travel Club*. I really hope you enjoyed reading about the adventures of Angie and Patty. In creating this story, I wanted to develop characters we all might recognise, and to show that it's never too late to follow your dreams. Don't worry if you're dying to find out what happens next – there's another *Mercury Travel Club* novel on its way!

I'd love to hear what you think so do follow me on Twitter or catch up with me on my website. Looking forward to hearing from you.

Helen x

www.twitter.com/Helen_Bridgett
www.helenbridgett.com